Death of a Succubus
Kim Bair

Facebook: kimbairauthor
Instagram: KimBairAuthor
Email: kimbair@proton.me
Website: www.kimbair.com
Telegram: kimbairauthor
Copyright © Kim Bair 2016
Ebook Cover Design by http://www.ebooklaunch.com

More books by Kim Bair:
Dead Shifter Walking, The Succubus Executioner Book 1
Demigod Down, The Succubus Executioner Book 2
A Witch's Fury, The Succubus Executioner Book 3
A Council of Betrayal, The Succubus Executioner Book 4
Death of a Succubus, The Succubus Executioner Book 5
Legacy of the Succubus, The Succubus Executioner Book 6
Creation of the Dual Shifter, The Dual Shifter Executioner
The Mel Files
Andy's Origin, The Andromalius Chronicles

Table of Contents

Chapter 1...1

Chapter 2..17

Chapter 3...26

Chapter 4...64

Chapter 5...72

Chapter 6...122

Chapter 7...141

Chapter 8...149

Chapter 9...155

Chapter 10 166

Chapter 11 189

Chapter 12 195

Chapter 1

It had been six months since we moved into the mansion.

"Logan, I'm not sure I'm ready," I whispered to him for the hundredth time.

He slung a meaty arm around my shoulders as we stood in Ginny's room gazing at her peaceful form, asleep in her own crib.

"I understand, but look at her, she's ready to be in her own room. Besides, we have the video monitor, and she's only a doorway away."

I grunted. I liked her in bed with us. I loved her small form curled up against us. But I had to admit, she was a bed hog.

"I can't believe this was a closet," I muttered.

Logan laughed quietly as we backed out of the room. "I can't believe you suggested turning it into a nursery."

Once I had seen Logan shirtless, sweaty, and with power tools, I'd have let him work on anything in the house, just to watch.

He laughed, his lips close to my ear, as he felt my memories. "Glad you enjoyed the show."

He softly closed the door between the rooms. He had also soundproofed our room, for obvious reasons.

I turned, looking at the warm cherry four-poster bed. I had laid my head next to him as pack leader and Mate for the past six months. The legal battles with Grams and Lorraine had been intense, but were finally coming to a close. We just had one more court appearance to make.

Grams had gotten Kitten. The manor was sold and I took control of the bank accounts. It wasn't perfect, but I at least wasn't poor anymore. Tomorrow we would finalize the paperwork.

But tonight...

I backed Logan toward the bed and his lion growled low at me.

"It would be a shame not to test the soundproofing," I whispered, an evil smile on my lips.

He dipped his head to mine, ending any other words I might speak. Strong arms snaked around my waist to cup my ass.

"We've had enough quickies in the shower," he muttered against my lips.

I smiled, pushing him onto the bed, following him down to straddle him. Logan relaxed against the plush California king mattress, his eyes never leaving me as I stripped off my top. Sizzling palms worked up my sides before unsnapping my bra and tossing it to the ground.

He growled low, arching off the bed to take one pink nipple in his scorching mouth. I ran my fingers through his caramel locks, exhaling a ragged breath, tilting my head back. My hips moved against him, my body craving him.

With a boost of his hips, he flipped our positions and I laughed, "I never get to be on top."

He nuzzled the larger of my two mate marks and I inhaled liquid fire. "Cheater!" I accused, breathless.

He chuckled, not bothering to deny the charge.

He leaned back and stripped me of my yoga pants and undies. Dropping his head down, he laid a trail of kisses up my calf. I flexed my ankle, smiling. His enjoyment of the situation flowed along our mate bond.

Moving along the back of my knee, he nipped the delicate skin there and I yelped, trying to twist out his grasp. He chuckled, not releasing my flesh. I wiggled against him, wanting him, needing him. Part of that was the mate bond, but honestly, for great sex, I didn't give a shit.

His lips toyed over my hipbone and I shifted, trying to get his heated tongue to the good stuff. His hands secured my hips, keeping them still. I growled.

He ignored it.

"Logan," I warned. Patience is not my strong suit; he of all people should know that.

He smiled as he lowered his head between my legs.

"Finally," I exhaled.

He tilted my hips before taking one long, leisurely stroke. I grunted, my hips twisting against his grip. My mate mark heated up and I bucked against him as he delved deeper into my depths. Every movement was perfect, my own pleasure seeping into our mate bond, giving him expert guidance.

Logan pressed against the tightly wound bundle of nerves and I exploded in one ear-shattering scream.

He smiled, and while I gasped from the pleasure seeping into my limbs, he chucked off his clothing. He covered my body again, driving warmth into me where his tongue had just ravished.

I bucked, curling around him and his sure, fast thrust. He paused, nuzzling the mark again. I dug my nails down into his back. He hissed, drawing his thighs under my own, pinning my hands over my head. He thrust again as our fingers interlaced.

I tilted my hips and he hit all the right spots. My arms tried to arch off and wrap around him, but his strength and positioning kept me immobile. That just made it hotter. While I had never liked giving up so much control in the bedroom, Logan knew me in ways no other lover had. He could sense my hesitation before the words would leave my lips.

Knowing my train of thought, he relaxed his hands, bringing my arms around his neck. I held on to him, crying out as his powerful thigh muscles thrust in perfect harmony with my vibrating body, driving me father into bliss.

My body clenched around him, a gasp leaving my throat before a cry followed, pleasure ripping though my limbs. Wholly engrossed in my own pleasure, I never heard Logan's own cry before he collapsed on top of me.

I sighed, shoving him over so I could breathe. He pulled me close, his overheated body smearing sweat all over me.

I ran small circles over his back until his breathing evened out and his arm became dead weight over me. Looking up at the ceiling and realizing I didn't feel tired, I rolled over and watched Ginny sleep on the monitor also.

I was restless. I needed this bullshit with Grams resolved so I could finally move on.

The Supernatural Council had been running smoothly under Ali and Grant's new rule. We protected those Supernaturals who lacked the massive clan of the shifters or Houses like the vampires. At least, we tried. My band of fellow executioners traversed the eastern US keeping order and delivering justice. I hadn't been out lately and it bothered me. My identity throughout the years, ever since I was sixteen, had been based entirely on hunting, killing, and removing threats. If I wasn't that person anymore, I feared what that meant.

Don't get me wrong, being there with Logan and the kids, it was nice. Really nice. I just couldn't help but feel it would be short-lived for me. I didn't get to be happy, at least that's what I'd told myself every other time life shit on me.

Here I was, unable to sleep again, wondering if I was really cut out for staying in one place. Often I just felt like I was playing a part.

Maybe Grams had just shaken my confidence in who I had become, or maybe she had reminded me of who I really was and always would be.

Either way, I pulled out my current book to pass the time. Logan always woke up if I left, and both of us not sleeping was never pleasant.

...

"Hey, wake up," Logan urged, shaking my shoulder.

Rolling over, I groaned, "What time is it?"

"Seven, we've got to leave here in thirty minutes." He kissed my cheek, his stubble scratching.

I nodded. "I can't wait until we are back on normal hours." I sat up with a groan, squinting to see Ginny still asleep in her crib on the monitor.

"I can't believe she slept through the night," I pouted. My midnight companion no longer needed me.

Logan laughed, shoving me out of bed. With a grunt, I made my way to the bathroom.

I showered quickly and slipped into the pinstriped pantsuit Logan had laid out. I also couldn't wait until leather and yoga pants were my normal again.

I crept toward Ginny's room, finding the door open and an empty crib. Turning, I headed downstairs, following my nose to the scent of what I was hoping was French toast.

Laughter greeted me as I walked down the lengthy hall and into the kitchen. The sheer size of this home, or mansion rather, was mind-blowing, easily double that of my beloved manor. I suppose that made sense since we had shifters and kids here all the time. Jerry turned his dark form from the stove, a blue and white striped apron over his black suit. He handed a plate to Mark, who in turn handed it to me.

I inhaled deeply, taking it over to the long, farm style table that sat sixteen.

Logan sat across from me, trying to feed Ginny peas in her highchair.

"She doesn't like those," I grunted at him, still half asleep.

"She needs her veggies," he countered.

I rolled my eyes and sent my irritation along the mate bond.

4

"Today is the day!" Jerry proclaimed, interrupting our silent communication.

I smiled as he and Mark sat with us.

"It most certainly is," I agreed, my stomach growling.

"Fork," Logan commanded, yet again disapproving of my eating habits.

I glared at him, dumping syrup over my French toast before picking it up and taking a gooey bite.

"Do not get that on your outfit," he growled at me, annoyance slamming into the bond.

I licked the syrup off my fingers.

Jerry and Mark both cleared their throats at our display.

I laughed, cleaning my hands with one of Ginny's wet wipes before picking up my fork.

"Better?"

He grunted, right before Ginny smacked the spoonful of peas all over his outfit. I laughed hysterically, along with Ginny.

Logan wasn't nearly as entertained.

"Feed her, I have to change," he growled.

I nodded, heading to the fridge for her sweet potatoes.

Logan re-appeared a few minutes later, adjusting his tie. A knock changed his trajectory, as he headed back up the hallway to the front door.

"That's Katie, for the baby," I crooned to Ginny. Katie was Ginny's sitter and along with being well versed in several impressive hand-to-hand combat disciplines, she was one of the few people who could get Ginny to sleep without an hour-long screaming fit.

Katie came in, dropping her purse off on a chair and draping her coat over it.

"My Ginny bean!" she exclaimed. Ginny squealed, holding her hands out to Katie.

I laughed, depositing my plate into the sink. "It seems we aren't needed anymore."

I dropped a kiss on Ginny's cheek.

"We should be back before lunch, Katie," Logan said, pulling on his suit jacket. He dipped down to kiss his daughter.

Mark and Jerry followed us to the mudroom outside the garage. As I stopped, slipping on my uncomfortable shoes, I noticed the longing in their eyes when they looked at Ginny. Their multiple applications to adopt a baby, infant, and toddler had all been rejected. I wished I could help, but even my hands were tied.

We all filed out to the SUV for, hopefully, our last day of court.

The case with Lorraine had been tied up months earlier. Logan stayed true to his wishes and didn't allow Lorraine any visitations, nor did he offer her any funds as compensation. The contract she had signed after Ginny's birth was binding, and though her attorney threw out the fact that Logan was a hairy shifter, so was Ginny.

Things finished up quickly after that.

Grams's case had taken longer. While my attorney, Sophie, was an impressive beast to be reckoned with, my own temper had called it an early day more than once.

I stared out the window, drumming my fingers on the armrest.

"It will be fine, Olivia, relax," Logan instructed me, picking up on my nerves.

I grunted. I'd relax when this was over, and then I might kill Grams.

Tommy had begged me not to and that was the only thing stilling my hand. That and her mastery of the legal system, demonstrated by her naming of the annoying Governor Hash as her beneficiary.

Logan parked in the underground parking garage. I slipped out of the seat, my hands flexing, uncomfortable with my lack of weapons.

Logan slipped his hand in mine, tugging me along at his breakneck pace, literally, given the shoes I was wearing. "It's almost over."

I sighed, "Can't happen soon enough."

He squeezed my hand, feeling my turbulent emotions and offering his silent support.

Jerry and Mark followed close behind us.

We walked that way into the courtroom, Logan only releasing my hand to let me go up front with Sophie. The swinging gate closed behind me and I took a seat.

"Have both parties signed the agreement?" the judge began. He was about done with us as well.

"We have," Sophia stated, tapping the documents in front of her.

The judge leaned forward, pushing his glasses down his nose to look at both teams intensely.

"Are there any problems with the signed documents?" he asked cautiously.

"No," Sophie answered.

The judge turned to Grams's counsel. He cleared his throat, standing. "No," he confirmed.

"Both parties have copies of said agreement?" the judge asked.

"We do," both attorneys answered.

"Well, praise Jesus, we are done," the judge announced, banging his gavel.

I turned to Logan, smiling. He returned my expression, reaching over the half wall to take my hands. I closed my eyes. I was free of Grams's betrayal. A weight was lifted off of me and I exhaled, a smile playing over my lips.

I turned to Sophie, her face betraying none of her emotions. She stood gracefully. "I expect prompt payment," she informed me, before turning to shake hands with the opposing counsel and gliding through the swinging door to the exit.

I stayed seated, watching Grams speak with her counsel before also heading out behind him. A part of me still wondered why. Why she had turned her back on me? I had trusted her and her attempt to release the names and address of every Supernatural we protected still stung to my core.

But this was a happy day. I pushed those dreary thoughts away, going to Logan's side as we also exited the courtroom. I never wanted to see her again.

Outside, I pulled a deep breath of fresh air, letting my mind fully accept that I was free of Grams. I laughed heartily.

Sophie, outside waiting for us, laughed as well, her cold demeanor left behind for a few minutes. I hugged her tightly in an uncharacteristic display of affection.

"Enough, woman," she grunted. I released her, standing a moment before I jumped at Logan. Pain laced my back, forming a pattern of three bursts in quick succession. I tried to draw a breath, my back arching, my body falling forward.

My knees hit the pavement, grinding rocks into the soft flesh there. I tried to break my fall, but my arms wouldn't respond to my commands.

My eyes rounded and my voice was gone. I tried to warn Logan, tried to tell him to run.

A single tear dripped down my cheek as my body went limp. My vision darkened. The breath I desperately needed, denied.

Even the wailing screams couldn't rouse me from the darkness.

...

"Olivia!" Logan yelled, the sound torn from his very soul. He watched Olivia's face change from joy and relief to pain and confusion. Red spots blossomed on her blouse, a blouse he had picked out himself for her. Disbelief and searing heat exploded inside of him, flowing along the mate bond.

He watched her reach down and touch the sticky blood seeping through her chest before her gaze found his. She tried to breathe. Logan watched her try, felt her panic when she couldn't.

"Olivia!" he bellowed again. Time slowed as he reached out for her, her sea green eyes wide and unseeing. His heart constricted as she fell against him limply. He clutched her closely, turning and tearing his expensive Italian suit at its knees in his attempt to block any other potential shots with his own body as they fell.

Jerry screamed a word in a language Logan didn't understand.

"Move!" Mark bellowed, reaching under Logan's arm to help him up.

Logan wasted no time scooping up Olivia's body easily. Feeling the warm blood making her back slick, he moved her inside. Turning to look, he saw Jerry holding an opaque shield in place as he ran to join them.

Logan laid her down on the cool marble, tearing off his jacket to press against the three bullet holes gushing blood out onto the floor beneath her.

"She's not breathing," Logan whispered. He lifted his head, seeing Mark and Jerry rushing in with Sophie.

Jerry's knees gave out as he ran, sending him sliding to Olivia's head. "She's not moving," he whispered.

"She's not breathing," Logan repeated, a numbness creeping into his chest, tightening and shortening his breath.

Jerry braced his hands on either side of her head. Pale light glowed around her face. "Don't you fucking die on me," Jerry hissed, holding her head. "Don't you fucking die, Olivia," he wheezed, his voice broken.

"Keep it together, Jerry. You are no good to her like that," came the stern voice of Mark, the only one keeping his head.

She couldn't die, it wasn't possible. Logan's heart refused to acknowledge the scene in front of him.

"She needs a hospital," Mark stated. Looking outside, he turned back to Logan. "I'm going to get the car, and we are going to get her help."

The numbness was creeping down Logan's legs, causing him pain. "Go." He charged the word with an unspoken order.

Mark shifted and was gone, loping out of the glass doors, shredding clothing as he went.

"Don't die, don't die," Jerry chanted, salty tears slipping down his chocolate skin.

Logan silently added his own chant, exactly the same as Jerry's.

The SUV crashed into the glass windows. Logan moved to cover his dying mate, glass shards cutting his skin. He looked at Jerry, who nodded silently before Logan scooped Olivia up. Jerry kept his hands at Olivia's temples, stumbling over his own feet and the debris.

"Move!" Logan yelled. Sophie threw the back door open before getting into the passenger seat herself.

"Drive!" she yelled, as soon as Logan had laid Olivia's bloodstained body across the seat. Jerry's hands wavered but never left, the light dimming but constant.

Sophie continued to bark directions and before Logan could grasp what was happening, Olie was being pulled away from him. He bellowed, his lion pressing against his skin, fur rippling down his arms.

Mark pressed against him, forcing him back. "Let them work! Let them work!" Logan's mate was moving farther away from him. Logan tried to dislodge Mark again. He succeeded in pushing him along the hospital tile, his bare feet squealing. Somewhere he had found gray sweats.

Jerry was still at her head, chanting, before they turned the corner and Logan lost sight of them. His knees gave out. The only reason he didn't fall was his leverage against Mark. Mark changed his forward push to support for Logan instead.

Logan couldn't help anymore here, but he could find the fucker responsible.

"Get us back to the courthouse," he barked, pulling away from Mark. He was not weak. He was the leader of the entire US Shifter Nation; falling apart was not an option. Olivia wouldn't have allowed it.

Mark blinked, confused, and Logan turned his full Alpha stare at him. Mark was quick to obey, even if he didn't understand. Logan supposed that Mark expected him to harass the nurses, demand to be by Olivia's side for the next hours or days.

He couldn't be idle. He couldn't watch helplessly, but he could kill.

Casting a glance at Sophie, he commanded, "Stay with her."

Sophie raised an eyebrow, but said nothing of Logan's order before she nodded.

Mark cast careful glances at his Alpha as they climbed back into the SUV. The scent of Olivia's blood clenched his stomach and his jaw.

Thanks to Olivia's impressive guards, Logan was able to block himself off from the rest of the pack, because he knew. He knew in his soul what the numbness creeping up his back and into his arms was.

Olivia was dying.

Clenching his jaw, he slammed the door shut, breaking the handle. He looked down disdainfully at the piece of plastic before tossing it into the back.

"Where do you want to go first?" Mark asked.

"We need the bullets. From there we need to figure out where the shots were fired from. I have no delusions about being able to catch the person still there."

Mark nodded, maneuvering the large SUV impressively around traffic, red lights, and a police barricade.

The police officer guarding said barricade waved his hands, yelling demands.

"Who do you think you are?" one of them yelled as Logan stepped out of the car.

Logan turned his fierce gaze onto the small human, pulling himself up to his full height and glaring down at him. With an audible gulp, the officer stepped back. Logan scented his fear and his lion enjoyed it.

Mercer came around from the driver's side with Mark and a host of uniformed officers hot on his heels.

Logan inclined his head, making no move to hide or explain the blood coating his hands and expensive dress shirt.

Mercer wasn't stupid. He took one look at the Alpha and averted his gaze.

"Everyone get lost," Mercer ordered. The officers around him opened their mouths to voice their shock and disapproval of the order. "NOW!" Mercer repeated, charging the word with urgency.

Logan took a step closer to Mercer. That action had the officers scattering. Mercer stood his ground, his eyes flicking up to Logan's before they moved to a spot behind his head.

"How is she?" Mercer asked, braving the angry shifter.

Logan's beast bellowed in his chest, wanting to tear down every building, destroy every living thing. Nothing was worth it as his mate lay dying.

Ginny, the soft whisper of her name gave him sanity and he clung to it.

"She's in surgery. I just got off the phone with Jerry," Mark answered.

Mercer nodded, but Logan hadn't moved.

"She will be okay," Mercer tried to reassure Logan, who could scent the lie.

"Have you recovered the bullets?" Logan asked, his stone face revealing nothing, at least that's what he hoped.

Mercer blinked at him. Logan wasn't about to repeat himself.

"I have them," a voice called out behind Logan.

He turned, his hand outstretched. Blue placed the thick plastic bag in it. Logan looked at the three bloody bullets that had torn through his mate.

His lion beat against his control, but with a shake of his head, Logan refocused on the bullets in front of him. He opened the bag, inhaling deeply before passing it to Mark.

"What do you scent?" Blue asked, unafraid to meet the Alpha's gaze.

"Blood, but not only Olivia's, wood, and salt. Mark?" Logan asked.

Mark took another long inhale. "There's something else, something faint." He inhaled again, holding the breath. "Jerry uses it sometimes, but I can't, I can't place it."

Mark looked lost and worried. Olivia had been a constant companion to him. She had risked everything to visit The Oracle and find Jerry.

Mark handed the bag back to Logan, not meeting his gaze for an entirely different reason this time. It was selfish to think only of himself. If Olivia died, ... he shut down that train of thought.

11

Even Olivia injured would be felt across the packs. It probably already was, but Logan couldn't bring himself to connect with them. The Council would be lost without her, he had no doubt. Despite her best efforts and plans for it to function at the same level without her, it never could.

Logan reached out, taking the bag with his left hand as his right extended to Mark's upper arm, gripping it reassuringly. Mark's gaze jerked up to Logan's own before he nodded and looked away.

Logan turned back to Blue. "Do you have a plan?"

Blue nodded. "I'm taking those to Gunner for him to examine."

Mercer cleared his throat, coming to stand near the aggravated lion. "We have labs that can help with that."

Logan raised an eyebrow. "Whose lab?"

"The St. Ann Police Department. This case has been given priority," Mercer replied.

"When did you start working for the police department again?" Logan asked suspiciously.

"After The Conferences. It seemed they needed someone on the force to handle the occasional Supernatural since the other guy got himself killed," Mercer answered with a shrug.

Logan sealed the bag shut, pressing the plastic together with unnecessary force before he handed it to Blue.

"Blue, take those now," Logan commanded. "If we find anything else we need analyzed, we will let you know."

Blue nodded and headed away without another word.

Logan turned to Mercer. "Do you know where the shots originated from?"

Mercer's mouth was turned down as he ran a hand over his blond hair, cropped short again. "Not yet; we are looking. There are four possible roofs we have identified. Olivia—" His voice cracked. "Olivia could have determined it faster. She's taken out snipers from these rooftops before."

Logan nodded. He had heard of that. When the shifters and vampires came out of the metaphorical closet, Olivia had run the first meeting with Hash. She had literally captured, hog tied, and locked up the snipers Hash had set up on the rooftops before they knew what hit them.

She was fearless and selfless. He wasn't going to lose her.

"I want to see all the possibilities," Logan demanded.

Mercer nodded, "Let's go."

...

They started out on foot, Mercer, Logan and Mark. While the use of their vehicles would have made the process faster, the roads had been shut down and cars blocked their way.

Logan's phone rang. Without breaking stride or looking at caller ID, he pulled it out of this pocket.

"What?" he barked.

"Is it true?" Tommy whispered.

Shit.

"Olivia was shot, she's in surgery right now," Logan relayed, feeling badly about forgetting the kids.

"What hospital? I'm going," Tommy demanded, sniffling.

Logan paused. He had no idea what to do, how to handle this, nor any clue as to how Olivia would have handled it.

"No, you are to stay in school until transport arrives. Just because someone injured her, that doesn't mean they won't be coming after the you and the kids as well."

"I'm not a child!" Tommy yelled. "I can help!"

Shit.

"You're right, Tommy, you can. Your first priority is to be sure no one else attempts to leave early. The second is, I need you to monitor police communications for any reports, calls, anything that mentions the shooting and Olivia."

Tommy gave a small laugh and the tightness eased in Logan's chest. "How do you think I found out about the shooting?" Tommy asked.

"Oh. Well, keep it up, document it all and let me know if anything strange pops up. I want a full report tonight."

"You got it, boss. Can we see Olivia after?"

"Yes, we will see her after."

"Okay," Tommy agreed.

Logan hung up with a heavy sigh. He hoped he had done the right thing. Olivia utilized Tommy's skills without hesitation, but he was still a teenager and depending on him sat wrong with Logan. Still, he needed all the trustworthy help he could get.

Olivia would also beef up security.

Logan dialed on his phone. "Hudson," his cousin answered.

"Wake up, and get your shit in order. You are needed in St. Ann," Logan commanded.

"Fucking hell man, what is going on? I can sense the pack threads are upset."

Logan hesitated, hating that he had to go back into this.

"Olivia has been shot, she's in surgery."

Hudson dropped something. "WHAT?" he screamed. "Who DARED to harm the Mate?!"

Logan nodded, glad he had thought to call. He needed to not be the only riled up animal in the city. "I don't know and I'm trying to find out. I need you here to help me protect the mansion. I have no idea what else we can expect."

"Do you want the rest of the Compass Alphas? Not that you have assigned an Alpha for the North yet."

Logan growled, he didn't need that reminder. "No, just get yourself down here, now."

With that he ended the call, hanging up only to dial again.

"About time," Becky answered, chomping on her gum. Logan didn't bother asking if Tommy had told her the news, or if she was also monitoring the police reports. It didn't matter.

"Increase security at the mansion. I want shifters and the Council taking turns protecting the children."

"Done, what else you got for me?"

"Nothing right now."

"Kay, then I'm also going to continue monitoring bank transfers in case this was a paid-for hit."

"Good thinking." Logan hung up.

He needed to call Alec, but they had just arrived at the first of the four buildings. It would have to wait.

Steel and glass met his stare, reflecting his locked jaw and twitching lip. What it failed to capture was the beast inside Logan, demanding blood, thirsting for retribution, and climbing the walls inside of him. The numbness had stopped spreading, but it remained locked around his heart. He rubbed his chest, feeling Olivia's blood drying on his shirt.

"Do you want to change?" Mark asked him, paying close attention to his actions.

"No, not now," he answered, turning from his thoughts to follow Mercer through the glass doors.

Inside, uniformed police officers were guarding the stairs and elevators. Annoyed business men and women were waiting impatiently.

"What does it matter that a Supernatural got shot? She's not one of us." Logan picked up on the whisper.

"I heard it's the bitch leader of The Council. The whore deserved it," another whispered.

Logan didn't realize he had stopped following Mercer. He stalked toward the soft human in the brown suit who was whispering about his mate being a whore.

"You should mind your tongue, before I remove it from your head," Logan stated.

Mercer hung back, but Mark was right at Logan's side.

"In case you missed it, shifters have exceptional hearing, and that whore who deserved to be shot is his mate. I'd suggest groveling for your life."

The soft human's face lost all its color.

"I — I — what I meant was —"

"Grovel," Mark repeated, stepping forward.

The human's knees hit the ground. "I'm so sorry, please forgive me."

Logan stepped back, looking at the scene he had caused.

The humans weren't worth it. He rationally knew that, but he wasn't operating on rationality right now. He was driven solely by primal instincts. Instincts that were craving blood.

Logan gave thought to spilling the humans on the highly polished floors, but a warming sensation in his chest stopped him.

He turned to Mark. "Call Jerry," he demanded.

Mark pulled his phone out and put the ringing call on speakerphone. As a group, Logan, Mark and Mercer carefully moved into the elevator. Here's hoping Mark's service doesn't crap out, Logan thought.

"Is she awake?" Logan asked when Jerry picked up.

"No, but her brain waves just came back on line, or are registering again. I don't know the terminology. I just know she isn't brain dead."

Logan listened carefully to the silence. "She's on a breathing machine?" he asked.

"And a feeding tube," Jerry confirmed.

"But she's not brain dead. She's alive." Mark covered his face, drawing a ragged breath. His other hand held the phone, shaking.

"She's alive, the bleeding is stopped. We are just waiting for her to wake up." Jerry's voice was ragged with emotion.

"She's going to wake up. I can feel it," Logan said, his confidence in the statement sewn into his bones.

"That's great news," Jerry whispered.

The elevator ding announced they had hit the 15th floor. Logan moved out, following another uniformed officer to the stairwell marked, "Rooftop."

Mark finished up his conversation with Jerry and they cleared the three levels of stairs easily.

"Don't wait for us," Mercer called from below, winded.

Mark gave Logan a small smile. "I hadn't planned on it."

"I heard that," Mercer muttered.

Logan pushed open the door to the roof, sunlight blinding him for a moment.

Chapter 2

The red moon overhead cast everything in shades of maroon, reminding me of thick, dark rivulets of blood. I turned a full circle, finding it was all the same wine color. The monochromatic landscape played strange games with my mind.

Where was I?

I looked down at myself. My dress pants and blouse were gone, replaced by a black, skintight dress that flared out at my knees.

"What the fuck?" I muttered, running my hands over the unfamiliar material.

I'd have to say it was a kickass dress, although if I had to do any actual ass kicking, I couldn't see it as an asset. Tumbling rocks behind me had me spinning. As another maroon rock skittered at my feet, I could see no source for the displaced object.

Maybe I was dreaming. This sure as shit didn't feel real. What was the last thing I remembered? I searched my brain, chewing thoughtfully on my lip, tapping my foot against the flat slate rock at my feet. I was in my own little valley, surrounded by sharp edges leading up into who knew what.

What was the last thing I remembered? I searched my mind again. I was with Sophie and Logan; we had finally signed the documents with Grams. I jumped in front of Logan and — pain bubbled at my chest and I put a hand to it, expecting it to come away with blood.

Nothing. Only the smooth feel of my skin and the silk of the dress. I knew that feeling, though, I had been shot. Ugh, how lax was I getting, that I didn't check for snipers on the rooftops anymore? Hadn't that been Hash's go-to the first time around?

Idiot!

Whatever, I'd do better next time. You know, pending getting the hell out of here, wherever here was. I sighed, no time like the present to slice and dice my hands and legs. I wished for my leathers.

To my surprise, the first jagged rock I clutched didn't hurt me, didn't cause me pain. I looked down at my skin, finding it unmarred, so I slammed my hand against the rock. Still nothing. Well, if this was a dream world, I liked it. I traversed easily out of the pit. As I looked down, it almost reminded me of a lotus flower. A pissed off lotus flower.

Shading my eyes, I turned, at first seeing nothing but flat red slate. Then, far in the distance, I made out the barest outline of a building. I set my sights on it and started walking.

...

Logan blinked the sting of the midday sun from his eyes, moving to the left to allow Mark room to stand also.

When his sight no longer held sunspots, he moved with careful scrutiny to the edge. He looked down until he found the courthouse and changed his viewpoint, carefully watching the ground and the edging for any clues.

He and Mark were halfway through their first walk when Mercer and the other officer arrived.

"Find anything?" Mercer asked.

"No," Logan growled, taking another walk around the perimeter.

Still finding nothing, he looked to Mark, who shook his head.

"Let's go to the next one," Logan demanded.

On the stairs down, Mercer asked, "Logan, do you think the shots were meant for Olivia?"

The question caught him off guard. Logan stopped mid-step, Mark bumping into him from behind.

"What?" he asked, his mind already replaying the question back to him.

Logan turned to Mark, searching his face.

"Olivia laughed, she hugged Sophie..." Logan's voice faded.

Mark picked up, "She jumped towards you."

"That's when she was shot," Logan stated, shaking his head before continuing down the stairs.

That vision would forever haunt him. The pure look of panic and pain in her sea green eyes. Her throat trying to work. The pain flooding their mate bond, the confusion at her body not responding. They were all images that would torment him, awake and asleep.

Logan answered Mercer's question, "No, I don't think those shots were meant for Olivia. They were for me."

Guilt rode him hard, even though logically he knew there was nothing he could have done. Nothing he could have sensed to prevent it. His lion knew only that he had failed his mate. Logan listened to his sorrowful cry.

"Do you have anyone who wants to kill you?" Mercer asked.

Logan turned toward him, calling the elevator with one rough push. "Yes, I have shifters who are upset at me mating a succubus. I have vampires pissed at me for mating a succubus. I also have humans pissed at me for taking Lorraine's child from her. Not to mention Grams." He hissed her name.

Mercer cleared his throat, looking away before picking a spot on the plaster behind Logan's head.

"We're not — things aren't—" Mercer ran a hand through his short hair. "I'm not happy with what she did to Olivia anymore than you are. I love that girl. She saved my granddaughter's life. She continues to save it everyday she teaches Mindy to cope or shares a terrible story from her own past." His voice broke. "We all need her, Logan."

Logan's heart constricted. He reached out, his large hand resting heavily on Mercer's shoulder. "She will wake up."

Mercer looked down, drawing a long breath.

"What's a succubus?" the uniformed officer asked.

The elevator announced its arrival and Logan moved inside, turning, his thick arms across his chest, to watch the rest follow him in.

"In human lore, they are the devil who takes the soul of men and women during sex," Logan began. The officer gulped. "In reality, they are similar to humans, except they are sensitive to emotions. If you are feeling angry, they can take the anger. If you want to feel happy, they can help. Not to mention the sex is fantastic," he added.

He thought back to the night Olivia had been his date to some formal function or another. She was beautiful in her navy blue dress, every curve on her body highlighted in the formfitting fabric. He had been too angry with Lorraine that night to compliment her on it.

Truthfully, Logan had been angry a lot back then. It was that night with Olie that brought the constant frustration to his attention. His relationship with Lorraine had eaten away at him, a slow moving cancer. He never recognized the changes in himself or the packs until one ruby haired vixen showed him the errors of his ways.

With each slight touch, Logan had felt the heavy burden of his life lifting. The gentle brush of her fingers against the back of his hand had sent heat directly to a place he hadn't thought of in conjunction with Olivia before.

In the soft glow, as a lock of red hair fell over her eyes and a soft smile parted her lips, he was now thinking dangerous thoughts. Thoughts that awakened the dormant lion within him.

Mine, his lion had thought, the first time he peered through Logan's eyes at Olie.

That response alone had Logan careful and guarded around her. In all his long life, he had never experienced such a powerful reaction to a female from his lion.

Olie had picked at his plate, maneuvering her fork around the bacon in the mashed potatoes, and Logan had watched the fork grace her lips, entranced by the movement.

Truth to be told, Logan was grateful when Lorraine showed up that night. At least his lion didn't demand to claim her as he had Olivia.

The elevator doors opened and it took Logan a minute to realize everyone was waiting on him to lead the way out. Pushing off the elevator wall, he heard the glass shift beneath his heavy weight.

"Next?" Logan asked.

Mercer nodded, "Follow me."

...

My footprints didn't leave an impression as I walked. I imagine I looked silly, stepping, jumping and looking back to check it. Nor did I leave a shadow, and I wasn't warm. I felt I should have been from the sun on my back.

The vague outline formed itself into a large building. It reminded me of a palace, straight out of Aladdin. I was holding out hope for a flying carpet. I'd absolutely had enough to do with the djinn. Unless of course this one wanted to grant me three wishes and then not kill me for freeing him.

As I approached, I noticed that a large picture window was broken. I steered myself toward it. It was probably a good idea not to hit the front door, considering I had no idea where I was. I have to say, I didn't remember any glass in Aladdin. I shrugged, maybe this place had embraced technology?

I used the broken shards to haul myself in, finding my hands and dress again unscathed. I needed clothing like this in the real world.

Huffing, I stood straight, brushing imagined dust off my hands onto the dress. I took in the red glow of the unused nursery room. Dust had settled heavily against the wooden crib and matching rocking chair. I crossed the room, looking down on the chair. Gently, I pushed it, a vague sense of déja vu settling over me as it moved.

"He won't like you in here," a deep voice muttered from the shadows.

"Who is he?" I asked, impressed I didn't scream first. I'll admit, I jumped.

"The Magician," said the voice, coming into the light. A giant greeted me, heads taller than my own 5'9" height. Dark hair interlaced with silver covered his entire face and body. Two large horns curled upward and a dark green tunic covered his body, with thick black leather crossing his chest. He snorted.

"What are you?" I whispered, taking a step closer to him.

He tilted his enormous face. "I am Doyle, the minotaur."

"Impressive," I breathed out. "I wish we had your kind at home. You must make excellent security."

He huffed, "We do." He extended a hand that ended in thick, dark claws, swiping through my middle.

I didn't move; my brain felt foggy and slow as his hand moved through my torso.

"What the hell?" I whispered, looking down. Pressing my own hands against my stomach, I found my body firm to the touch.

"So that's what he meant," Doyle the large Minotaur stated. "Follow me," he ordered.

Did I have a choice?

Down dark stone hallways we traveled, with everything cast in a red glow. The high ceilings and stairs had more shades of red than I could have dreamed possible.

We arrived at an arched door Doyle pushed open. More stone greeted us as cream light from the candles gave a reprieve from all the red.

"I don't remember asking for trespassers to be brought to me, Doyle," a hunched figure spoke. I couldn't see more than his back, his attention drawn to whatever was in front of him.

"She isn't really here," Doyle answered. Minotaurs, taking cryptic to a whole new level.

The Magician dropped whatever he had been so carefully attending to with a metallic thud. "What did you say?" he asked, turning. He ripped off the magnifying glasses that were secured over his head with a leather strap, tossing them onto the wooden workbench.

"I tried to remove her and my arm passed right through her," Doyle said. I wondered if he was smiling under all that fur; his tone certainly sounded smug.

Stepping closer, The Magician analyzed me. I returned the favor, his black hair streaked with silver reminding me of Doyle. He was dressed in a Victorian style black jacket with the tails hitting below his knees. The suspenders and button up white shirt were clean and dated.

"What?" I demanded. I was used to being appraised and inspected, but his perusal of my body unnerved me.

"What's your name, girl?" The Magician questioned.

I raised an eyebrow, crossing my arms over my chest and pushing out a hip. "Olivia, who the hell are you?"

"Watch your mouth," The Magician scolded, his eyes snapping up to my own. I blinked, surprised by the similarity of color.

"Who are you to give me orders?" I asked, moving my hands to my hips.

The man smiled, sea green eyes looking into my own, and I fought the urge to shift uncomfortably.

"I am your father," he announced proudly, holding his arms wide, chest puffed out. My brow furrowed.

"Bullshit. I don't have parents." Denial seemed to be my safest answer, even though what Bob the Fae had said kicked around in my head.

Your father has great expectations for you.

A cold chill took up residence in my spine and I fought the urge to give into its shutters. What the fuck had the small Fae known about me that I didn't? I had dismissed his words, finding no use in speculating about whether I truly was lab created as Selena claimed.

But if I wasn't, and I'm not saying I believed him, but if for a second I entertained the thought that I actually had parents, why the fuck had Selena ended up raising me?

He took another step closer to me, his arms still out, and I backed up. He was looking for a hug, a warm embrace between kin. My face closed down.

He dropped his hands and I could see the hurt in the unshed tears glistening in his eyes. He moved on from the emotion quickly, though, rubbing his hands together.

"So daughter, what brings you here?"

"If I am your daughter, why didn't you raise me?"

His face fell, his valiant attempt at normalcy dwindling.

"You were born here," he began. I was waiting for, In a galaxy far, far away, and the music to start playing. He turned from me, picking up his discarded items on the workbench, placing them gently on shelves above the space.

He sat down, turning back to me, his eyes cool and calculating.

"You were born here, in the land where the succubi have been trapped for almost two centuries. I sent you through the portal with Selena in the hope that someday, some way, you would find your way back to us."

"Selena," her name came hissing off my lips with venom. "You willingly gave an infant to Selena?"

He looked at me, clearly uncertainly.

"Yes," he answered. Well fuck, at least the asshole was honest. Fuck. Did I believe him? My gut said yes.

I took a step closer to him. "Did you know what she had planned for me?"

"No."

"Well, let me tell you. The bitch had me raped, beaten, and tortured until I was her perfect fucking solider."

His entire body stilled, his eyes widening.

"And you gave me to her," I scoffed, turning away from him, hurt and betrayal lacing through my heart in ways I'd never dreamed of. Not believing I had parents was better than this pain.

I rubbed my forehead, pushing down the tears and the pain.

I turned back to him. "Well, I'm fucking here now, how do I leave?" My voice rose in an attempt to mask my pain.

Apparently, my abrupt change in topic caught him off guard. His mouth opened and shut, sealing into a thin line.

Finally, he came out with, "Do you know what happened before you woke up here?"

"Yeah, I was shot. Pretty sure I was or am dying." I rubbed the back of my neck. I needed to get back to Logan. He was stable and he loved me. He hadn't abandoned me.

I was holding out hope The Magician's story wouldn't hold up. Maybe this was all a clever hallucination. My subconscious was fucked up more than I'd previously thought if I was dreaming of such betrayal.

"Shot with an arrow?" Doyle asked.

"No, with a gun, a really big gun, three times," I answered, turning to look at him. His deep set eyes were glowing with red.

"Doyle is your guardian," The Magician stated.

"I don't need a guardian. I've managed just fine on my own," I retorted. Doyle growled. "Not to mention that you tried to slice me up when we first met."

"I could never hurt my true charge. It was a test," he replied with a shrug, like attempted murder was no big deal.

"Alright, back to the topic at hand, how do I get back?" I turned to The Magician.

He stood, running a hand absentmindedly over his workbench before looking at me.

"We have to create a portal. Your soul went back to the place of your birth under extreme stress; since we can't recreate those conditions with just your soul, we will have to utilize other methods," The Magician answered.

Doyle grunted next to me, "That is dangerous."

The Magician shrugged, "She wants to get back to Earth."

"As do you," Doyle stated.

My hackles rose. "Will opening the portal allow you to travel back to Earth as well?" I asked.

The Magician shifted slightly. "Yes, it will."

"Who trapped you here?" I wasn't dumb.

"The witches." He spat the species with venom and it was hard to deny the family resemblance, although I was still trying, or perhaps still undecided.

"The witches aren't powerful enough to trap an entire race in another dimension," I countered.

"Really?" That tidbit of information interested him.

"They can't even open a portal to the Fae without a blood sacrifice."

"It must have been powerful blood," Doyle commented.

I rubbed my chest. "It was."

"It was your blood?" The Magician questioned.

"It was."

"What happened?"

I sighed, really not wanting to get back into it. "They loaded me down with their magic and bled me out."

"I'm surprised it didn't work," The Magician commented.

"It did." I avoided their eyes, choosing to look out a narrow, tall window toward the back of the room.

"Who came through?" The Magician asked.

I turned my gaze to him, debating if I needed to tell him anything else.

"Luharposn and Bob." I tried to keep my voice neutral. I'm fairly certain I failed.

The Magician caught it. "You don't care for them?"

"Bob has always been kind in his own way to me, but Luharposn and I have a history. It isn't a pretty one," I admitted, not willing to divulge any more painful details.

The Magician nodded, deep in thought.

I wanted a topic change. "Alright, what do we need to get the portal open?"

Chapter 3

It was the third building that finally yielded results. Logan stood on the rooftop, looking down where Olivia's blood on the sidewalk in front of the courthouse looked so small, so minor.

"Whoever it was must have left in a hurry, not to pick up the shell casings," Mercer commented, taking in the rooftop scene.

Logan nodded silently in agreement.

"There are no smells up here," Mark commented, inhaling deeply. "The wind should be leaving a trace of something."

"Wolfsbane," Logan stated, his thick arms crossed over his chest.

Mark looked at him. "Why would a sniper leave wolfsbane?"

"Because he or she knew Logan would find this spot, and whatever his heightened senses picked up would be a vital clue," Mercer supplied.

Logan nodded, watching the sun drop lower on the horizon.

"Let's get the shells to Blue," Logan commanded, turning away. The scene held no additional clues and his beast needed action.

Mark nodded, taking the thick plastic bag from Mercer and using the end of a pen to drop in the, hopefully, helpful clues.

They turned as one unit, heading back to ground level and to the SUV.

...

The uniformed police were gone when they got back to the front of the courthouse. Mercer paused for a moment as Logan opened the passenger door of the vehicle. He had too much on his mind to safely drive anywhere.

"I'll call you if I hear anything from the uniforms that canvassed the area," Mercer said.

Logan nodded. "I'll let you know if anything changes with Olivia."

Mercer nodded, emotions thick in his throat. "I'd appreciate that."

Closing the door, Mark looked over at Logan. "Where do you want to go?"

"To the hospital."

They made the drive in silence, parking this time in an actual spot before making the short walk to the automatic doors.

Logan and Mark both began breathing shallowly. Hospitals wreaked havoc upon their sensitive shifter noses. They didn't bother asking for directions, they could smell Olivia in the massive building and swiftly took the twisting turns.

Everyone watched them carefully. Nurses stopped their conversations and doctors whispered for security. Neither Mark nor Logan acknowledged any of it.

"It's the blood," Mark whispered to him. "And my lack of clothing, not to mention shoes."

Logan reached down, touching the now dried blood Olivia had spilled out onto him.

"I had forgotten," he admitted.

Mark nodded. Turning the corner, they both saw Jerry seated outside what could only be Olivia's room.

"How is she?" Mark asked. Jerry stood to greet them. Logan looked through the glass window, coldness seeping into his body.

He moved through the doors to her, not hearing Jerry's response.

He knew she was on a breathing machine, he knew she had a feeding tube. Those were facts Jerry had relayed earlier in the day.

But seeing her, with a tube shoved down her throat inflating her chest, knocked his heart into his ribs with a painful cadence.

Logan watched the breathing machine inflate her lungs again. She was so still. So little when not telling him how to handle his business and causing a constant ruckus in his life. The room felt so empty without her vitality in it.

She couldn't die.

He couldn't lose her. He wouldn't lose her. He searched internally for the confidence he'd held earlier. His chest was warm, no longer numb. She would wake up.

His mate would return to him.

Logan reached down, running his hand over hers. He never realized how small they were, how delicate and petite, how slender her long fingers. Or how much she needed lotion after all the poopy diapers she had changed.

He smiled at that thought. He may have known her body inside and out, but the small detail of her hands had escaped him. It wouldn't anymore.

"Logan, I'm sorry to disturb you, but the kids are calling from the mansion," Mark stated behind him.

Logan nodded. "Jerry, do you need a replacement?"

Jerry shook his head. "I got a few more hours in me."

Logan nodded. "I'm going to head back to the kids and start bringing them over in shifts. They will want to see her and they will find a way to do it without me if I don't."

"I can stay with Jerry," Mark offered.

Logan nodded, "I'll be back soon."

...

Logan opened the garage door and the screaming he had heard in the car boomed to full volume.

"You can't keep me here!" Tommy yelled.

Logan entered the kitchen and followed the noise to the living room.

"Kid, stop it. Logan wants all of you to stay safe. Stop twisting. Dammit, Mindy, do not bite me!" yelled Caleb.

Logan turned the corner and Tommy looked up at him from where Caleb had him pinned.

"Get off of me!" Tommy screamed, desperation in his voice.

Logan nodded and Caleb released him. Tommy flung himself at Logan. "Is this her blood?" he yelled, frantically pulling at Logan's shirt. Tommy was going to be tall; already he came to Logan's chest.

"Yes," Logan answered. He looked at the room filled with grieving children. Some were sniffling, others had a murderous glare.

"Is she okay?" Tommy whispered, hope making his voice soft.

"Sit down, Tommy. I've been on my feet in these damn dress shoes all day." Logan guided Tommy to the couch, sitting in the armchair and turning to meet each gaze watching him closely.

"Olivia was shot three time with special bullets that I believe were meant for me and not her."

"What was special about them?" Tommy asked.

"I could smell blood that wasn't Olivia's, wood, and salt. Mark picked up on something else. We sent the bullets with Blue for testing at Gunners."

Tommy grunted, nodding. "Gunner delivers results."

"Glad you approve. The rooftop the sniper shot from was on top of a rundown apartment complex. No one saw anything that they will admit to."

"We need a vampire to glamour the truth," Connie called out. "Or let us try."

"That's a good idea. Remind me to call Mal when we finish here. My first priority is to keep everyone safe. No one will be doing any investigation without backup. Olivia will have my head when she wakes up if anything happens to any of you." Logan stared particularly hard and long at Tommy.

Tommy shrugged, shifting in his seat.

"She's not awake?" Mindy asked in a small voice.

Logan pulled her into his lap. She leaned against his wide chest. "Where is Mercer?" he asked softly.

"Running down a lead, he dropped me here after school," Mindy confided.

Logan nodded. "Good, this is the safest place for you."

"She's not awake?" Tommy repeated the question.

"No. When she was shot, I felt a numbness soaking into my limbs from my chest and I know ... I know it was her dying." Shocked gasps met his confession. "But later, when she was stabilized, that numbness turned into warmth. That's how I know she is going to wake up. She is going to live."

There wasn't a dry eye in the house as he assured them, and himself, that Olivia The Executioner and Mate would live. He only hoped he wasn't lying.

"Can we see her?" Mindy asked in a small voice.

"Yes, we are going to go over in groups. I have to warn everyone, she is on a breathing machine and a feeding tube." Nods met his words. Everyone sat up in their seats, anxious to see her. "I'm going to take the younger kids first since they need to get to bed earlier, older kids last."

Bear walked down the stairs, a pissed off kid in tow. "These children are some of the most talented escape artists I've ever seen," he commented, releasing the pissed off teen. "If you want, Logan, we can caravan down there, Caleb and I can both drive."

A wail sounded from above and Logan jerked his attention to Katie coming down the stairs, her tear-soaked face unable to hide any emotions.

"The poor little dear has been all out of sorts today," Katie said, sliding Ginny into his arms. She clung to him, letting out a squeak before snuggling down against his shirt.

"Dammit," Logan said, looking down at his bloodstained shirt.

"Katie—" he began.

"On it," she said, heading back upstairs for a new shirt.

Mindy reached out and patted Ginny's back.

"Let me change and we will head out," Logan stated. Nods met his command.

He hoped he was doing the right thing.

...

"The feather of a griffin?" I repeated to The Magician.

"Correct, that is the hardest item to obtain. If we can get that, the rest will be smooth sailing," he confirmed.

I nodded. "Where does said griffin live?"

"Two days travel from here. We will pack up and leave at first light," The Magician stated.

"This isn't light?" I asked.

"No, this is night, day is much worse."

"Awesome."

"In the meantime, we need to find you accommodations for tonight."

"She needs to sleep here, it's the safest place for her," Doyle stated.

"Certainly not the most comfortable," The Magician countered.

"She is a soul. She does not feel cold nor heat nor hunger," Doyle reminded him.

"I suppose you are correct," The Magician agreed, moving farther into the long room.

I followed and he dusted off the blanket on a cot.

"It's not much," he admitted, rubbing the back of his neck.

I shrugged, "I've slept on worse."

He sighed heavily.

...

The kids took it hard seeing Olivia in that condition. Logan questioned if he had done the right thing again. Olie never kept anything from them. She always said they had walked through hell, there wasn't anything they couldn't handle.

This, seeing their idol weak and unconscious, was looking to stretch those limits.

...

I expected the dust to settle around me in clouds when I sat down on the cot. It didn't. I sighed, rubbing my head. I expected the dress to pull and bind as well; it didn't.

So how the hell was I going to grab a griffin feather if I didn't even impact the world around me? Depend on the possible father figure who sold me into slavery? Or the minotaur who claimed to be my guardian? Neither option sat well with me.

I reached down and rested my hand on the cot. Tingles spread up my wrist, to my elbow, and up my shoulder before my arm passed through the cot.

Hmmm. But I was sitting on the cot.

I had expected to sit on the cot. Maybe if I expected to fall through... My ass started tingling. Okay, okay, I expect to sit on the cot!

Too late. My ass hit the cold stone floor. The tingling across my chest where the cot passed through me had me pushing up, you know, just in case it got stuck there. That would be a fun look. I turned, looking at my butt, seeing dust there.

"Nice," I muttered.

The dress felt tight around my waist, excellent progress. I looked toward the door, an itch to explore nudging me. My trust toward The Magician and Doyle was limited.

So I walked to the door. Okay, I didn't trust them, but I wanted to.

I expected my hand to land on the cool metal door pull. I smiled when there was no tingling as I pulled the door to me. I checked the hallway, seeing the torchlight illuminating pools of stone pathways and no living being. This was dangerous, I could admit that. I was in a world—dimension—I knew nothing about. Venturing out on my own could prove deadly.

I hesitated on that thought, but distrust pushed me into action and I slipped out the door. We had come from the left, so I went right, pulling the door closed behind me.

I took the dimly lit hallways slowly, trailing my hand over the rough stone, trying for more control over my transparent form. My feet moved silently over the hallway, which was beginning to curve to the right.

A sharp right turn in the hallway came next, but I continued forward into a huge room. The floor had been polished until it shone from the candlelit chandeliers hanging from the exceptionally high ceiling. Wine pillars surrounded the space and heavy gold accent pieces were displayed between the pillars.

I moved in front of one, two bodies, intertwined. The more delicate of the two figures smiled in glee, while the other grimaced in pain. I took in their interlaced bodies; there was only one thing they could be doing. I looked to the next figure before I scanned the room, finding it still empty.

I waited a moment, straining my ears to hear any warning sounds. Hearing and seeing nothing, I moved down the stairs and to the next gold piece.

Again, one figure smiled, her head thrown back, breasts perfectly captured mid bounce as she rode the man beneath her. He was restrained, his mouth opened, head turned away.

I'm all for woman power, but this looked violent and not consensual. Had I wandered into a female dominated world? Pending, of course, that my mind wasn't actually playing tricks on me as my body healed.

I crossed the large room, scanning constantly, until I reached the opposite end and another statue. This one had the female poised over two men, each looking fairly miserable.

I sighed. I needed to get home. Moving up the three steps, I edged into the darkness tinged with red. More statues dominated the walls, this hallway in far better shape than the one I had come from. I stilled, hearing noises from ahead.

A woman cried out in what I assumed was pleasure. I paused, debating. It certainly didn't seem like I should go any farther, especially since I had a fairly good idea of what was going on.

Yet something pushed me forward. A deep set need to know, to be able to dismiss the grotesque statues as poor attempts at art. I hugged the shadows, staying close to the walls, expecting to ghost through them, hoping that made me invisible.

It didn't. I was delusional.

Torchlight flickered and more moans met my ears as I crept closer to the noises, crouching down. Gold everywhere blinded me—the walls, the statues, inlaid into the bed. Even the man who was restrained on the maroon and gold bed had gold chains around his wrists and ankles.

He didn't appear to be in distress; if anything, he was eagerly awaiting the woman, who was fiddling with a contraption I didn't understand.

She turned and my breath caught in my throat. Pale, porcelain skin, strawberry blond hair, and full lips. If The Magician was my father, I was betting she was claiming the role of my mother.

I had seen enough and backed quietly away.

My thoughts were so consuming that I ceased exploring and went back to The Magician's makeshift room for me. I wasn't sure I wanted to see any more. I was happy with my life, happy with Logan, with our new home, with Ginny and the kids. All this could do was dampen my joy.

I sat back down on the cot and dust billowed up around me. I coughed, great, I was managing this expectation thing better than I'd realized.

...

Logan took a silent carful of kids back home, with Bear and Caleb following. While his shirt was new, he could still scent Olivia's blood on his skin. He didn't want to wash it off.

Still silent, the three carloads of Olivia's children filed back into the manor, not making conversation, just taking to their rooms.

He didn't know what to say to them, he had no words of his own.

"You two staying on?" Logan asked.

Bear shrugged. "For a few more hours, until our replacements get here."

Logan nodded, heading to the pantry for a protein bar. Bear cleared his throat. "What?" Logan asked.

"Have you given any thought to who is trying to kill you?"

Logan sat down heavily on the bar stool at the island. "No," he answered, unwrapping the bar.

Bear moved around to the other side of the island, watching Logan closely. "I know I am echoing Olivia's paranoia, but my money is on Zachariah."

Logan crumpled up the empty wrapper, watching Bear. "Why?" he asked when his mouth was clear.

"Olivia said he threatened to take everything from her. Now that you are her mate, you are a very big part of her world. She has already lost Grams."

"That had nothing to do with Zachariah," Logan denied.

"Nothing that we know of. You know how damn crafty the vampires are. He was probably the one who sent those threatening photos."

"Or Hash did to get closer to Grams."

"Maybe, but do you think Hash thought of those threats by himself?"

"Humans can be just as dark as we can."

"I know. I'm just saying we will need a target if she dies."

Bear's words froze Logan's insides and his lion pushed to the surface. "She isn't going to die."

Bear was smart enough to look away. "We need a target when she wakes up. We need someone to pay for attacking the Mate."

Logan took a deep breath, his eyes turning back to orbs of caramel. "We will, and when we do, we will have solid proof."

Bear nodded, turning to head away. "Wait a second, Bear," Logan said. "I need someone to take over as Compass Alpha of the North."

Bear turned back, surprised. "Are you asking for recommendations?"

"No, I'm asking if you are interested."

"Logan—" Bear began.

Logan held up a hand. "I don't give a damn about your sexual preferences."

"But Olivia."

Bear just let it hang out there. He had slept with Logan's mate, before she was his mate, granted. Logan's lion wanted to kill Bear, and maybe that was why he was sending him away.

"Olivia has a past, as do I. Answer the question." Logan was being intentionally short. He didn't want to discuss Olivia's past or his own.

"Uh," he cast a look at Caleb, entering the kitchen behind Logan.

"You can take Caleb, but he is too young to be your Beta."

Bear bristled at that. "Not to mention he's submissive," Logan added.

Bear nodded. "Can we talk about it?"

"It's okay, Bear. I don't really want to be your Beta, anyways," Caleb admitted with a shrug.

Bear sighed, watching his friend. "I accept."

"Good." Logan tossed the empty wrapper in the trash. "You leave tomorrow."

Logan went upstairs, at least one item off his plate. Pulling out his phone, he called Hudson. It went straight to voicemail. Hopefully that meant he was en route.

He scrolled through the other messages he had missed, cringing in guilt when he saw Darren's, Call me.

He sat down heavily on the bed, Olivia's scent wafting over him, before dialing.

"Are you okay?" Darren asked when he picked up.

Logan drew a breath to say he was fine, but hesitated. He wasn't fine. His mate lay in a coma with a breathing machine, he didn't know who was out to kill him, and he hadn't said good night to Ginny.

He cleared his throat. "I'm fine," he lied. At least Darren wouldn't be able to pick up on the dishonesty over the phone.

"I'm going to ignore that lie." Or not. "How is Olivia?" Logan could hear Kass in the background, trying to shush a fussing Harrison.

Logan scratched his head. "She's in a coma with a breathing machine. But she's stable."

"Is she going to wake up?" Darren asked.

"I think so. When she was shot and dying," Logan forced the distasteful word out, "I could feel a coldness from the mate bond, but once she was stable, it warmed back up."

"That's good," Darren exhaled. "She's going to wake up," he repeated, believing it more.

"I hope so. We took all the kids over to see her tonight."

"Was that wise?"

"I don't know, but they're resourceful. They would have found a way down there if I hadn't taken them."

Darren grunted. "That's true enough. Who is trying to kill her?"

"I don't think it was meant for her. I think it was meant for me."

"Who the fuck is trying to kill you?" Darren yelled.

"Language!" Kass scolded from the background.

"I don't know. The bullets were specially designed. Blue took them for Gunner to review."

"What do you need me to do?" Darren asked.

Logan rubbed his forehead. "I don't know what my next move is. The rooftop where the shooter was has been laced with wolfsbane."

"Wolfsbane?" Darren repeated. "That's what the asshole who tortured you used."

Logan's back arched, his lion pressing dangerously close against his skin. He still hadn't healed from that attack completely. But for his packs' sake, he did a damn fine job of pretending.

"Correct," Logan confirmed.

"Do you think it's the same person?"

"Possibly, Bear seems to think so. He thinks its Zachariah."

Darren grunted, "It certainly makes sense."

"We need proof before we go after a European Master Vampire."

"I know," Darren agreed. "How do we get it?"

Logan sighed, "The Oracle."

"No, it's too dangerous. You said Olivia almost didn't make it out."

"I know. It's a last resort, but the packs will need someone to pay for Olivia's wounds."

Darren sighed, "Let's cross that bridge when we get there."

"Tell him about Anna," Kass said from the background.

"Right. Sophie called Kass, it seems Olivia's will and power of attorney have been activated by her being in a coma. Anna has been named head of The Council until she wakes up."

"Who the fuck is Anna?" Logan growled.

"I don't know. She was also referred to as Seven in the paperwork."

"Seven," Logan repeated, rolling the name around on his tongue. He knew that name. Olivia had told him about Seven being with her when she escaped from her private hell.

"Do we know anything more about her?" Logan asked.

"Only that she lives in New York and will be arriving in two days."

"She's not an executioner?"

"Not that I'm aware of."

"Wonderful."

...

Logan slept poorly alone in the bed. He ended up going to watch Ginny as she slept peacefully in her crib, catching a few hours in the rocker. He woke up with an awful crick in his neck.

Ginny stood wobbly at the side of the crib, babbling to him.

He picked her up, holding her close for a moment before setting about changing her diaper.

Downstairs, the children had all gone to school as usual, and there was no sign of Bear or Caleb.

Mark, however, sat at the long kitchen table, drinking coffee.

"How's Jerry?" Logan asked, sitting Ginny in her highchair.

"Exhausted. I finally got him to leave and get a few hours of sleep last night. He feels so guilty about everything."

"There's nothing to feel guilty about. He didn't shoot her."

Mark sighed. "I know. I told him that, but he keeps thinking that if he was a more powerful mage, he'd be able to heal her wounds."

"He kept her alive, that's more than we could have done."

Mark nodded, staring down into his coffee.

"So, I hear Bear is moving?" Mark changed the subject.

"Yes, I need a unified front."

Mark nodded, "He's a good choice."

"I would have preferred sending you."

Mark choked on his coffee. "Olivia already asked me."

"I know, she told me."

Mark nodded. The silence stretched out between them as Logan fed Ginny a puréed vegetable medley.

"Blue called. He wants to meet us at Gunner's this morning," Mark told him.

Logan nodded, finishing the last of his breakfast as Katie walked through the front door. Ginny squealed and Logan was relieved to see that Katie didn't look like she was about to burst into tears again.

...

The morning found me dressed and sitting on The Magician's stool, waiting for them. At least I was assuming it was morning. Instead of everything being bathed in red, it was now yellow. I had found clothing in a cupboard, changing into brown pants and a white shirt with matching boots. The clothes were a little big, but far more comfortable than the dress.

The door finally creaked open and The Magician looked at me, startled. "How did you change? And how are you able to move the stool?" he asked as I turned back and forth.

"I expect to," I answered cryptically.

Doyle laughed behind him.

The Magician pulled down on his tailed coat, casting a knowing glance at Doyle.

"She is a fast study, like her father," Doyle commented, pushing The Magician out of the way so he could close the door.

I tapped my fingers on my bicep, my arms crossed over my chest.

"Speaking of you being my father," not that I believed it, "why can't I do magic?"

"I bound it."

"Why?"

"Unchecked and untrained magic is dangerous."

"Do you plan on unbinding it?"

He sighed, resting his bag on the workbench and pushing a roll and cheese at me. I snatched the food up, still watching him for an answer.

"It is a very painful process."

"I've been through worse. It would be nice to have an added tool in my arsenal." Instead of it just showing up randomly in near-death situations.

The Magician only nodded. "Also, how do you obtain power? Are you like the witches who eat hearts?"

He recoiled in distaste. "No! We are nothing like those vile witches. We are born with our powers, like all Supernaturals. Witches are no better than dabbling humans."

I couldn't disagree with that, well, except for Jerry.

I finished my quick meal. "Do I get any weapons on this trip?" I asked, as The Magician added a few items to his backpack.

"I didn't bring any for you. I hadn't expected you to be so corporeal."

"We can stop by the armory," Doyle informed me.

"Armory, lovely." I am a girl who loves an armory.

We went the opposite way from the realm I had explored in the night. I wasn't mentioning the unnerving statues or the eerily familiar woman I had stumbled upon. Having a father, or potential father, was enough; I didn't need to add a potential mother. Especially since my gut warned that she wasn't as kind as him.

Doyle led the way and we encountered no one on our walk. He opened a sliding iron gate, motioning me in. I stepped inside and whistled.

"Impressive," I whispered, gingerly touching a broadsword hanging on the wall, next to the double-headed battle axes and knife-tipped spears. There were no guns to note, but I did find a crossbow.

In front of the knives section, I selected a leg holder for a long dagger and a cross body scabbard for throwing knives, which made me feel very Rambo. I accessorized with two thin swords, strapped to my back.

My father looked at me strangely. Doyle nodded approvingly.

"What?" I asked. "I don't have powers. I've had to rely on my strength and cunning to keep me alive."

My father bowed his head. "Forgive me, you have done an excellent job protecting yourself."

I grunted, not comfortable accepting his compliment.

"Let us head by the kitchen as well," Doyle commented, picking up a backpack for me that already had a bedroll attached.

"Thank goodness, bread and cheese are not enough to sustain me."

The Magician looked over at me, surprised.

We continued to travel away from the chamber I'd discovered the previous night, rounding a corner into a noisy, delicious smelling kitchen. A woman with a rolling pin was beating dough, yelling out orders.

"What are you two doing here?" she asked, taking a second look and noticing me with them. "Who is the harlot?"

Awesome, even in a different dimension, I'm still a whore.

"A fellow practitioner," The Magician lied easily. We had that skill in common, although mine was due to environment, I think.

I wiggled my fingers at her in a wave. She looked me over critically, leaving her rolling pin on the massive ball of dough.

"Don't you try lying to me." She stepped closer to me than I would have liked. "That's your daughter. That's HER daughter," she hissed before slapping me.

I stepped back, cupping my cheek. "Nothing good can come of her being here," she continued.

"Hit me again, bitch, and I'll make that prediction come true," I warned her.

She turned her attention back to me. "What did you dare say to me?"

I took a step closer to her. "You heard me."

"Vile creature," she hissed as she reached out to push me away. I captured both her hands, my fingers pressing into her plump wrists. I enjoyed her wide-eyed look of panic before I shoved her away. She landed on her ass.

"That was me being nice, not that you deserved it."

She pushed off the floor, yelling, "She is just like her mother. Heartless and cruel. You should have killed her when she was a babe!"

Oh, I'd just about had enough out of her. "Listen here, you loud-mouthed, foul woman, YOU slapped me first. If you don't want retribution, keep your hands to yourself."

She tried to spit at me; I saw the tilting of her chin, the drawing in of her cheeks. I hit her across the jaw, snapping her head up before she hit the stone ground.

The Magician watched me closely. "We didn't come here to cause problems," he reminded.

Doyle grunted, whether in agreement or in appreciation of how I'd handled it, I didn't know.

"I got manhandled for the first sixteen years of my life, it won't happen again," I spat at The Magician.

He inclined his head, relenting. "Let's get our provisions."

I left with a bag heavily loaded down with food. No one said shit to me after I took out the head bitch.

I stomped off across the flat red earth in silence for a long time before The Magician spoke.

"You haven't asked about your mother," he ventured, his voice soft.

"I saw her last night. I saw her statues, she's not someone I'm going to like," I informed him.

"You left the safety of my workroom?" he asked, shocked. He jogged a few steps to walk next to me, his tails billowing out behind him.

"I did."

"You could have been captured."

"It's hard to capture air," I retorted. Not that I had any idea how fast I could turn it on or off.

He scoffed, "As a soul, you are pure energy, and there are those here who prey on that. They could capture you easily."

I shrugged, "They didn't."

"You shouldn't take such risks."

"My life, my decisions."

He sputtered, having no answer for that statement. Finally, he drew a long breath. "You are her daughter. You are part succubus."

He said it like I was going to be surprised.

"I know, that part of me wasn't bound." Yeah, still pissed about that.

He said nothing again for a moment.

"How do you manage it?"

"Fine, I have exceptional guards, which I can thank Selena for, so I don't influence whole rooms like I could."

He nodded. "But you can influence emotions?"

"Only those that are already present. I can pull also, and sometimes sense the emotional charge in the room."

He and Doyle shared a look.

"And sex?" God, that was awkward.

"It recharges me, helps speed up my healing."

"Do your partners..." His voice trailed off.

"Geez, twenty fucking questions. Yes, my partners can feel my emotions as long as it's consensual."

He cleared his throat. "And their souls?"

"Still in their bodies." I sighed, "I'm not a demon."

I was, however, part magician, apparently.

"I know that," he bristled. "But your mother..." His voice lost its momentum again.

"What, she can suck souls during sex?" I stopped my stomping to turn and look at him. My turn to be surprised.

"Yes," he answered.

"Huh. Nope, it's never happened. Although with your magic, I can kill with a touch."

"How has that happened?" He sounded honestly curious.

"It's usually in life or death situations. I can push emotions into a being and short circuit them."

"But you don't have access to it at any given time?"

"Nope, I usually have to be bloody and beaten for that trick to work."

He nodded, not adding anything further.

We lumbered over the red earth and I watched Doyle's back, black fur rippling over substantial muscle.

"How much farther?" I whined.

"A day and a half, probably more with your slow pace," Doyle answered.

Ugh. I was so bored and insulted.

...

Logan drove with Mark out to Gunner's compound an hour outside of town.

He couldn't help but think of the last time he was out here with Olivia. She was deadweight over his shoulder, her plump ass within biting distance.

He recalled how warm she was, not fighting him even as he threw her over his shoulder, a dead giveaway something was wrong. Settling her on the thin mattress, he couldn't help but stroke her cheek gently, looking into sea green eyes that were far too dilated after their encounter with The Oracle. The way she gave him that dopey half smile melted his resistance, sending him unconsciously leaning closer to her ruby red lips.

He knew what those lips tasted like, knew what her body felt like against his own. Those sensations haunted his dreams. The raw power in her kiss.

"Why are you being so nice?" she had asked, tilting her head up at him.

He had smiled, pulling back his affections. Olivia was as rough as they came, ruthless and cunning, but her emotional state was delicate after the breakup with Blake. He knew that. He also knew that he wanted this enough that he had to be patient, to be sure he wouldn't just be a rebound. No one else had stood by his side, had protected what was his without question. No one else gave him as much shit.

His beast may have claimed her first, and fear might have kept Logan from leaving Lorraine and pursuing her sooner, but his mind and heart agreed, she was going to be his.

Lost in his own memories, he thought back to Olivia and the enchanted room. Getting her into that room had accelerated his plans, dangerously so.

He had envisioned their first time together, dreamed about it and thought he had it planned out fairly well. There was a certain amount of pressure trying to woo a succubus who excelled at sex. Even Blake couldn't seem to leave her alone.

All of that had gone out of the window. With the added push of the enchanted room, he lost all rational thought. He only knew he needed to claim her, to make her his forever.

He had and the aftermath had badly shaken his core. Olivia had tried to stop him; he hadn't listened. She had told Jerry it wasn't rape and that eased his conscience some, but not entirely. He hadn't obeyed her wishes and it still bothered him that he had lost control that badly.

His mind wanted to travel down that path of thought, but their arrival at Gunner's ended the perusal of his memories.

He clambered down the metal ladder into the bunker, blinking a moment and letting his eyes adjust.

"You've arrived," Blue called out from the darkened back.

Logan moved toward the sound of Blue's voice as his vision returned to normal, Mark's footsteps behind him.

"What did you find?" Logan asked, seeing Gunner behind his massive wall of computer screens.

Gunner turned, pushing up his wire rimmed glasses. "You're not going to like this," he warned.

Logan flicked his gaze to Blue, who just smiled.

"What?" Logan repeated.

"The bullet was composed of iron, sea salt, frankincense, along with wood from the tree it came from, and—" Gunner hesitated, drawing a breath. "Infant blood."

Logan's lion roared to the surface and he tightened his jaw, keeping his beast under control.

"Infant. Blood?" Logan asked.

Gunner nodded. "It might not have been enough to kill the baby."

Logan pulled a chair up next to Gunner. "Can you trace the blood?"

Gunner rubbed his eyes and Logan noted the stale scent of sweat as those bloodshot eyes turned to meet the Alpha's. "I've been trying. None of the databases thus far have yielded any leads. Besides, infant DNA isn't something that is widely recorded."

Logan nodded, crossing his arms over his chest. "Keep digging into it."

"Was that the part I wasn't going to like?" Logan asked.

"Oh, no. Blue wants to shoot you," Gunner admitted.

"What?" Mark exclaimed.

"I want to test the makeup of the bullet in you, less the infant blood. I think someone did quite a bit of research constructing it," Blue stated.

"They used iron, not silver," Mark pointed out.

"Why would someone need to research how to kill a shifter?" Gunner added, leaving unstated that decapitation or extreme blood loss would do the trick.

"Someone who didn't know," Logan guessed. "But that doesn't explain how the person knew to leave wolfsbane."

Logan stood, pulling up his shirtsleeve. "I assume you have a bullet?"

Blue smiled, pulling out his sidearm, caressing it. "All locked and ready to go."

"You can't be serious?" Mark asked.

Logan shrugged, holding out his arm. "It's a small caliber, it should heal instantly."

"Unless there is some truth to the bullet being well researched," Blue countered.

Mark threw his hands up. "Fine."

"Do it outside," Gunner warned, reaching out to protect his high dollar electronics.

No one missed the show as they hurried up the ladder outside.

"Not by the cars," Mark groaned, leaning on the SUV by Gunner.

"I can't believe he agreed to this," Gunner whispered to him.

"Me either," Mark agreed, not bothering to whisper.

Logan watched Blue smile as they faced off. "I have to admit, I'm going to enjoy this."

"Get on with it," Logan muttered.

"Are you sure I can't convince you for a chest shot?"

"No."

The gun echoed loudly as Blue pulled the trigger. It took all of Logan's control not to move, and when the pain laced his upper arm, it took all his control not to kill Blue, who walked up nonchalantly, inspecting the wound.

"The healing is delayed," Blue noted with detachment.

Logan stopped growling, looking down at his arm. Indeed, while the hole was sealing around itself, the bullet having gone straight through, it would stall every few seconds in closing. Blue turned Logan's arm and the wounded shifter hissed.

"Don't be a baby," Blue chided.

"If Olivia wouldn't be upset, I'd end you," Logan hissed back at him.

Blue smiled, looking the pissed off shifter in the eyes. "You wouldn't dream of pissing her off that badly."

Logan growled.

Mark and Gunner came over, Gunner snapping pictures of the wound and pulling out a swab before looking fearfully up at Logan.

"Go ahead," Logan bit out.

Gunner nodded, taking the swab quickly and sealing it in a glass container. He continued to take pictures until the wound had healed, leaving a small white mark behind.

"That is interesting," Mark admitted.

"Why are new ways to kill shifters popping up?" Logan mused. "Someone is coming after us as a whole." It wasn't enough that his own people were betraying him. Sage's double cross had stung Logan deeply. He had appointed her to protect the North and she had sold out her own kind for money and power. It was a miserable reminder of his failures as Alpha.

"Not someone, some race," Blue corrected, his face drawn in anger.

"You believe it's the vampires as well?" Logan questioned.

Blue's piercing gaze shot to Logan. "I know it is. Those blood suckers have always done more harm than good."

"It could just be Zachariah after Olivia," Mark added.

"No, the vampires never do anything without planning and support. One House would never go rogue. It has never ever happened in their long and sordid history," Blue stated with full confidence.

"Not a fan of the vampires?" Gunner asked.

"No," was the extent of Blue's answer. "I have no idea why Olivia has been so tolerant of them."

"They pay the bills," Logan stated, flexing his arm.

"If my math is correct, with the caliber of bullet used, you would have bled out from three hits before your body could heal, due to the delayed healing," Gunner stated, pushing his glasses up his nose. His gaze flicked nervously around the group. "And for the record, I agree with Blue, the vampires are not to be trusted. None of my other clients kidnap me for my services."

Logan couldn't argue with that logic.

"You should be thanking your lucky stars she saved you," Blue said, his eyes glossy as he addressed Logan.

"I'd have traded places with her in a heartbeat, if it meant she wasn't harmed." Logan answered, not liking Blue's tone.

"Then you would be a fool. While she will be able to bounce back from this, you would have left your mate and child alone. How long do you think a succubus would last against the challenges the shifters would levy?" Blue chided.

Logan growled, "No one would have killed her."

Mark reached out, placing a hand against Logan's arm. "As much as it pains me, Blue has a point. Your death was carefully planned out. She is hard to kill."

Logan didn't care for this conversation. "Is there anything else, Gunner?" he asked.

Gunner shook his head.

"Let's go," Logan commanded.

...

"Seriously, how much longer?" I groaned. The backpack was heavy and I was sweating. I was really wishing I wasn't so fucking corporeal. Not to mention, this was day fucking two.

"We are almost there," Doyle stated. I could tell by his tone, he found this amusing. The landscape had been repetitive, flat red rock until we hit the mountains of even redder rock. I was wishing for flat after that. We scaled the often sheer rock face until my fingers were sliced and I was having flashbacks to visiting The Oracle.

At least there was a prize at the end with her. A griffin feather seemed pretty easy. How solidly could those things be attached, anyways? I was surprised they weren't just collected at random, since they were needed for spells.

"Let's make camp here. We can continue the rest of the way after we eat," The Magician stated.

I crashed down, leaning against an outcropping of rocks.

"So, are griffins the same here as in my world? Head of an eagle, body of a lion?" I asked, pulling out a chunk of bread.

46

"Yes," The Magician answered.

I shrugged. "How did griffins end up here, anyways? The witches' target broader than just magicians and succubi?"

"It was far broader. Any clan that aligned themselves with the succubi was seen as a threat. The minotaurs, griffins, mermaids, and unicorns were all locked away."

"Oh man, you are going to make so many of the kids happy when they hear mermaids and unicorns are real."

"You have children?" The Magician asked, sitting forward, attentive to my answer.

"No, Selena sterilized me. I can't have children." I let that sink in for a moment, seeing his disgust and disappointment.

He shook his head. "I can't apologize enough for that decision."

"I take in other children, other succubi like me who have no families, who are forgotten about by everyone else," I told him.

"How many do you have?"

I shrugged. "Living with us, fourteen. Another six in college or working."

"That is quite a brood," he commented.

"Unwanted children are my specialty."

He grunted. I might have been adding salt to a wound, but I didn't see it as undeserved.

"You didn't take any jerky," Doyle commented, holding out a piece to me.

I shook my head. "Thanks, but I don't eat meat."

That shocked him, which was a funny look on a minotaur.

"Such a lovely picnic party," cooed a voice above me.

The Magician's head jerked up, his body tensing as he slowly stood. Doyle growled, which I have to admit was an impressive sound.

I looked up, into the beady eyes of the griffin. A long, curved beak was poised inches from my head.

"Hey, you speak," I commented.

It regarded me, its head shifting from side to side.

"You are not of this vile world," it commented, inching closer.

"True, I'm trying get back to my own world and need one of your feathers," I informed it.

The griffin stood, jumping down in front of me.

47

"Why would I help you leave here if I cannot?"

"Goodness of your heart?" I tried.

It preened its feathers, ruffling their lemon and russet silken appearance.

"I suppose The Magician didn't tell you our feathers only come off in death."

"Fucking shit, no, he did not." I stared pointedly at The Magician.

"I had planned on telling you," he stated.

The griffin laughed, "Who are you to him, my dear? His latest conquest?"

"His daughter," I stated flatly.

That got its attention. "Daughter, no, it cannot be," it whispered, peering closer at me.

"Well, I am just going off of his word. I suppose this could be an elaborate hallucination."

"How did you return? Where is the portal?" The griffin stomped closer to me.

"My body is in my world, my soul here." I shrugged, I didn't understand it.

Apparently, the griffin did, as it nodded in thought. "You are a fool to think you can reunite the two," it asserted, turning to The Magician.

"My power is plentiful to complete such a small task," he answered.

The griffin tsked, which was a weird sound from a beak.

I reached up and yanked on its feathers. They didn't budge, but the griffin did spin around.

"Maybe we can just cut it off?" I backed away from the snapping jaws of the griffin. "Dude, do not make me kill you!" I yelled at it.

"You can try, pretty," it hissed at me, continuing to snap its jaws. I rolled back, pinned against the rock. I pulled a throwing dagger from across my chest, rejoicing in its cool metal touch, flicking it toward my target as soon as I grabbed it.

It bounced harmlessly off the griffin's thick coat.

"Fucker," I groaned out, annoyed.

Doyle groaned and the griffin's eyes widened in surprise before it was tossed away from me. I hustled to Doyle's side, looking down at his hands. Rivulets of blood dripped from his fingertips into the dusty red ground.

"Shit, Magician, can you do something about that?" I asked, palming more knives, moving my body in front of Doyle.

"I don't need healing or protecting," Doyle grunted, pushing me aside.

"Fine," I ground out.

The griffin screamed, launching over the top of the rock face, claws extended. I threw the knives with all my nonexistent strength. One stuck and orange blood oozed from the wound.

"Score one for me," I smiled, before I flung myself forward and out of the way of her destruction. I felt fairly confident in calling it a she now; there were no dangling bits that I could see, and as she had soared overhead, I tried aiming for dangly bits.

Doyle caught the brunt of the hit, her claws raking across his midsection. He pushed her back with impressive strength, his stomach bleeding freely.

I cast a quick glance at The Magician. He was screwing with little packets of who-knew-what. I growled, having the distasteful feeling of being used.

I opted for a sword, using the rock to launch myself onto her back from behind, my legs locking around her neck. The bitch, yeah I decided she was totally female, launched into the air.

"Whoa, this is not cool!" I screamed as Doyle's massive form grew smaller.

Bending at the waist, I held the blade against her throat. "Down, bitch."

She cawed at the open sky and if I wasn't so freaked out about flying, it might, almost, have been slightly exciting.

She rolled and I used both hands to hold onto the blade around her neck. What happens to body-less soul beings when they fall? I didn't want to find out. The blade didn't cut into my hand, although it should have. I can't say I wasn't loving not getting hurt.

I pulled the blade up, warm liquid spilling over my hands.

She flew straight up into the sky. Seriously, not what I was after. A popping noise deafened my ears and suddenly we were still. I relaxed my grip on the steel, turning to see that the distance between us and the ground was dwindling rapidly.

The Magician looked strained, fighting against the will of the griffin. At least, I assumed from his pained expression that he was the one responsible for our sudden change of direction.

"Use the sword and cut her feathers off. It will be enough," he ground out through clenched teeth as the griffin hit the red dirt in front of him.

I relaxed my grip. Twisting to the left, I sliced a handful of feathers off before I slipped off her back.

"It was that easy the entire time?" I grunted, going behind him to check on Doyle.

Doyle's wounds were healing, looking more like scratches than life threatening wounds, although he was going to need a new tunic.

I picked up my discarded bag, shoving the griffin feathers in it before securing it to my back.

"How long can you keep her like that?" I asked, helping Doyle up.

"A while, let us head down the mountain," The Magician stated.

I picked up Doyle's pack, shifting it on my shoulder before following him down the mountain.

"This was his plan all along," Doyle informed me, moving quickly for one still healing. "He never planned to put either of us in harm's way."

"Did he tell you that before or after we were attacked?" I questioned.

"Before," The Magician said behind me.

The griffin's cry had us all moving faster.

"How far before she stops trying to kill us?" I yelled.

"I don't actually know," The Magician mused.

"Wonderful," I groaned. The downward force of air above us had us all looking up.

"Get down!" my father yelled, before covering my body with his own.

I felt his weight leave, his cry next to my ear.

"Dammit," I hissed, dropping my bags and running back up the rocky hill. I scrambled up to the top, tracking the griffin's progress. I pulled a dagger, throwing it as I ran. It landed in her underbelly, lodging there. She cried out, still holding my father in her claws.

Learning her lesson on flying above me, she changed her altitude, dropping next to the mountain. It was a smart tactic, leaving her hide exposed to only one side.

I added a burst of speed before vaulting over the edge, clamping down on the scream that tried to force its way past my lips.

The winged asshole didn't change course. I pulled my sword and, with the help of my basically suicidal momentum, pierced her thick, feathered hide just behind her skull. It would be a killing blow for most Supernaturals; hopefully my luck would hold here. I clutched hard to the sword hilt, her scream making me want to cover my ears. She angled her body skyward, sending my sword slicing down her back.

I had to be close to killing her. Such a desperate move was foolish and instinct-based.

Her body went slack with a final cry. We had one moment of perfectly balanced stillness in the air before it all came crashing down. My fingers still clung to the sword, as though it would afford me some sort of protection.

It didn't, and I will admit I screamed before I blasted apart against the hard packed dirt below us.

I thought it would hurt. I had no idea how much. I bounced several times against the dense ground, my body seeming to split apart and form back together with each ricochet against the red dirt.

I came to a stop, terrified to even try moving, breathing shallowly, tears staining my face. A groan from far behind me had me pushing up to make sure the griffin wasn't moving.

It wasn't. I went back to lying on my stomach.

"For the love of the seven hells!" my father cried out. "Did you even think that through before you jumped off a cliff and almost killed yourself?"

He stomped closer, his shadow falling over me. "Can't kill me. I'm just a soul," I grunted back.

"Oh, smart. You don't even know if that's true." He hauled me up.

"I'm still alive, aren't I?"

He put an arm around my shoulder, having no response for that.

"Let's get you back."

...

"What's our next move?" Mark asked in the SUV, driving back to the mansion.

"The newborn blood," Logan answered. "When Tommy gets off of school, we will have him find all missing and deceased infants and see if we get lucky."

"Lucky how?" Mark asked.

Logan shook his head. "I don't know."

Back at the mansion, Logan gave Katie the rest of the day off. He needed some time with Ginny. She rolled around on the living room floor, shoving her balls and yelling until Logan rolled them back to her.

Mark and Jerry were with him. They were all waiting for Tommy.

"Logan! The next time you text with no details, I'm cutting school!" Tommy yelled out, slamming his backpack against the kitchen table, walking in with his laptop under his arm.

"No, you're not," Logan reminded him.

Tommy gave Ginny a kiss before settling down next to Logan on the couch. "Hit me."

Logan sighed. This wasn't the type of thing he wanted to involve a kid in, even a genius kid.

"Logan, I can handle it," Tommy said to him, pulling out his laptop. Damn incubus emotional sensors. "Olivia trusted me to handle things because she knows all the shit I've survived."

Logan smiled at Tommy, nodding. "I need you to look up all missing infants and infant deaths."

"What's the time frame?" Tommy asked.

Logan groaned, "Is there a way to track that?"

"Eh, maybe, maybe not." Tommy's fingers flew over the keyboard. "Local?" he asked.

"I don't know," Logan said, feeling worse and worse about the situation. "It's a long shot."

Tommy patted Logan's knee. "It's okay. I'll find it," he offered, before retreating to his room.

"We need a break," Jerry whispered.

Logan agreed, but he didn't know what form it was going to come in.

"How does Olivia usually do this?" he asked, rolling the ball back to Ginny.

Jerry laughed. "She usually just pisses people off until they come after her directly."

Logan huffed a laugh. "I think it's time to pay a visit to the vampires."

Mark and Jerry both smiled.

"I need a few hours to prep," Jerry said, rubbing his hands together.

"How hard are those silver chains to make?" Logan asked.

Jerry huffed, "I can do it, but I can't do it by tonight. Nor will I be any use after I complete them."

"When this is over, I want a pair made. I have a feeling they will come in useful," Logan stated.

Jerry nodded and Mark threw him the keys as he left.

Logan sighed, rolling the ball back to Ginny.

"Should we call ahead?" Mark asked.

"No, I think the element of surprise will serve us well. I do think we should have backup. Where the fuck is Hudson?" Logan asked, pulling out his phone.

"Logan," Hudson answered.

"Where the fuck are you?"

"So it's a long story, but I'm visiting my friend, and I do believe I have a lead."

"Get to the new house, now," Logan growled. "We are paying a visit to the vampires."

"Yes! This shit is getting good."

...

"Are you certain you don't want to see Olivia again?" Mark asked cautiously.

Ginny was asleep and Ali had her monitor. She and Grant occupied the other end of the house, where it was quieter but they could still be close at hand if the children needed anything.

Logan watched Hudson arrive, pay the cabbie, and pull out a backpack before sauntering up to the gate.

"I'm certain," Logan answered. He couldn't see her like that again, unable to inflate her own lungs or feed herself. His hope would dwindle, and he needed to be strong, for the packs and for the children.

"Certain of what?" Hudson asked.

"That your intel needs to be exceptionally fantastic for you to be so late," Logan growled.

"Easy, cousin," Hudson teased. Logan glared at him as they walked to the SUV, Logan sliding into the front seat. Mark was driving and Jerry was in the backseat, completing his final preparations as Hudson hopped in next to him.

"What's that smell?" Hudson asked, wrinkling his nose.

"Hex bags," Jerry answered with an evil grin.

"What are hex bags?" Logan asked.

Mark groaned.

"Hex bags are old magic. It takes time for them to work, but they cause bleeding from the eyes, electrical shortages, and double vision," Jerry stated gleefully.

"Don't forget itching, uncontrollable itching," Mark added.

Jerry laughed, "I almost forgot about that one."

Mark shivered and Logan cracked a small smile.

"Hudson, what is this intel you seem so proud of?" Logan demanded again. He didn't enjoy repeating himself.

"I found Raphael."

Logan turned in his seat to see Hudson's smiling face.

"How?" Mark asked.

Hudson shrugged. "Let's just say Olivia isn't the only one who has tech geniuses working for her."

Jerry laughed, "Well, she's the only one who has a fifteen-year-old tech genius working for her."

Hudson cut a glance to Jerry. "Fifteen? That seems a little young for this line of work."

Jerry shook his head. "He's an old soul."

Logan cleared his throat, not wanting to get into it. "What did Raphael say? And if I have to keep prompting you, it's going to hurt."

Hudson leaned forward. "First off, that he was very sorry to hear about Olivia. Second, that he will be keeping in touch from now on and third, he doesn't think the attack on your life was vampire related. He does think that the vampires will try and eliminate her now that she is injured."

Logan growled, "Olivia is well guarded. Does he have any idea who is after me?"

Hudson shifted in his seat. "Yeah, and you are going to be pissed."

Logan turned, piercing Hudson with his gaze. Hudson quickly took an interest in the passing scenery, avoiding eye contact.

"Hudson," Logan growled.

"I've been having an uprising, a small issue in Idaho." Hudson pulled on his t-shirt collar. "It hasn't caused much trouble."

Logan groaned, turning back around. "Hudson," he warned.

"Right, well apparently, I should have been paying more attention to them. Raphael was pretty convinced that is where the attack originated from."

Logan leaned his head back, taking a deep breath. "Hudson, I should kill you."

"Yeah, I know," Hudson reluctantly agreed, his good humor gone.

"If you weren't related to me, I would." Hudson breathed a sigh of relief. "But don't think for a second this is over. I will think of a fitting punishment for your lies."

"I didn't technically lie," Hudson tried.

"I'd stop talking now," Jerry warned, next to him in the backseat.

Hudson grunted, taking the hint.

Logan drummed his fingers against his knee.

"How do you want to handle the guard gate?" Mark asked.

"Can we run it?"

Tommy's voice came on over the speakers. "I wouldn't recommend it. They have a shoot first, ask questions later policy. Not to mention the tire spikes will ruin a quick getaway if you need it."

"Tommy," Logan began.

"I can override most of the tech, but I'd suggest not getting violent at the gate," Tommy continued.

"Tommy," Logan tried again.

"Plus, I have located Tate and Mal, and you told them Mal is off limits, right?" Tommy steamrolled over him.

"TOMMY!" Logan bellowed.

"What?"

"How long have you been listening?"

"Since you left he manor," Tommy answered.

"Do you see a problem with that?" Logan tried.

"Nope," Tommy answered.

"Oh, and Hudson, I'm pulling satellite photos now, so if you can narrow down where the rebels are, I'd appreciate it," Tommy added.

"It's not a town, but I think I have coordinates I can send you," Hudson answered, shifting in the backseat for his phone.

"Wonderful. Alright gents, be nice," Tommy warned as they approached the gate.

Logan growled, looking over to Mark. "I had no idea," Mark said, not meeting his gaze.

The guard at the gate was a vampire, as Logan expected at this late hour.

"Alpha, what can we do for you?"

Vampires, always politically correct. "We are here to see Tate and Mal."

The guard nodded. "Did you have an appointment?"

Logan just stared at the guard.

"Let me just make a few calls." The guard pulled the thick glass closed.

"Who is Mal?" Hudson asked softly from the backseat. Based on the fact Logan couldn't hear the guard, he thought they were safe to speak.

"Olie granted her protection for saving Ginny," Logan replied. "That protection extends to the shifters as well."

Hudson whistled. "That is one well protected vampire."

The guard opened the thick glass. "Mal will meet you at the front door."

The wooden guard gate slid up smoothly and they parked without incident.

Mal was anxious, pacing on the front steps of the Centennial Compound, with black clad security behind her.

Seeing Logan moving toward her, she broke away from the guards on the steps, running into his arms.

"I'm so sorry, Logan," she whispered. "I swear, I haven't heard anything. I didn't know," she pleaded rapidly with him.

Logan stopped moving but watched the guards carefully as he wrapped his arms around her.

"I know, Mal." He could scent the truth in her words and it eased his worry slightly. "What you did I can never repay," he assured her, his voice soft against her ear. "You have the protection of the packs as well."

Mal's body sagged against him. "Thank you," she whispered.

That deep relief had him questioning what was really going on inside these walls.

Mal pulled back smiling, before she turned to embrace Jerry and Mark. Hudson extended his hand with a charming smile.

"I can't believe we haven't met before," he oozed, bringing her hand to his lips.

Mal raised an eyebrow at him before looking at Logan. He just shrugged. Internally, he questioned if he was making the right decision letting his cousin keep his head. Once it got out that Hudson's incompetence had resulted in the

Mate being shot, others would question Logan's strength for not taking care of the problem.

He was going to have to remove him from the job of Compass Alpha, that much he knew. Wonderful, now he had another spot to fill.

Mal disengaged from Hudson. "Come on, Tate wants to see you guys."

Logan followed Mal through the twelve-foot-tall solid oak doors. Inside, the sconces gave off limited lighting. Logan didn't need it.

Jerry stubbed his foot.

"Damn lighting," he cursed under his breath.

"Here, take my hand," Mark offered behind Logan.

Mal led them up a grand staircase, carpeted in black, with an iron handrail. The pillars were twisted metal, jagged points jutting out between them, perfect for staking vampires. Logan turned his gaze, taking in the painted portraits of Centennial House's past. Vampires sat poised, looking out from cold, vicious eyes.

Logan turned his attention to Mal and the head of the staircase. Vampires watched them with hunger, their eyes sunken in, their faces drawn, their clothing hanging loosely on sickly bodies. Low growls issued from their throats.

Logan stopped at the top of the stairs.

"What is going on here?" he demanded.

"We are starving," a blond vampire said, stepping forward.

"Why?" Logan asked.

They all cast furtive looks at Mal, who, for the record, was not starving.

"Come Logan, let us talk with Tate." Mal tried reaching out to him.

Logan stilled. Mal didn't look malnourished, but she also had the succubi to feed off of.

Logan turned to the blond. "Stay here. If Tate doesn't give me the answers I want, I'll feed you my blood to know what is going on."

The entire vampire population surged forward slightly, the blond bobbing her head in rapid agreement.

Mal swallowed, a gesture she didn't need to do anymore, before continuing to walk, her posture stiff.

"You sure that's the best idea?" Hudson whispered.

"It's what Olivia would have done."

Mark laughed. "She would have demanded answers before moving on. She could get shit done."

"And turn everything on its head," Mal said with warmth.

Mal opened a black door, carved with tightly woven details Logan didn't bother to look at before following her in.

The door closed solidly behind them. Logan had no doubt it was soundproofed. If not, Tate should have been looking a fair bit more upset.

"You have our deepest condolences for Olivia," Tate began, bowing his head slightly.

"Save it, she's not dead. I can't say the same for your House," Logan snapped out.

Tate's eyes widened before he looked over at Mal. She shrugged, tactfully looking away.

"What concern is that of yours?" Tate questioned.

Logan scoffed, "It shouldn't fucking be any, but both our species are out of the closet. I don't need your entire House starving and waiting to kill humans."

Tate slammed his fist down on the black desk with carvings matching the door. "None of my people have killed any humans."

"They will," Logan answered with absolute certainty. "If you think your House will choose death before killing a human, you are delusional. You have a ticking time bomb on your hands."

Tate turned away, facing his bookcase with the same black artwork. Fucking vampires and their love of black and blood red.

"The situation is far more complicated—"

"Save it," Logan interrupted. "If I have learned one thing from Olivia, it is that shit is never that fucking complicated."

"And a healthy love of swear words," Mal added with a smirk.

Logan gave her an answering grin. "Secondly, if you cannot take care of your own, I will."

He turned his laser focus back to Tate. "So Tate, let's try this again. What the fuck is going on?" Logan demanded.

Tate slammed both his fists against the bookcase before turning back to Logan.

"Zachariah is decimating my House." Tate's voice broke and Mal moved to him. He stopped her with a hand.

58

"Kill him," Hudson suggested.

Tate laughed. "Kill a Master European vampire, who is older and stronger than me? Aside from the repercussions from the other Houses, how do you expect me to defeat him?"

"Olivia could do it," Jerry whispered.

Everyone turned to him. Logan's heart constricted painfully. She would have figured it out with a straightforward approach that left everyone impressed.

Jerry looked up, blinking rapidly.

"I had planned on approaching her when she got back in town after The Conferences," Tate admitted, his hands braced on the back of his black chair, head bowed.

Logan rubbed a hand over his forehead. "How is he stopping your house from feeding?"

Mal answered for Tate, "The blood bank driver won't deliver here anymore after the last three were killed brutally, even with our armed guards on high alert. We've hunted at Halfling, but no bloodletting is allowed on the property. When we try to take our snack home, both the vampire and the human are killed. Our families, who we went to as a last resort, have been brutally destroyed." Mal's voice broke on the last word.

"Everyone is terrified," Tate said, lifting his head up. "I can't protect my own House."

Logan sighed, "What are you willing to give up, Tate?"

"Excuse me?" he asked.

"You heard me," Logan answered.

Tate stood up straight, crossing his arms over his chest. "What do you want?"

"The loyalty of your House to Olivia and me," Logan stated. He knew he was asking a lot, but Olivia had asked much from him and she always delivered in return.

"So we can be your personal lap dogs?" Tate hissed.

"So you can live, idiot," Hudson added.

Logan smiled. "He's not wrong."

Tate turned to Mal. "Is this your doing?" He knocked over a stack of papers on his desk. "You have all the protection, all the food you need. Are you trying to make us slaves to the shifters?"

Mal stood forward, her eyes ambering. "I did what I did to keep myself safe, which you cannot do. Take the deal, Tate. It's the only way we avoid a mass murder."

"NO!" Tate yelled. "This is my House. I will take care of it."

"That's the wrong answer," Hudson said softly. "You are playing a dangerous hand."

"What does Zachariah want from you?" Jerry asked. Good thinking, Jerry, Olivia's voice whispered in Logan's head.

"The same thing you want. My House," Tate answered.

Logan scoffed, "You sell out to him, and we will kill all of you."

"This conversation is over. Show them out," Tate commanded Mal, waving a dismissive hand.

Her mouth opened and closed. "Tate," she pleaded.

"No, I'd rather sell out to a vampire than a shifter."

"That was the wrong decision," Jerry echoed, sorrow lacing his words.

Logan took a deep breath. "I couldn't agree more. You've made yourself a powerful enemy this day, Tate." He turned to Mal. "Our agreement stands. If you would like to come with us now, we will protect you."

Mal turned to Tate, searching his face, her eyes misting over. "Tate," she whispered again.

Tate shook his head. "I'll stay for now," Mal whispered, turning to Logan. "But I imagine I'll be calling in that debt soon."

Logan nodded. "We will see ourselves out."

Hudson opened the door and Logan walked out. The blond vampire stood there, her hunger making her drool, her eyes bright yellow.

"I don't want to leave you like this," he began, meeting their eyes to show his honesty. "I offered Tate a deal: he swears loyalty to Olivia and me, I make your feeding problems go away. He has decided to join with Zachariah instead. I am sorry, but to go against Tate's wishes would only put all of us in danger."

The blond's lip quivered. "What do we do?" she whispered, looking back at the closed doors.

"I'd suggest finding a new Master. How does it work with the vampires, if you kill it, you keep it?" Hudson asked.

"No, House Masters are appointed," the blond said softly.

"Can you rebel?" Hudson asked.

The blond shook her head. "They'll send an army to destroy us all. Even if Tate had sided with you, they would have sent an army, but belonging to Zachariah..."

Logan growled, "Not if I kill him first."

With that, they headed out. Logan had a target, actually he had two, and he was going to make sure neither of them lived to bother him again.

His group stayed silent on their march outside. Once the car doors closed, Hudson whistled. Jerry clapped and Mark just drove away.

"I hate the fucking vampires," Logan growled.

"Are you really going after Zachariah?" Mark asked.

"Yes, Olivia thought he was going after her. She read Nathaniel's thoughts that Zachariah was there when I was—" He left that thought unfinished. Everyone knew, and he didn't need to relive it. "That is enough for me. But first we deal with the uprising in Idaho," Logan added, turning to look at Hudson.

"You going to remove me from my position?" Hudson asked, grimacing.

"I'm giving it thought," Logan told him before turning back around. "Serious thought."

Mark cleared his throat. "Jerry, how did it go with those hex bags?"

"I left the itching one in Tate's office." He laughed gleefully.

"Tommy," Logan tried.

"Yeah boss," he said around a mouthful of food.

"What have you found on Idaho?"

"Nothing. I'm still waiting on Hudson's coordinates."

"I need you to find Zachariah as well."

"I've been looking for him since Olie told me he tortured you. The bastard has gone to ground," Tommy grunted.

"Hudson will be sending those coordinates now, let me know what you find. We are headed home." Logan ended the call; well, he hoped he had.

...

The walk back to the Aladdin-style palace was long. So freaking long. Like what the hell, why aren't there cars here?

61

I was pretty sure Doyle and The Magician were done listening to me bitch. Also pretty sure that I didn't give a shit.

"Finally." I flopped down on the cot, ditching my pack.

My father unpacked all the griffin feathers delicately. "These will fetch quite a price."

I pushed into a sitting position. "What else do we need?"

The sun dipped below the distant mountains, the never-ending red glowing everywhere.

"Tomorrow, daughter," my father, The Magician, stated.

"You can't even tell me what it is?"

He turned from the door. "So you can wander the halls again in search of it?"

I huffed, he had a point. "Don't even think of locking that door."

"I'd never restrain you, my daughter. You can wash up through there." He waved a hand and a door in the stone opened.

"Neat trick," I said. I turned back, seeing them both gone.

I went and checked the door, finding it unlocked as The Magician had promised.

They were fucking lucky.

I headed into the stone opening, finding a claw foot tub full of steaming water. I sighed, alright, that I could get used to. Could I wash in my soul state? Guess I was going to find out.

...

Lying heavily in their bed, Logan sighed as he listened to Ginny's baby monitor and the white noise machine, his arm behind his head.

Things at the Centennial House hadn't gone well, at all, they'd gone straight to Hades, quickly. Logan had pushed Tate right into Zachariah's arms. No, that wasn't right. Tate was weak as a leader; his inability to protect his House was going to cause everyone a nightmare.

How could Logan fix it? How could he feed an entire houseful of vampires?

The only option he saw was posting patrols around the House, waiting for the vampires to lose their shit. Unless Tate really did take Zachariah's deal. The house would be fed, wouldn't it?

Fucking vampire politics. His numbers were not never-ending, and those currently protecting his house were missing work and their lives to be sure everyone was protected.

At least Hudson had been able to track down Raphael. That was an unexpected bonus. Let's hope the self-proclaimed "protector" lived up to his name.

Actually, maybe Raphael would watch Centennial House. It wasn't a terrible idea. Why was Zachariah entrenching himself in that House, anyway?

Did it matter? It wouldn't to Olivia, but it did to him. This couldn't all be because Olivia killed his vampire child who had kidnapped Tommy, could it?

His thoughts circled around, until finally he slept.

...

I stared out the narrow window, so fucking tired of the color red. I wanted caramel eyes and dark blond hair. I wanted pizza and dessert. I wanted to be whole. I wanted my mate. Drawing a breath, I turned away from the window.

I missed Logan, his emotions flowing along with him, his protective nature, his snoring. Okay, I didn't really miss his snoring. But I probably wouldn't complain about it, maybe, for a while.

Chapter 4

Morning came, chasing away the darkest red and steeping the miserable expanse of dirt in pale yellows. I sat up, rubbing sleep from my eyes. I needed to get back to my body and back home. This little game of scavenger hunt needed to pick up the fucking pace.

I went back into the same stone room to splash cool water on my face before I dressed in yesterday's clothing. Or four days ago's clothing or whatever. I slouched onto the cot, picking up my pack to eat stale bread and hardened cheese.

I really missed pizza.

The door opened, but it wasn't Doyle or The Magician—my father.

A slight woman in a pale blue dress blinked her large brown eyes at me. She looked down the hall before looking back at me.

"What do we have here?" she asked, her voice high-pitched and grating. The pitch didn't match her soft outward appearance.

I raised an eyebrow, not letting my eyes flick to where I had laid my daggers.

"Cat got your tongue, my dear?" she asked, closing the door behind her with a sway of her slim hips.

I leaned back against the wall, keeping my hands relaxed in my lap. My daggers were hidden under the crumpled up black dress I was using as a pillow. Some habits are impossible to break. I was glad I hadn't placed my trust in the wards The Magician had placed. I was also slightly disappointed.

Logan had been pissed to find my daggers in the mansion with Ginny in our bed. I argued, all the more reason to keep weapons close by. He didn't share my logic, but of course, he grew claws.

I tilted my head at her as she sat down on The Magician's stool, tapping her olive fingers against the wooden top.

"Oh, come on now, you can tell me, my dear. How a sweet thing like you wandered into The Magician's clutches?"

I narrowed my eyes at her. I could feel her power wash over me, trust and safety bathing my body.

"Nice try," I told her dryly.

Her eyes narrowed at me. "Why, he has picked up quite a rarity. I wonder if the Queen knows," she taunted.

The door opened again and The Magician walked in. He ignored the woman sitting on his chair, although her posture went rigid, fear leaking off her pores.

My father handed me a plate with eggs and toast. I inhaled deeply before digging in. Doyle closed the door, not moving his large body from in front of it as he crossed his hairy arms over his repaired green tunic.

"Has she bothered you at all?" The Magician asked me.

"Nope, just being nosy," I said around a mouthful of food.

The Magician nodded before turning to face the woman.

"Delores, what do you think you are doing in my workroom?"

I couldn't see her through his back, but the quiver in her voice was evidence enough that my father was a powerful force to be reckoned with. Nice. If I was throwing my lot in blindly, at least I was throwing in with a powerful ally, even if he might be the bad guy. Based on my mother, I was picking between shitty and shittier.

"The Queen wishes an audience," Delores stated, changing the subject.

"Really? Why would she wish that?" The Magician asked.

"She heard about the griffin feathers," Delores answered, quite compliant.

Doyle rumbled, "It was only a matter of time."

"Yes," The Magician agreed, "I suppose it was."

"Leave us, we will present her after she eats and dresses." The Magician waved a dismissive hand and Delores sprang from her borrowed seat, fleeing the room. Doyle lumbered to the side, his deep set eyes watching her intently as she fled.

The Magician occupied her abandoned seat, turning gravely serious eyes upon me. "I was hoping to avoid this meeting."

"Who is the Queen?" I asked, setting my empty plate down.

"Your mother, the most powerful succubus," Doyle answered.

"Great, will she know I'm her daughter?" I asked.

The Magician and Doyle both shrugged. "She has given away many children over the years. I'm not sure she cares of the blood relation. She only cares to assess your power, whether you are a threat to her," The Magician explained.

"Ah, so I need to be very, very corporeal."

"Yes," they answered in unison.

I picked up the black dress I had been using as a pillow. "Any chance you can magic this wrinkle free?"

He smiled and the dress floated up, in perfect condition.

"That's handy." I went into the stone room to change, running damp hands over my hair, trying to tame it into something presentable.

"Let's get going. I can't imagine the Queen has an abundance of patience." If she was anything like me, or I suppose, if I was anything like her.

The Magician cracked a smile. "That she does not. Let me do the talking."

"Gladly," I grunted. I knew the shit my temper and mouth got me into.

We turned right, and my steps slowed as we headed to the sunken, polished room. This time, a golden throne sat at the head, occupied by a woman who looked damn similar to me, staring daggers at me. Well, hello to you too, mother.

"Magician, so good of you to join us," she purred, her strawberry blond hair piled high on top of her head. A delicate golden crown intertwined through her locks, chandelier earrings with red diamonds drooping heavily from her lobes. Around her neck twisted more gold, in the form of a serpent. I was curious if it was real.

"What can I do for you, my Queen?" he asked, his tone bored. He didn't bow, standing instead with his legs braced wide and his hands clasped behind his back. Doyle hung back to his left and I mirrored the position on his right.

I wished I had daggers.

"I heard you've obtained quite a collection of griffin feathers," she taunted, crossing her legs, her wine dress sliding up to her tan hip. Apparently, underwear wasn't a thing here, or at least it wasn't for her.

The Magician stayed silent, but I caught the twitch of his lip from the corner of my eye.

The Queen stood, her jewelry chiming together, her dress opening up to drape over her amble bosom. She descended the steps, her bare feet kissing the polished stone. She ignored The Magician, staring into my eyes.

"And what do we have here?" she crooned. I stared into her eyes, trying hard not to compare our noses or our large eyes and full lips. I saw the intelligent gleam in her gaze, calculating and savvy, but what I felt was a coldness.

She walked around me slowly, her delicate feet adorned in matching gold chains. I cringed, feeling her eyes appraising me. Coming around, she brushed a hand against my bare shoulder. I felt the push of compliance into me before she stopped back in front of me, her wine skirt flowing elegantly behind her.

"Who are you, my dear?" she asked, a smug smile on her lips.

I stared at her, blinking once, lips sealed. She placed her palm against my exposed neck, wrapping her exquisite digits around my throat. She tried pushing compliance again. I felt the barest flick to obey her before I brushed it away.

"I said, who are you?" Her eyes looked nothing like my own, anger darkening them.

I took a step forward; she held her ground and I smiled.

"I'm a decision come to haunt you," I whispered, proud of my clever words.

Fear flashed in her eyes for only a second before she shoved me. "Foolish child, you will not speak to me that way!" Obedience hung heavily in the air.

I braced myself on a step back before shoving her back. "Bitch, I do what the fuck I please," I hissed.

We squared off, circling, and I was really wishing for daggers to cut my bitch of a mother down to size. A small part of me cried, I'll admit. I had hoped for some sort of sorrow or joy at finding me. I wanted an apology for being discarded.

But instead I was now about to brawl with the bitch. The anger seared my insides and I rejoiced in it.

"Enough!" The Magician commanded.

The Queen stopped moving, but I didn't take my eyes off of her.

"Who she is does not concern you," he continued to boom.

"The griffin feathers do," she hissed, turning to storm in his face.

I fought a protective instinct to guard him. He was a big boy who could take care of himself, but I needed him to get home. Plus, my mother had wounded me; I wanted the opportunity to return the favor.

"Yes, the griffin feathers do," my father admitted. He examined his fingernails.

The Queen held her head high, having won that round. I gritted my teeth, watching her sway back to her throne. She sat grandly, assistants fluffing out her minimal dress.

"How do you plan on repaying me for the death of such a fine creature?" she asked smugly.

"An elixir of course, to magnify your already powerful charms," The Magician answered.

The Queen leaned forward, exposing her chest. "I'm listening."

"Of course, it will take some time," he continued. I'll say this for the man claiming to be my father, he had patience, cunning, and vampire-like political skills.

She leaned back in her throne. "I care not for the time, Magician." She waved her hand dismissively. "We have nothing but."

I didn't look at The Magician. Not all of us had ample time.

He inclined his head, turning to face me. I watched him closely, preparing to turn.

"Oh, and daughter," my mother began. My father's face drained of color before he turned to face her. I steeled myself, ready for a brawl. Doyle at my back had the same thought, standing close behind me. "How did you get away from Selena and back to us?"

My father reached for me, probably to silence me as I stepped closer to her. "Selena is dead."

The Queen hissed at me, "You lie."

I smiled, "No, I don't." I was happy to piss her off with the truth.

She stood, her jewelry smashing together. "Selena has been a vital part of our survival here. You wouldn't dare kill such a powerful vampire and someone we depend on."

"She's been dead for almost eight years. Apparently, you've been surviving just fine without her," I answered, crossing my arms over my chest. I couldn't believe this was my mother. She was a disgusting piece of work, even if she was beautiful.

The Queen narrowed her eyes at me. "And what do you know of this? Are you an expert on our survival?"

"Your gold jewelry states all is well in your realm," I answered.

She sneered at me, "You know nothing."

68

"I know enough." I took a step forward. "You are a heartless, selfish leader, who sold her child to a monster."

"Children," my father amended.

"Sold your children," I repeated, shaking my head. "I have no need for you and less respect. Save your pathetic mind games for someone who gives a fuck."

She stepped down from her throne and my father groaned. "How dare you speak to me in such a manor? I will have your life."

I smiled. "Many have tired, none have succeeded. Least of all a spoiled brat."

"I am the Queen Succubus!" she roared, holding her hands outstretched. The air vibrated and I knew she was pushing fear into the air. Her minions behind her bowed, trembling. The Magician stiffened his stance next to me.

"Oh, enough!" I yelled. I felt for my shields, wrapping them around my father and Doyle, who was growling lowly behind me. "You can't hurt me and you can't influence me. I am your daughter and apparently that has afforded me some protection against your insanity."

"Get her out of my sight!" she screamed. Doyle picked me up, tossing me over his shoulder.

"This isn't over!" I screamed back. I was going to end that bitch.

"No, it isn't." Her voice followed me down the hallway.

Doyle set me down inside The Magician's workroom. I was raring for a weapon.

"What is wrong with you?" my father hissed, backing me against the wall. "Why did you taunt her like that?"

"Because I can," I answered, pushing his hands off of me. "I am no slave. I am no servant. I have paid for my freedom in blood and pain. No one, least of all some selfish bitch, will take it from me."

He rubbed his forehead, groaning under his breath. "She is going to have you killed," he warned, sharing a worried look with Doyle.

"She can try. I'm not easy to kill."

The Magician nodded. "Right. Let's get ready for today. We are heading to the Oasis for a shadow lark."

"Is that a bird?" I asked, picking up my clothing from the day before.

"A plant, actually," he answered, turning to his workbench.

I nodded, moving into the stone bathroom to pull off the black dress, leaving it in a pile on the floor.

"You need to strengthen the wards," Doyle said.

I slowed down my dressing, wanting to hear their conversation.

"I am aware. Lilith will send her best mages to break down my protections," The Magician said. I stopped dressing, my head tilted toward the ceiling. My mother, The Queen, was named Lilith. I closed my eyes. I don't believe in coincidences; my money was on her as the inspiration for the biblical demon whore who sucked out the souls of men. Good to know I'd been fighting against the stereotype she created for my entire life.

I finished dressing, picking up the black dress and laying it back on the cot.

"How many more ingredients do we need to break through to my dimension?" I asked, securing the blades across my chest.

"Anxious to return now that you have poked the giant?" The Magician asked.

My movement stilled and I turned to him. "I am not afraid of her. I have faced worse and survived. I am anxious to return to my mate and my life."

"Mate?" My father straightened up at the word.

"You have a mate?" Doyle asked as well.

I rubbed the back of my neck, wishing my mark was still with me. "Yes, I have a mate. I have a Council that I rule and my mate is the Alpha of our country."

"You are a Queen in your own right," my father said, sitting back down with a look of wonder.

I furrowed my brow at him. "I protect those who can't protect themselves. I defend the defenseless, the weaker, those our society has cast out and deemed unworthy. I am not a Queen. I am an Executioner. Being mated to Logan just happened."

"You miss him," Doyle observed.

I strapped the long dagger to my thigh, replying, "Very much," before meeting each of their gazes. "Nothing will stop me from getting back to him and the children."

The Magician nodded. "We have a handful of items left to procure. The hardest was the griffin feather. It should hopefully get easier from here."

I nodded. It didn't matter, easier or harder, I would obtain it all.

"How long will the portal be open for?" I asked, slinging my pack over a shoulder. I was hoping we were heading to the kitchen again. I had eaten most of my food.

"Only a short time," The Magician answered. "You will have to go through in an orb." He closed the door behind us, laying his hand on the worn wood. Symbols flared to life before they dimmed.

He flexed his hand, continuing toward the kitchen. "An orb?" I questioned. I wanted to know how Delores had gotten in through that door, but the answer could piss me off and I needed him, at least for now.

He nodded, casting a look around us. I took the hint and tabled my questions.

In the kitchen, the same woman eyeballed me as I took my provisions.

"I heard you had quite the conversation with your mother," she commented, casting a sly smile as she kneaded dough.

I groaned, "Yeah, we agreed to kill each other." I sniffed the bread in my hand before looking at her.

She laughed, "You have nothing to fear from me. I'd appreciate a change in leadership."

I grunted. I wasn't corporeal anyways, could poison hurt me? Guess we'd find out.

"The food is safe," my father informed me, loading his own pack.

"That's what I said," the cook sneered at him.

"Let's go. I've had enough bickering for one day," The Magician stated. I groaned, following Doyle out.

Once the palace disappeared from view, I picked up with the orb conversation. "Why do I have to travel in an orb? How will I get into an orb?"

"Easily, you are a soul. The space you consume now is because, as we've established, you expect to. But you don't need to. You must be contained when we travel through the portal, or we risk losing you. There will be nothing to hold onto to keep you with us," The Magician answered.

"How do I get back in my body?"

"I will break open the orb over your body. Your soul should be pulled right back in."

I nodded, not taking issue with the "should." It was a gamble, but one I was willing to take.

71

Chapter 5

Logan looked over the reports from Tommy.

"They're gone?" he repeated.

Tommy shifted the images on his three large computer monitors. "As far as I can tell. Granted, their shacks are well hidden, but I haven't seen any movement in the past twenty hours."

Logan rubbed the back of his neck. "We are going there."

Hudson grunted from the doorway, "Idaho?"

Logan growled, "Had you properly taken care of this, I wouldn't be cleaning up your messes."

Hudson averted his gaze. "I guess this is your time to prove why Logan shouldn't kill you," Tommy offered helpfully, turning around in his chair and taking a bite of his red vines.

Logan pulled the remaining candy from his hand. "Breakfast," he commanded.

"Oh geez, the nutrition police are after me." Tommy rolled his eyes, bumping playfully into Logan before heading downstairs.

"You were able to get ahold of Raphael?" Logan asked, following Tommy downstairs.

"I left a message," Hudson replied.

Logan nodded, hearing Ginny's babbling as the children got ready for school.

"Are we going to visit her?" Hudson asked.

"Yes, before we leave. Kass and Darren will be dropping off Hannah and Harrison and coming with us to the hospital."

"Three kids, that seems like a lot for Katie."

"Ali and Grant are here also."

Hudson nodded, finding a place at the table and picking up the plate. Logan kissed Ginny's messy cheek. Tommy was busy shoveling eggs into his mouth, trying to talk over the other kids. It was loud and messy. Logan couldn't imagine going back to his life before the children, the noise, and Olivia.

"You want me to call Mark and Jerry?" Hudson asked, filling his own plate.

"No, I already texted them. Jerry needed a few hours to prep."

"It's strange having a witch on board. I'm surprised you allowed it."

Logan turned to Hudson. "Who Mark loves is none of my concern. Jerry is an excellent asset to the packs and a loyal friend."

"To Olivia," Hudson threw in there.

"Who is my mate, so tread very fucking carefully or I will rethink my stance on not killing you," Logan growled.

Hudson smartly did not make eye contact as he moved to sit down.

Tommy watched them both closely. "You need to me to stay home?" he asked.

"No, I do not want to hear about it from Olie that I let you miss school."

Tommy smiled. "Yeah, she'd have your ass. But hey, don't tell her about the car trick. I want that to be a surprise."

Logan rolled his eyes. "No promises."

The kids left the mansion in protected vehicles thirty minutes later. Logan snuggled with Ginny for a moment before handing her off to Katie, who was wrangling Harrison and Hannah.

"I'm going out of town for a few days, so I'll need you here."

Katie nodded. "I got your message. I came prepared."

"Good. You have Ali's number if you need help with the kids?"

"I'm here," Ali called, pulling her hair up into a bun, her Star Wars pajama bottoms flapping with her quick step.

"Good. Kass and Darren will be back in about an hour. I will be in touch after we touch down in Idaho."

Ali nodded. "Go get 'em tiger!" she said, quoting a cereal commercial.

Logan laughed, "I'm a lion."

"Oh crap, right, my bad," Ali backtracked.

Logan kissed Ginny again and headed out.

Kass and Darren were waiting in the car. Kass had said it was easier if she didn't go in. The kids were less clingy.

"Ready?" he asked.

Kass looked sick but she nodded, sliding in the back. Hudson was smoking a cigar in the front seat. Logan stopped looking at him through the glass. Hudson smiled and waved.

"Darren, stay in the car," he warned, before ripping Hudson's door open.

He was surprised; it spoke volumes to Logan's lax attitude over the years that Hudson didn't see it coming.

Lifting Hudson out of the car by his throat, Logan smashed the back of his head into the drywall, creating an indent. Logan was close to killing him, his beast was demanding it and he tightened his grip. Hudson flailed under him, kicking and coughing.

"I am going to say this once. You will not smoke in, near or around this home, around the children who occupy it or my guests. Your behavior has cost me greatly and if you continue to think so selfishly, I will cure my problems by your death."

Logan dropped him into a pile.

"Get in the car," he commanded. Hudson coughed, putting the cigar out before hacking and stumbling into the car.

"Sorry," he wheezed as his throat rebuilt itself.

"You should have killed him." Kass's voice reached Logan's ears. He looked in the rearview mirror in surprise.

Her face was drawn, eyes red and puffy. "She would have. If the situation was reversed and his mistake left you dying in a hospital bed, she'd make him suffer for weeks, drawing out his pain until he knew nothing but the sound of her voice and the feel of her blades."

Logan bowed his head, starting the SUV. "I know," he answered Kass. "I'm removing him as Alpha of the West."

"You what? I thought you were thinking about it?" Hudson whined.

"I have been thinking about it, and I've decided the best place for me to watch you is here," Logan growled.

Hudson crossed his arms over his chest.

Kass leaned forward. "Be grateful Olivia isn't awake yet."

Hudson cast a look back at her. "You seem pretty confident in her torturing abilities."

Kass smiled and something feral peaked out. "She's gifted, and I've been lucky enough to see her in action."

"She is," Logan agreed. "The woman knows her way around a blade. Rumor has it, the last time a male pissed her off, she skinned his manhood alive before making him eat it."

Hudson covered his crotch, the blood draining from his face.

"You are alive because you are an exceptionally talented and dirty fighter. We are going to need that in the coming days," Logan said. He wasn't sure if the explanation was for Kass or his own beast.

"But your manners could use some work," Kass added.

"Right, sorry about that. I forgot not all Supernaturals live forever."

"No one lives forever," Logan stated.

The rest of the drive to the hospital was silent.

Logan led them to Olie's new room, a private room with a shifter guard by the door. She nodded as they headed in.

"Holy fuck," Hudson whispered. "I didn't know — I didn't know it was this bad."

Kass sobbed silently, clinging to Darren's strong embrace.

The breathing machine inflated her lungs. Logan still felt the warmth inside of him, but he didn't know if it was more or less than before. He just knew she wasn't there.

Kass stepped forward, cradling Olie's hand, raising a shaky hand to stroke her pale face and oily hair.

"Hey beautiful, you come back to me. We all need you here. Hannah and Harrison need you, I need you." Kass shut her eyes tightly. "Please Olie, please come back." She bowed her head before turning back into Darren's arms.

Darren helped her outside with a last look at Olie's prone form.

"She's so tiny," Hudson whispered. "From the way the kids were talking I thought — I didn't — I figured she was fine."

"She's not." Logan said, moving to take her hand as Kass had. He pressed a kiss against the cool palm, not bothering to speak. He would find whoever did this and make them suffer. Olie wasn't the only one who had studied torture.

He turned and Kass's words weighed heavily on him. Would Olivia be disappointed he hadn't killed Hudson?

The shifter in question followed him out. There was no point in sitting and watching her still form, it only drove him closer to losing his grip on his humanity. His lion was powerful, but not rational. Killing everyone and everything wouldn't help, at least not until he found the rebels.

The ride back was silent. Logan dropped Darren and Kass off at the mansion. He watched the garage door close with a sense of finality before backing the car out of the driveway again.

"You got everything?" Logan asked Hudson.

"Yeah, I'm good," he answered, his thoughts clearly preoccupied.

Logan grunted, heading to the airstrip.

The owner of the private hangar was a shifter, and after he heard about the humans bugging his aircraft, security had been increased. Logan showed his hangar ID to the new guard gate before he was allowed passage.

Logan parked the car roughly and he and Hudson got out, without luggage, heading to the plane.

"What is your Beta doing?"

"Looking for a new job."

Logan nodded, boarding the plane.

"Where are Mark and Jerry?" Hudson asked.

"They need more time. They are going to meet us out there," Logan answered.

Hudson nodded.

...

"I feel like Link in Zelda," I huffed, continuing on the quest to get me back to my body.

"Who is Link?" Doyle asked.

"It's a video game Tommy plays. You control this character called Link to gather all these items to do shit with." I hadn't actually played past the first level, so I didn't know what the end game was. "Okay, so once we gather all the ingredients for this spell, you cast it, shove me into an orb and we three walk to where my body is?" I asked.

"Correct, only you will be carried, not walking," my father stated. "The spell will be pulled to where your physical body is."

"Probably in a hospital," I'd bet. Oh man, that was going to be fun, waking up with a minotaur in tow. Logan was going to freak! I smiled at the thought of being reunited with him, and every part of my soul-infused body ached.

"But no one else can follow us after we three go through?" I clarified, thinking of the hell on Earth my mother would create if she was able to get through.

"Correct, the portal will be open for a very small window," The Magician confirmed.

So I could leave here and never see my mother again. It seemed fitting that she rot in this hellhole. Pending I didn't get the opportunity to kill her first. If I had to choose between getting out of here or killing her, I was picking freedom.

The red earth sprawled out in front of us and my feet were dragging before long.

...

Logan was working through his massive pile of emails on the plane when Ali's image popped up, requesting a video conference.

"Hello?" he said.

Ali was not on the screen, but a wine-colored redhead with vibrant, ice blue eyes was.

"Who are you?" Logan growled lowly.

"I told you," Ali said from the background.

"I am Anna," she stated, appraising him. There was something familiar in her gaze. "Olivia's will has appointed me as Head Executioner while she plays in dreamland. I thought you should know we are moving her to your house."

"She needs to be near a doctor," Logan growled, leaning forward, his hands digging into the leather chair.

"No, actually, she doesn't. I verified with the doctor overseeing her care that there is nothing more they can do until she wakes up. Her body is healing, at an exceptionally slow rate, but I believe once it is stable she will wake up. Aside from the non-existent medical reasons, I don't like being spread so thin at the manor. If someone is trying to kill you, obtaining your daughter is a particularly easy way. I have increased the guards here and brought some of my own." She sounded smug. Logan was debating turning the plane around.

Anna regarded him for a moment. "Just be glad I am not following through with her wishes to be taken off life support."

"WHAT?" Logan bellowed, his claws tearing through the leather chair. He stood, throwing the computer off his lap.

Hudson tackled him. "We are on a plane!" he screamed over and over. Logan thrashed in his grasp, destroying chairs and Hudson's flesh alike.

Logan threw him across the airplane, damaging another seat and shaking the plane dangerously in the process. His shoulders shook from repressing the shift. His mouth crowded with his fangs, he tipped his head back and gave his lion voice, a terrible, fear-inducing roar.

He looked into Anna's smug face on the floor, tilted at an angle. "You do anything to harm her, and I will end you."

Anna smiled. "Spoken like a true mate. Don't worry, I don't plan on harming Olie. If I did, I'd have to take this gig on permanently. That just sounds awful."

Anna leaned forward, brandishing perfectly polished teeth. "Take care of your problems in Idaho. I won't be running the shifters while you are gone."

"Put Ali on," Logan hissed, pulling the laptop off the floor, far too loaded up with adrenaline to sit back down in the ruined chair. He heard Hudson groan in pain, but his gaze didn't leave the monitor.

"Hey," Ali said, pulling the laptop toward her.

"Has she harmed anyone?" Logan demanded.

She cast a glance over to where Logan guessed Anna was sitting. "No, but she has upset the majority. She caught Tommy sneaking in to see Olie. She didn't handle it well."

"Did she hurt him?" Logan asked, willing his claws to retract so he didn't damage the laptop.

"Not physically. But whatever she said to him had him scared silent."

Logan growled, "I'm coming back."

"No, it's okay. We've got it under control. Whatever her faults are, she is exceptionally good at security—and functions just like Olie," Ali added in a whisper.

"We were raised together. Of course I am like her. Except for her love of children, I never had that problem," Anna informed them both. Her bored tone dripped from the screen.

"We can handle this, Logan," Ali reassured him.

He nodded. "Verify that what she said about Olie's health is true. If the doctor has any concerns, do not move her, do you understand?"

"Crystal clear. I just wanted—" Ali pulled a breath. "I wanted you to know where she was going to be," she said, her eyes brimming.

Logan nodded, "Keep me informed."

Ali nodded before Anna popped into the screen, hanging up the call.

Logan closed the laptop with excessive force, tossing it into his ruined chair. He listened to Hudson groan again, his gaze flicking to him as he sat up, apparently regaining consciousness.

His mind was swept back to when the sex tape was released, and he felt himself sucked into the memory of that day.

Logan looked on from the side of the stage where Olivia was barking orders, her sex tape having been released in front of all the shifters who sought arbitration. He was going to find out who had released it, and he was going to kill them, slowly.

Darren had found the recording and shown it to him shortly after their dinner with Olie and Kass. It was heartbreaking to watch. It was also the first chink in Olivia's armor Logan had ever seen. She never showed weakness. She was a ruthless killer who enjoyed her profession.

Yet somewhere beneath that thick exterior, she was still a vulnerable woman. He had overlooked that fact; his lion never had.

As the challengers for her seat at his side formed a long line, she cast a look of pure determination at him. He inclined his head ever so slightly to ask if she wanted him to stop it. She shook her head, able to read his body language easily, calling the first participant up.

She was determined and stubborn to a fault. He tried to remind himself he was engaged, but watching her, hands on her curvy hips and rounded ass, he was having a hard time.

...

"When you said oasis, this was not what I had in mind," I told my father, looking at the expanse of jungle in front of us.

"There is a wide stream that feeds all this vegetation. We need to make our way to the bottom and follow said river until the sun kisses the sky. That's where we will shall find what we seek," he answered.

"Could that be more cryptic?" I grunted, taking the first tentative step down into the steep ravine.

Doyle lumbered next to me, the lose dirt sliding under his massive weight.

"Be careful," I warned.

"I do not fear falling," Doyle stated.

I rolled my eyes, "Whatever."

I swear my fucking father glided down, without any dirt staining his brown trousers or black jacket. Doyle and I, on the other hand, had red dirt smeared everywhere. At the bottom, the ground was painfully moist and I rubbed my hands against a tree trunk just to get the clumps of dirt off. Doyle did the same with his entire body.

"Alright, try to stay dry. We will have to bunk here tonight and temperatures can drop quickly," my father informed us.

Awesome. In case anyone was wondering, I'm not the camping type.

...

The plane touched down a few hours later.

"See about having the repairs made while you wait," Logan instructed the crew. They all nodded cautiously.

Hudson was waiting for him at a rented jeep. "She reminds me of Olivia."

Logan was jerked out of his thoughts by Hudson's words. "Who?"

"Anna, she has the same demanding authority that gets obeyed or people get killed."

"I hadn't thought of it that way."

"Certainly Olivia pissed you off at first?" Hudson asked.

Logan thought back.

"She's always been a handful," he admitted.

Logan would never forget Olivia, half dead on his couch, ready to take down the Puppet Master when Steven had been foolish enough to challenge Logan in his home.

She had already give up so much to find him and end his killings. Blake had drained her within inches of her life. But even that didn't stop the predator inside of her from rising to the challenge of killing the bastard.

His lion appreciated that and pressed dangerously close to the surface. He commanded Olivia to run and she did taking Lorraine and hiding in his room.

It was a terrible decision for her. In his territory with her scent lingering on the air, it only pushed his lion closer to the surface, his fiancée forgotten for the warrior with sorrow in her eyes.

He stalked closer to her, needing to touch her, needing to claim her. He doubted Olivia knew how lucky she was that Lorraine picked the moment when he dropped his mouth to her neck in inhale deeply, to fling open the bathroom door and run to him.

"Boss, you hear me?" Tommy's voice broke through Logan's memory, coming over the speaker system of the Jeep.

"How did you—wait, no, actually I don't want to know," Logan amended. "No, I didn't hear you."

"I said there has still been no activity at the site Hudson is driving to. Hopefully, they left a clue behind of where they went," Tommy informed him.

"Tommy, did you meet Anna?" Logan asked.

Tommy went silent. "Yeah," he answered cautiously.

"What did you think about her?"

Tommy sighed. "She's smart, cunning, and expects to be obeyed. Where Olie granted us slack, she demands perfection. It's going to be a rough time until Olie wakes up."

"Did you hear Anna's theory on it?" Logan asked.

"Yeah."

"You don't believe it?"

"I have a hard time accepting intel from a person I just met on a subject as important as Olie."

Hudson whistled. "How old are you again, little man?"

"Old enough to know your porn collection is disturbing," Tommy retorted.

"What the fuck?" Hudson hissed, before turning to Logan. "He didn't really?"

Logan laughed, surprising himself. "Oh yeah, he really did. There are no secrets to be kept digitally from Tommy."

...

The bottom of the jungle was thick black mud; not brown, but soul-sucking black, absorbing the light and warmth. My father continued to glide along, while Doyle and I were pulled into the sticky mess.

I gripped the side of a tree at one particularly deep trench that was threatening to take my shoe with it. I ripped it free with a grunt.

"Oh look, the sun is setting," I observed, pulling myself up on a low hanging branch to breathe. My feet were heavily laden with the disgusting fucking mud.

Doyle rested against another tree, snorting, "You've said that before."

I groaned, "Seriously, it really is setting." I pointed as the yellow light shifted into an auburn glow.

"Indeed it is," The Magician stated. He clapped his hands and the oncoming night exploded with color in brilliant hues.

"Whoa," I muttered, looking down at the mud. Yeah, it was still black. The tree I was sitting on was veined, neon yellow and green running under its surface. I looked over to Doyle as pink and purple orbs glided around his head. He huffed out a breath, stirring the orbs.

My gaze shifted to my father and I had to blink several times. Small blue pinpoints of light surrounded him, lifting him off his feet and wrapping around his body.

"That's cool," I whispered.

"You have no magic," Doyle commented, looking inquisitively at me.

"That's what we are seeing?" I asked, looking down at my own orb-less body.

Doyle nodded, looking over to my father. "She needs her magic."

"I know," my father agreed. "But until we get her back to her body, that can't happen."

Doyle grunted. I had a feeling this wasn't the first time they'd had this disagreement.

"So now that we can see the glowing orbs, what next?" I asked.

"Now we should be able to see the shadow lark," The Magician stated, turning around, or rather floating as his blue orbs turned him.

I huffed out a breath, looking across at the stream. "Wow," escaped my lips. The movement of the water, combined with the multitude of shades of blue, was peaceful, calm and refreshing. Painfully unlike the red desert above and the black shit mud below.

"In its simplest form, magic is just energy; magic users have the ability to manipulate said energy," my father instructed.

I nodded, "Good to know."

"The shadow lark is pure energy, which is why it can only be been seen at sunset with magic present. But I don't see it."

"It appears it has found us," Doyle commented, pointing toward the stream.

I turned and saw that from the midst of the blue orbs dancing above the water, a perfectly white light had appeared. It transformed in front of my eyes into a lily. Whether it happened because that was what I expected to see or because that was the form it actually existed in, I wasn't sure.

"Wonderful," my father breathed. He used his magic to glide over to the lily, leaving the water perfectly unblemished. He reached down, hesitating once before reaching to pluck the plant.

His hand passed through the flower. "What in Hades?" he whispered before trying again. Again, the plant disappeared, the intensity of the white petals dimming each time. I held my breath.

"Stop," Doyle commanded. "Only the worthy can pluck it."

The Magician stood. "Be my guest." With that, he glided back to the shore.

"You wanna try picking the flower?" I asked Doyle, my gaze riveted to the spot that held a piece of my freedom.

"It appears as a flower to you?" Doyle asked.

"A lily."

"Then no, I think you are the one it wants," Doyle answered.

I sighed, slipping off my branch. While it wasn't comfortable, it did keep me out of the black mud of hell. I crashed down and sunk to my ankles, not bothering to lift my feet out as I slowly slurked toward the river. At the bank, I left behind the mud, the sand shifting under my feet and darkening from my muddy contribution.

I kept pushing forward, wading until the sand dropped off, swimming the rest of the distance in the crystal clear waters.

The icy touch of the water was bone cold; such a great time to go corporeal. I felt it pulling at my energy as my head dipped under the surface, sending a chill to my core.

"Beautiful," I heard beneath the water. I pulled back up, gasping a breath.

"Be careful!" My father screamed.

I raised a hand to them behind me, hoping to convey that I was indeed alright. Then I reached forward with the hand to touch the large, trumpet-looking flower.

"Not so fast, my pretty," a voice whispered next to me.

"No! Leave her be!" my father screamed. The panic in his voice had me groaning before I was pulled under.

I looked down at the arms wrapped in scales, holding me securely around my middle, drawing me down into the icy depths.

"You can breathe," she whispered, her voice echoing in the water.

I grunted, not being the trusting kind. She laughed, pulling me down farther, orbs of colors flying by my head. My lungs were at capacity. I struggled against her, seeing a gold tail under my feet. Eventually, my body gave in to the raw need to breathe. I expected the water to choke me, but I inhaled sweet air. My body relaxed and the arms disappeared from around me.

I turned, testing out my underwater swimming skills. "Mermaid?" I asked, smiling like a fool.

She nodded her purple locks, her hair flowing around her heart-shaped head perfectly. Golden scales trailed along her temple and down her throat.

"This is so cool!! The kids at home are going to be so pissed I got to meet a mermaid and they didn't."

She raised an eyebrow at me and I shrugged. "So what's up?" I asked.

"You are not scared," she commented.

I shrugged, "I got a lot going on right now. Being terrified of you seems like too much work."

"You are unique."

I huffed, "Yeah, I get that a lot."

"I mean that as a compliment."

"Thanks."

She blinked blue eyes that matched the ever-changing blue of the river.

"You may have the power of the shadow lark on one condition: you free us as well."

"Free you as in transport you to Earth?" I asked.

"Correct."

"Do you feed on humans?"

"Disgusting, no."

"Do you lure them to their deaths for fun?"

She shrugged, "Sirens do that."

"They're reformed. Now they seduce over beer."

The mermaid blinked at me. "But we need men to mate with."

"Do you kill them after you mate with them?"

"No."

"So, trust me when I say you will have no problems finding men to mate with. In fact, we can even build you a swim up bar, although I guess the whole breathing thing is going to be an issue," I mused.

"We can breathe air above water just as we do below."

"Oh good, that's easy. Wait, The Magician said when the portal opened I'd be taken to my body, and how did you know that's what I was after, anyways?" Seriously, delayed suspicion just because she had a cool tail.

The mermaid smiled. "What else would you need the power of the shadow lark for?"

"I have no idea."

"Neither do I."

"Okay, so back to our original issue, my body is probably in a hospital and not near a body of water."

"The magician can open a portal again," the mermaid confided.

"Shit, really?"

"Yes, really. Once you have our swim up bar built he can summon us through."

"Alright, I agree, but I have conditions of my own."

"Name them."

"In my world, you follow my rules and if you start killing, maiming or fucking with the humans I will hunt you down and kill you. Trust me, I'm very good at my job," I smiled.

"You are a peacekeeper between the races?" Geez, everyone was out to make me sound like a hero.

"No, I am an Executioner."

The mermaid shrugged, "I agree."

"How do I—" My jaw was wired shut as pure energy or I guess magic infused every square inch of my body. I vibrated with power, my eyes rolling back in my head.

When my eyes were working again, I was lying face down in the fucking mud.

"I'd rather be tased," I wheezed, pushing myself up.

"Here she is!" Doyle yelled. I was pulled into his hairy embrace. Too tired to fight it, my head flopped on his shoulder.

"Daughter, daughter?" My father's panicked voice reached me.

"I'malive," I slurred, using my muddy hands to wipe at my muddy face.

Hands moved quickly over me, checking for ailments. I heard my father's relieved exhale.

"I thought you'd drowned, my magic couldn't reach you."

"Turns out, the mermaids want out, too. I agreed to open a portal for them after we get back and I build them a swim up bar." My eyes were staying closed.

"Swim up bar?" my father questioned.

"Later, I need to sleep," I groaned, finding my eyes not cooperating.

"At least she successfully obtained the shadow lark," Doyle observed.

"I never dreamed she would be able to hold such raw force," my father's voice drifted to me.

I'd like to note that he didn't take issue with opening the portal again.

I awoke sometime later on a dry bed of leaves to a mouthful of mud and a small fire crackling. I groaned, spitting dirt out.

"Fucking mud," I grunted.

"How are you feeling?" my father asked.

"Like I got kicked by a horse," I admitted, rubbing my chest with gritty hands.

"That is to be expected."

I nodded. "You didn't tell me that once you left here you would be able to open portals back here." Did I need to be worried about him bringing others to my world behind my back?

"I can open many portals. It just depends on the proper ingredients. I will honor the deal you made with the mermaids."

My eyes closed, the pressure in my head mounting, I groaned, "Thank you. Do you have somewhere I can dump this energy?"

"You can do that?" My father asked, surprised.

"Yeah, I can push pretty well."

"Here," a glass orb was slid into my hands. Behind my closed lids, I saw the brilliant, clean, white power. Slowly untangling it from my own energy, which I was guessing was my life force, I pushed it into the glass circle.

It creaked, filling to capacity as the tiny orbs bunched together tightly.

The pressure in my head instantly cleared. "Much better." I blinked a few times, my vision adjusting to the dark night.

"Food?" Doyle asked.

"Food," I agreed. I'd never been so depressed about my food options before, as he put cheese and bread into my hands yet again.

"Let me tell you both about pizza," I began.

Logan got out of the jeep cautiously, filling his lungs with the clean scent of the Idaho woods. Undertones ruined its perfect allure—oil, fire, and blood.

Hudson came around the front of the vehicle.

"Split up?" he asked.

"No, we stay together. We don't know what we are walking into." He couldn't believe he was going over survival basics.

Hudson nodded, following Logan's path. He was headed toward the blood; it called to his lion and he knew the worst of this place would be there. Logan rolled his neck, cracking his knuckles. His lion was present, pushing against the seams of his clothing and heightening his senses.

Hudson matched his pace. Logan could sense Hudson's beast pushing against his control as well.

Up a hill they marched, fueled by their superior genetics, neither slowing down nor increasing their breathing. They passed shacks with greasy sheets flapping in the breeze as doors, the waft of stale food and body odor overwhelming.

Cresting the top of the hill, Logan looked down to the pit of blood below.

"Fuck," Hudson hissed.

Logan ground his jaw together, staring down on the hundreds of animal carcasses.

"Please tell me you didn't allow your entire territory to hunt like this," Logan growled.

"No — holy — fucking NO!" Hudson stuttered. "Sure, we hunt, but we use everything. We eat all we can, and we've got craftsmen who take the hides and bones." Hudson turned back to the fly-infested flesh before them. "This is, this is wastefulness."

"It's undisciplined." Logan turned back to the huts, inhaling. "They've created shifters here."

Hudson jerked around. "What? How do you know?"

"Newly made shifters love to hunt, need to hunt to balance their beast. We train our minds and hone our mastery of that instinct from the beginning, to ensure a higher level of control. They indulged the hunger."

"What are we going to do?"

"Kill them, kill them all," Logan rumbled.

He went into the first hut, ripping the soiled sheet from the makeshift doorway, the wood creaking under his assault. His eyes took just a breath to adjust to the dim light.

"Gah, what is that smell?" Hudson asked behind him, stumbling back out.

"Feces," Logan stated, moving deeper into the shelter.

He pushed over the handmade cot and it fell apart. He bent down, tossing the ripped fabric around.

Nothing.

Logan went back out, inhaling the fresh air. "Check the rest of the cabins, there has to be a hint here as to where they went."

Hudson nodded, moving to check the shack on the other side of the makeshift road. Logan didn't break his stride, storming into the next foul smelling lean-to.

Hours later, Hudson called out, "Here, I found something!"

Logan tore out of the shack he was searching, running to Hudson. He was behind the line of huts in an actual house. Logan's step paused as he took in the glass windows, the chimney, and the hose bib in front of the house for running water.

Hudson stood in the doorway, the doorframe broken in.

"What did you find?" Logan asked, resuming his quick pace.

Hudson handed over an open ledger. "They've been buying property."

Logan ran his hand over the aging pages. "Let's get back to the car and call Tommy."

...

Something had woken me up, my eyes snapping open. Holding the breath in my chest, I listened intently.

Nothing.

The fire had dimmed substantially and the night air felt cold against my cheeks. I was loath to toss off the warmth of my blankets, but something was there.

Moving my right hand, I checked the blades across my chest, finding their familiar touch reassuring.

"Not yet," Doyle muttered on the opposite side of the dying fire.

My gaze flicked to him. I kept my mouth shut and my body still. I didn't want to alert whatever was out there that we were keen to its attack. At least the throbbing in my head had diminished with a few hours of rest.

"Keep the girl alive for the Queen," a voice instructed, before I was kicked from behind.

"Ouch." A little warning would have been wonderful. I didn't waste time trying to untangle myself from the thick blankets, rolling to my side and freeing an arm to throw a knife blindly. It landed in a thigh.

"She stabbed me!" the offended party yelled.

I stood, throwing off my blankets. "You didn't think kidnapping me and killing my friends would end well, did you?"

"No one defies The Queen's Guard." A white blond stepped forward into the flickering light of the dying fire.

If he and his band of assholes hadn't been working for the deranged Queen, I'd have appreciated their well-defined physiques; apparently the cold wasn't bothering them at all. Twin pieces of leather crossed over the chests and short skirts covered the essentials.

"The Queen's Guard is not an enemy to take on lightly," my father warned, standing up and brushing nonexistent dust from his shoulder. He probably slept on magic. I cracked my neck, feeling the muscles beginning to tighten up.

"That's great. I'm not one to leave my enemies alive. They tend to try sneaking up on you."

"Do you have any friends at home?" Doyle asked, rumbling next to me.

"Yes. I have plenty." I was almost offended by that comment.

"Plenty of enemies I'd imagine, also," Blondie added smugly.

"That's how I know I'm doing something right," I snarked back at him.

"Did you obtain the shadow lark?" Blondie asked.

"Bite me," I told him.

His eyes roved over my body. "That is a tempting offer, daughter of the Queen."

"Oh, come on, that is not what I meant," I groaned, crossing my arms, annoyed.

"We will not go with you," Doyle growled.

"That is a poor decision," Blondie stated.

"Add it to my list," I grunted, pulling more throwing knives.

"I get the girl," barked the asshole with the leg wound I had inflicted.

I sent a dagger at his chest. He caught it.

"Impressive speed," I muttered, pulling a sword, matching his own sword pull. They had sent three scantily clad blondies to match us.

That was just insulting.

I twirled my sword, stretching out the muscles in my wrist.

"You hold that sword like you almost may know what you are doing," the injured blondie taunted.

I smiled. "Come closer and I'll show you all the pretty ways I can dice up your body."

He huffed out a laugh. "Your strength is not in weapons."

I lunged, wiping my blade around with deadly precision to slice through both crossed pieces of leather, leaving a wet trail of blood behind.

He was shocked, reaching down to touch the red liquid pooling from his body. I lunged again, not giving him the time to recover. If this was all the Queen's Guard had to offer, I'd march in and take the crown off her head. Not that I wanted it.

He dodged, a blur. Fuck, even vamp speed wasn't that fast.

"How did you get so skilled with a sword?" he whispered in my ear from behind.

I snapped my head back, connecting with the soft cartilage in his nose. I was done talking.

"Harlot!" he screeched.

Apparently, in any dimension, being female and a bad ass was an insult.

I turned, kicking out, aiming for his chest. His hand cradled his nose, his body arching forward. My kick landed against his sternum, knocking him back, away from the fire.

"You fuckers need to learn how to take a beating." Decision made and shared.

He moved again, just a blur. I spun back to the dark night, an eerie howl splitting the blackness. I stepped forward, I knew that howl.

"LOGAN!" the scream left me. My feet moved before my brain could convince the rest of me that Logan had not somehow managed to cross the veil between our world and this one. I left behind the meager light from the dismal fire and with it, any additional protection.

I stopped. My legs and heart demanded to go on. My chest inflated and deflated rapidly, denying my most basic need to find my mate.

My fingers clenched around the handle of the sword and I hissed out a breath, my shoulders stiff.

"You will pay for that," I whispered to the night.

A whisper to my left had me turning. It was too dark to see anything. Footsteps to my right had me shifting my gaze there, searching the darkened woods, my feet slowly sinking into the soft mud.

I sighed, "This is pointless." I turned to trek back to the small pinpoint of light from the fire. Up the hill I pumped my legs, keeping my sword out. I could either flail around in the dark until exhaustion overtook me, or go back to the light and have a better chance.

I didn't get the opportunity to get that far. I could feel the Guard to my left, his emotions of glee and triumph alerting me to his presence. Whether that new skill was from the magic of The Magician or my succubus heritage, I wasn't sure. Nor was I going to analyze it at that moment.

I spun, bringing the tip of my sword up, thrusting it through his exposed chest. In the darkness I could see the white of his eyes widening in shock.

I took a step forward, letting the blade pierce through his back. Laying a hand on his chest, I pushed him off the sword, turning and continuing up the hill.

The howling had ripped open a vacant part of my soul. A part that Logan had filled with his mate bond, with his constant supportive presence. I needed that back. Having him inside my head and being a part of the packs had healed a few wounds I was too stubborn to even talk about. It was nice to have a guarantee. To know that no matter how badly I acted or broke down, he'd never leave. He'd never falter. I missed him, painfully so.

Doyle threw another log on the fire. "Where is your guard?"

"Dead, down in the shadows," I muttered, rubbing moisture from my eyes with the back of my hand.

"I'm sorry, daughter. I should have warned you of their ability to imitate a loved one's voice."

I shrugged, sitting down on my discarded bedroll, using the dirt and grass to wipe the blood off my sword before I stowed it.

"Why did you hear a howl?" Doyle asked.

"Logan is a shifter," I answered, my voice soft. "He's a lion shifter."

"Oh, yes," Doyle responded.

"That is the voice you miss the most?" my father asked.

I looked into the fire, unable to meet anyone's eyes. "There is a purity in his lion, a simplicity in our communication that leaves no room for misunderstanding. I find comfort in that connection."

My father clasped a hand on my shoulder and I jumped slightly.

"You will be home soon, daughter."

I nodded, brushing away more tears, drawing a deep breath.

"We have much time before dawn, try and get some sleep," Doyle muttered.

I rubbed my eyes and nodded, not lying down. Doyle slipped down under his bedroll and was asleep instantly.

I huffed, "That's a neat trick."

"He does not carry worry or stress like we do. Every situation is assessed and acted upon," my father explained.

"Must be nice."

"I have often thought so. He doesn't have regrets or wonder about what ifs."

I nodded, my gaze still on the fire.

"You should get some rest," my father tried.

"I don't sleep well."

"Why?" he asked.

My gaze cut to him, "Because I am haunted. Selena fundamentally broke something inside of me. I don't sleep much. I don't let people get close, but I kill. I kill without remorse and I need it. I need to end lives."

His gaze turned away from mine. Anger rode me hard at the injustice of the situation. What would my future have been like with a parent who cared?

"While you may have been trapped here for years, at least no one forced your hand. No one made you their slave," I hissed the word.

"I'm sorry. I did what I thought was best for you," he responded.

"How did you open a portal to send me through?" I asked, changing the topic. He might be my father, he may be helping me, but he gave me to a monster. I couldn't forgive that.

"I didn't. Selena had been working with the Fae; they provided her transportation."

I nodded, rubbing my hands together. "She ended up double crossing them and losing that relationship."

"She made quite a few mistakes."

"So did you."

It hung between us. My anger and distrust.

"You would have been trapped here," my father tried.

"At least I would have been loved. I wouldn't have grown up damaged."

"You would have never met your mate, either."

I wheezed out a breath. He was right. "That doesn't excuse your decision."

"No, it doesn't. I made the decision to send you through. Please believe me, it was not an easy one."

I lay down, tears seeping down my face. I didn't want to have this conversation. My heart was already shredded in my chest. I just wanted to go home.

...

"Alright Logan, Montana has nothing. No structures, no utilities, not even an amazon order. I feel confident in crossing it off the list. Well, right after I transfer ownership into your name."

Logan smiled, listening to the keyboard click on Tommy's end. Hudson turned the jeep, getting back onto the main highway.

"Wyoming is the same." The clicking continued. "However, Nebraska and Kansas both have buildings, utilities, and people out and wandering."

"Good work, Tommy. Get all the photos you can and send them over to me. I want to have eyes walking in there."

"You going to take backup?" Tommy asked.

Logan debated, rubbing his chin. "No, Hudson and I can handle it."

"Alrighty, boys. Oh, and Logan?"

"Yeah."

"Olie is being moved here tomorrow."

Logan clenched his jaw. "How's everyone taking it?"

"Fine." In his mind, Logan could see Tommy's shrug.

"She's going to wake up, Tommy."

"I know." Tommy paused before adding, "I just miss her."

"Me too, buddy, me too."

The repairs to the airplane were completed. Logan and Hudson took their familiar seats.

"We are going to Kearney, Nebraska," Logan relayed to the flight crew.

"Do they have a landing strip?" the flight attendant asked in a high-pitched squeak.

Logan turned. "I should hope so, or it's going to be a bumpy landing."

She nodded, heading to the cabin to relay the change of destination.

Logan drummed his fingers against the newly upholstered armrest and Hudson cleared his throat. Logan slanted his gaze to him.

"They just fixed it," Hudson muttered, not making eye contact.

"They can fix it again."

Hudson cleared his throat again. "It will be dark when we land."

"It will."

"Are we waiting until daylight to see them?"

Logan swiveled his chair to Hudson. "First, we are not seeing them. We are killing them. Second, are you scared of the dark? Must we wait until sunrise to make an appearance?"

Hudson swallowed, adjusting in his seat. "We don't know if everyone there deserves to die."

Logan blinked caramel eyes at him, flecked with espresso. "I am the Alpha, whoever attacks me dies."

"Well, yeah, I guess it is that simple," Hudson admitted.

Logan nodded, looking for the flight attendant. "You picked up dinner while we were out?"

"Yes, let me grab it."

Logan and Hudson dined on three steaks each, with potatoes, broccoli, corn and apple pie. Once Logan's stomach was full, he reclined in the seat.

"Get some rest, it's going to be a long night."

Hudson grunted, grumbling incoherently. Crash course in becoming a responsible alpha.

Logan pushed everything from his mind, Olivia, the packs, Anna. He pulled upon his beast to still his mind and rest his body.

The second the plane touched down, Logan sat up. The flight attendant hadn't woken him up to put his tray table and seat back in their upright positions, and he was grateful.

The cabin door opened and Logan scented cow manure on the chilly air.

"Will you be needing us again tonight?" the flight attendant asked, staying in the safety of the onboard kitchen.

"Give them a rest," Hudson muttered on an exhale.

Logan turned to him with a raised eyebrow.

"Whatever you think, Alpha," Hudson amended.

Logan turned his gaze back to the timid flight attendant. "Be ready to fly at eight a.m." She nodded, staying out of their way as they exited.

Hudson scanned the area. "Where the hell is the car?" he muttered.

A familiar black SUV took a corner quickly, leaving rubber on the asphalt. Logan grunted, a smile playing at the corner of his mouth.

The vehicle came to an abrupt stop and the passenger window slid down.

"Hey boss," Mark called out.

"We have arrived!" Jerry proclaimed.

Logan chuckled in spite of the worry heavy on his heart. Hudson slipped into the backseat, sliding over, and Logan followed him.

"We got snacks," Jerry announced, and Mark passed back the greasy bags.

"Excellent," Logan grunted, taking the food.

"Didn't we just eat?" Hudson commented.

Jerry laughed, "You haven't been around long enough, Hudson. We take our meals where we can get them, especially going into a fight."

"Yeah, we never know when some psycho is going to kidnap our asses," Mark grunted.

"Not anymore!" Jerry was downright gleeful.

Mark grunted, casting a look at Logan.

"I've perfected the anti-kidnapping hex bags!" Jerry did a little happy dance in his seat.

"Really?" Hudson asked.

"Well, hopefully I have. I plan on testing them out," Jerry amended.

"On who?" Logan asked. "Who's volunteering to get kidnapped?"

"No one's volunteering, but I do happen to know of one particular succubus who happens to get her ass kidnapped quite a bit," Jerry alluded.

Logan grunted, "I can't deny that logic. If they work, I want one for all the shifters and The Council."

Mark laughed as Jerry groaned, his shoulders slumping.

"You walked into that," Mark noted, continuing to laugh.

"I'm charging you a small fortune. It took me a week to make three," Jerry whined.

Logan shrugged, "We will see if they work."

Jerry groaned again.

The compound was a two-hour drive. Logan turned his gaze to the almost full moon overhead.

"Have you both seen pictures of this place?" he asked.

"Yeah, Tommy sent everything over, or rather they just showed up on my laptop. That kid is dangerous," Mark commented.

"He's brilliant," Logan stated.

"Terrifyingly brilliant," Hudson added.

"From what he sent over, it looks like there is only one building, with a sentry tower close to the road." The light from Mark's laptop shined around the edges of the seat.

"The windows looked to have bars as well," Hudson added.

"To keep them in or us out is the question," Mark commented.

"We will find out. There will be no mercy tonight. Anyone who attacks us will be killed," Logan commanded.

"You've clearly been hanging with Olivia for too long." A note of longing tinged Jerry's voice.

Logan grunted.

The GPS announced they were ten minutes away.

"Let's park around here," Mark said, closing his laptop.

Jerry grumbled, "I did not wear walking shoes."

"Good thing I brought them for you," Mark responded.

"I suppose," Jerry sighed, slipping the SUV into a thick patch of grass and trees.

Stepping out of the vehicle, Logan stretched, inhaling the crisp night.

"Fuck, it's cold," Jerry complained, pulling a jacket around his shoulders before changing his shoes. Over the thick fabric, he slid a messenger bag onto his shoulder.

He muttered a word, leaving a bag next to the wheel. Brushing his hands off, he smiled. "Don't be jealous of my skills."

Logan chuckled, "I'll try to keep it in check."

He appreciated Jerry's attempts at good humor. He imagined it must be draining. Olivia had become a fast friend to him, one who had proved her loyalty on more than one occasion.

Hudson led the way into the thick undergrowth.

"No flashlights, Jerry, hold onto Mark," Logan commanded.

"Oh, I got this." Jerry flipped down night vision goggles.

"We visited Myrtle's," Mark muttered.

"Yes, and you're lucky I left without that gorgeous sword."

"You can't use a sword," Mark reminded him.

Hudson stopped his forward movement, crouching down and waving to them to do the same. Logan moved next to him, inhaling deeply.

He scented the sentry's gunpowder and fear. The air was rank with fear.

With a hand he indicated they were to hang back. Logan stepped into the clearing, waiting for the light from the sentry tower to land on him.

The beam of light blinded him. Logan heard the gasps, followed by the readying of firearms.

"Do you know who I am?" he asked calmly.

"You're the false Alpha," a voice reached him. "Shoot him!"

"Wrong answer," Logan muttered, already on the move to the wooden ladder leading up to the sentry station.

He knew they would shoot down, having seen where he was headed. He waited a breath, steeling himself for the inevitable pain before starting up.

"Hey assholes!" Hudson cried, "Over here!"

Logan heard the feet above him shift to the window, looking down to the new threat. Pushing with all of his considerable speed, Logan stretched his long body, skipping rungs to arrive at the trap door. He slowed as he reached the door, anticipating it would be locked after the announcement of his arrival. Coiling his body under it, he paused for just a breath before pushing up.

The wood snapped under his assault, drowned out by the sound of assault rifles being fired at Hudson. He hoped the idiot was smart enough to run.

Logan burst through the broken wood, a piece raking down his back. He turned, facing the two shooters. Their wide eyes and trembling hands gave him all the time he needed to clear the distance between his body and theirs.

The guns went first, ripped from trigger-happy fingers. Logan felt a bullet pass through his shoulder.

He grunted, "Iron."

"We didn't expect you here. He told us we were invisible," one shooter stuttered out.

Logan raised one caramel eyebrow. "Who is he?" He didn't have Olivia's penchant for killing first and asking questions later.

The second shooter's hand itched to the holster on his hip.

Logan snapped his neck with one hand, careful to pull the bones away from his shoulders.

The first shooter peed himself. "Who is he?" Logan repeated.

"Our — our —— our alpha," the shooter whispered, turning his shocked gaze back to Logan. "He said you were weak, not worthy to lead us."

Logan grunted, "How many others are here?"

"I — I don't — I don't know, our main forces are at the base in Kansas, preparing for an attack against your home, once you move the whore."

Logan snapped his neck as well.

"No one calls my mate a whore," he told the dead bodies. A quick glance told him nothing of value was stored up here. Aside from the two men and guns, they had a card table, chairs, and beer. Logan headed back down.

Jerry was waiting for him, bent over and breathing heavily. "Your boy here is an idiot."

"They were iron bullets," Hudson shrugged.

"Next time, Jerry, don't save him. He is an alpha, he can make his own poor decisions," Logan rumbled.

Jerry straightened up, shocked. Hudson's mouth was hanging open.

"I didn't ask for help," Hudson tried.

"No, you didn't, but we are going into the enemy's lair. How valuable are you to me if you are shot up and need help?" Logan turned the fierceness of his gaze on him.

Hudson squirmed, "I wouldn't be."

"Exactly." Logan turned, stalking toward the building. He could hear people whispering, high and frightened. When he got to the door he paused, drawing a breath. He wanted to kill them all, fuck the conscience beating against him.

Olivia might call herself a cold-blooded killer, but he disagreed. She never killed anyone who didn't deserve it. She was the protector of the weak, and those in this building were exactly that. That didn't make them harmless, though.

"Listen and listen well. I am Logan, Alpha of the Shifters across the United States. Your leader has lied to you. If you choose to follow him, we will kill you. If you attack any of us, we will kill you."

"So join or die is our only option?" a teenager called out.

Logan's frown was deep. "Yes."

"Some of us didn't ask for this," tried an older voice.

"It doesn't matter. What's done is done. You are part of the packs now, either in life or in death."

Logan heard the muttering before he kicked the door in. All the adrenaline, excitement and fear in the air hit his beast hard. He growled, letting his lion seep into his eyes.

"Attack!" cried someone, and the entire room was moving. The first wave came at him in their human forms. Fodder for the slaughter. Logan's frown seemed permanently etched onto his face as he gutted one, throwing him against the wall before the next one came after him. They couldn't control their shifts, their animals demanding freedom from the cages inside of them.

Logan let his beast free, his back and hips changing shape as he went from walking on two legs to prowling on four. Long claws tapped against the carpeted floor. He threw his head back and roared; the Alpha had arrived.

Next to him a wolf stepped forward, careful to keep Jerry, who was muttering incantations, behind him. A large russet water buffalo stood on Jerry's other side. Hudson was handy to have in a fight, if for no other reason than that he was a massive shifter. Dumb, but massive.

Logan howled into the contained space before snapping his jaws at the foolish wolf shifter who tried to attack him. The crunch of bones in his mouth brought his beast joy. He spat what remained of the wolf out before charging after the next fool.

They were untrained and it was a slaughter. After watching their fellow wolves die bloodily and quickly, a few of them banded together, circling around Logan, who had pushed forward into their numbers.

Wolves were pack animals, after all. Logan's tail twitched and he waited for the attack, it was going to happen by his flank. He wasn't worried about these numbers, there was a reason he was the Alpha.

He watched the other wolves in front of him. When their attention shifted behind Logan, he spun, landing his fangs in the neck of the attacking wolf. Logan shook his head, separating the head from the body. He felt the warm blood dripping from his chin and he smiled before snapping his jaws.

The rest of the wolves attacked together. The last stand. Logan took a hit to his left flank, teeth and claws sinking in deep. He kicked back, dislodging the attacker. Once his back leg landed again, he reared back, swiping at the three wolves in front of him with massive paws. They were thrown forcefully back.

Logan turned his attention to the wolf who had reattached at his flank, peering over his shoulder at the young animal. He was scrawny, even in his wolf form, and Logan knew he couldn't be much past puberty. While it pained him, he turned, throwing the attacker off again. The wolf landed on his side, snarling up at Logan. Logan crossed the short distance, using his paw to crush the youthful skull with only his body weight.

At least it was quick. It was the only mercy Logan could grant.

"Logan, here," Jerry called out.

He looked around the large room, finding Mark and Hudson handling the few remaining shifters. He followed Jerry's voice.

"It's okay, no one is going to harm you," Jerry kept repeating.

Logan passed through the doorway, his gaze riveted to the hunched figure in the corner. Without thinking, he shifted back.

"What's going on?" he asked Jerry.

"Children," Jerry whispered on an exhale, looking desperately up at Logan. "No one attacked me. She's trying to protect them."

Logan nodded, his nakedness forgotten as he squatted down next to the terrified brunette. Her face was hidden beneath her arm, but a pair of dark brown eyes looked up at him curiously.

"Did you hear my decree?" Logan asked.

The woman nodded. "Please don't take my baby from me. Please don't hurt him."

Logan moved back. "No one is taking your child from you. I don't have any plans to harm either of you. You haven't attacked me, so unless you have plans of doing it later, I see no reason why we can't help you."

He waited for those words to sink in. He had been with Olivia when she coaxed people out from hiding before. While he lacked her ability to give the woman the feeling of safety, he knew Olie always waited, said their overworked brains had a hard time focusing on words at first.

Logan repeated himself. The woman's tremors subsided slightly. The little boy darted away from her.

"Don't let him into the other room!" Jerry cried out.

Logan caught him easily enough, swinging him into his arms. He expected fear, but instead the boy reached down and started pulling on his chest hair. Logan huffed, amused. He would be an alpha, Logan had no doubt.

The woman stood, her hands outstretched, as though any sudden movement might end the child's life.

"Is there another door?" Logan asked her.

She blinked at him, her gaze never leaving her child, before lowering her arms. "Yes, back through the kitchen."

The little boy leaned his arms out to his mother and Logan handed him off.

"Jerry, go with them. I want to check on Mark and Hudson," Logan commanded.

Jerry nodded, guiding them away from the bloody scene Logan walked back into.

Hudson had shifted back, looking down as a long gash healed on his side. "I don't suppose anyone thought to bring a change of clothing," he muttered.

"In the SUV," Mark groaned, cracking his back before stepping outside.

"What did Jerry find?" Hudson asked as Logan came even with him.

"A woman and her child," Logan answered.

Both of their gazes ripped to him. "They're still alive," Logan reassured. "He is bringing them around through the kitchen, so let's get something on before they catch up."

Mark threw a package of baby wipes from Jerry's discarded messenger bag at each of them. Hudson raised an eyebrow. "Seriously?"

Mark shrugged. "Tell me it won't be easier checking into a hotel room without blood smeared all over us."

Hudson shrugged. Logan knew it was a trick Mark had picked up from Olie. It worried him that Hudson had never encountered the problem. He needed to get someone covering the West immediately. He didn't relish other surprises waiting for him.

Jerry came around while Logan was pulling off the tags from his gray sweatpants. They were a little snug and very short.

Jerry laughed, "Sorry there, big boy, that's all the store had."

Logan grunted, "I appreciate the forethought. Are there car seats here? He is going to need one."

The little boy's mother looked up at him, shocked. "No, they didn't let us leave."

Logan growled lowly and the woman backed away. Jerry sent him an annoyed glare before talking soothingly to her again.

"Where are you from?" Logan asked.

She looked at him, startled, before looking away again. "Vegas."

Logan nodded. "I'd like you stay in St. Ann for a while until your control of your beast improves and you feel comfortable traveling home, being around family."

She looked at him for longer than a moment this time. "What?" she whispered. "I can go home?" she asked breathlessly.

"Of course, once you learn control."

She nodded, her entire body relaxing, a giggle pressing from her lips. "Thank you, thank you so much."

They sat the mom in the middle between Hudson and Jerry. Logan drove to a motel Jerry had picked out.

"I'm calling for room service," Jerry announced, dialing his phone.

"We don't have room numbers yet," Mark teased.

"I'll handle it. The usual?" Jerry asked. "Pasta, pizza, and the entire—" His voice cut off abruptly.

Logan knew what he was going to say, the entire dessert menu. Olie's favorite.

"Order it, Jerry, the kid will like it," Logan uttered, refusing to give in to his turbulent emotions.

"What did I miss?" Tommy's sleepy voice came over the speakers.

The woman yelped, holding her son close.

"We raided Nebraska, but the main forces are going to be in Kansas," Logan began. "We were able to save one adult and one child."

"Okay, you need me to arrange transportation for them? I think Alec was in your area."

"How do you know that, Tommy?" Hudson asked.

"The same way I know you like bustyAsianbeauties.com," Tommy muttered.

Jerry laughed hysterically. "Oh, I needed that."

"Stay off my computer," Hudson growled.

"Make me," Tommy answered. Logan had a hard time not smiling, thankfully Tommy couldn't see him.

"Oh, I'll be back," Hudson threatened.

"You can't touch me," Tommy confidently stated.

"I guess we will see," Hudson growled.

"Bring it, bitch."

Logan pulled under the hotel overhang.

"Tommy, get ahold of Alec and let us know the results. We are at the hotel now," Logan interrupted.

"Got it. Tell Hudson the girl he has been texting just received his browsing history."

"WHAT?" Hudson yelled.

Logan laughed, "That will teach you."

"Fuck! The kid is right, he's untouchable," Hudson grunted.

"You can touch him," Logan heard Mark comment as he walked to the sliding door into the hotel, "but Olivia will kill you."

"I know," Hudson grunted.

The warm air from the lobby hit Logan and he inhaled the sweet smell of coffee. The girl behind the front desk licked her lips, letting her eyes rove over his bare chest and tight sweat pants.

"Hi," she perkily greeted.

"I need three rooms for tonight," Logan began, pulling out his wallet. At least he'd had the presence of mind to take it out of his ruined pants.

"Sure, I just need an ID," she chirped. "How are you doing tonight?" she added, grinning up at him.

Logan looked at her, her dyed platinum blond hair perfectly styled, her heavily made up eyelids with purple accenting her brown eyes. She smiled up at him, noticing his attention to her coral lips. He couldn't deny she was beautiful.

"I'm well, how are you doing?" he answered, giving her a small smile.

"I'm great now." She held his gaze for a moment before returning to her typing.

He would have invited her to his room before Olie, but now those sea green eyes and feisty smile were the only things he ever wanted in his bed.

Logan leaned on the counter, taking the room keys.

"Thanks, actually can I get four rooms?" Logan amended. He didn't want to share a room with Hudson.

"Yeah, no problem."

"And is there a room service order?"

She laughed, the sound wasn't unappealing. "Yeah, you ordered the entire dessert menu?"

Logan rubbed his temples. "Yeah, that was us." He gave her a half smile, noticing her eyes dilating and scenting her attraction. Man, he wasn't even trying to flirt.

She slid the last card over. "Feel free to call if you need anything. I'm off in an hour."

Logan smiled, "I'll do that, thanks." He'd have Hudson call, the boy needed to get laid.

Back in the car, Logan drove around to the back entrance. Only Jerry and Mark had bags. He handed out room cards, "Hudson, you should call the front desk."

"Why's that?" Hudson asked.

"Just do what the man said," Jerry groaned, rubbing his forehead.

"Why?" Hudson repeated.

"Man, you are dense," Mark grunted, picking up his and Jerry's bags and heading inside.

"What am I missing?"

"She was picking up on Logan. Since he's taken, he's sending her your way," Jerry told him, climbing the stairs to their rooms.

Logan stopped in front of the room sandwiched in the middle. "This is your room. I'm to the left, Mark and Jerry to the right, and Hudson across the hall," he told the female and her child.

"You aren't staying with us?" she asked, swiping her card. Logan opened the door for her while she held her son.

"No, I want you to trust us. We are only offering to help you, to make you part of our packs. Your safety is our prime concern. Anything happens, just yell and we will come." Logan met her eyes for most of that statement. She was going to be an alpha, too.

He reached out, placing a hand on her shoulder, squeezing gently. "Whatever you need. The food will be delivered to—"

The elevator dinged and Logan heard the cart coming down the hall.

"My room!" Jerry called out. "So come on over!"

She smiled. "Let us get washed up and we'll be there."

Logan nodded. "Do we have any other clothing?" he asked Mark.

"Nope, sorry, we can hit a store in the morning for everyone."

Logan nodded, smelling the steaks on the cart.

"I think I'll skip washing up," Logan smiled.

"What's your name?" he asked gently.

"Patti, and this is Dillion."

Logan nodded.

...

The morning arrived with me staring at the dying light of our fire. I sat up, rubbing the stiffness out of my limbs before finding a bush to do my business in.

When I got back, Doyle was up and handing out breakfast, you guessed it, bread and cheese. Ugh.

"What's next?" I asked when The Magician sat up, finally.

"Good morning to you, too," he grunted.

My patience was done. "We have the griffin feather, the shadow lark, what else is needed?"

My father sighed, "You have your mother's patience."

I grunted, "I am nothing like her or you. What I am I have forged for myself."

He was silent after that response. I was being harsh. I could see that, but I couldn't bring myself to care. Hating him would almost be easier than entertaining the idea of forgiving him.

Eventually, he blew out a long breath. "We have three more things to gather. The next from the unicorns, the second from the high desert, and the third from your mother."

I grunted, rubbing my forehead. "Seriously, the shit from The Queen is going to be the most difficult."

"I had expected it to be the easiest, honestly," he admitted. "I didn't expect anyone to find out about you. I held her favor highly."

"At great risk to yourself," Doyle added.

I huffed, "I'm not surprised. Your magic would feed her for a while."

He jerked his gaze to me and I plowed ahead. "I'm not stupid. I recharge from sex, it must sustain her as well." And possibly be how she soul sucks.

He shrugged, clearly not wanting to get into it. "It isn't her fault what she needs to survive."

"Agreed, but how she chooses to go about getting it is her fault. Something she did caused the witches to shove all of the succubi and their supporters into a separate dimension."

His lips thinned. "As if you know ANYTHING about that!" he roared at me.

I snarled, "I don't need to! She has proven her inability to care for her people. What more is there to know? She has one job! ONE! To protect her people. She has failed in that. Only her power allows her to keep her throne."

"Your Alpha does the same."

I scoffed, "My Alpha protects the packs. Yes, he keeps his title because he is the most powerful shifter around. But do not mistake power for leadership. If he didn't have both, he would have been removed. Because on Earth we believe in taking care of our own! You have no right to judge me. You sold me!" I hissed my last words, hatred seeping from me.

He opened his mouth to contest what I had said, but we both knew I was right. He sold me to Selena. He sold my innocence, my youth, my hopes and dreams. I wasn't sure I wanted to forgive that.

I drew a breath. "Look, right now we need to focus on gathering the supplies. I'll hold to my end of the agreement and get you two out."

He grunted, not looking at me.

"To the unicorns then?" Doyle asked, taking a large chunk of beef jerky.

"The unicorns," The Magician agreed.

We finished eating in silence before stowing our gear and heading out of the steep jungle. The mud from the previous night was now a dusty reminder that I tried to slap out of my clothing, hair, and face.

I gave up after the dust settled into my eyes and mouth. I walked side by side with Doyle over the red fucking clay, The Magician behind us, I assumed.

"You should be kinder to him," Doyle reprimanded me softly.

I snarled.

"It was not easy giving you up," he continued on.

"Of course not, but once I was gone, how long before he was back to himself?"

"That is not fair. Our world here is difficult."

"Everyone's world is difficult, Doyle. The difference is in how to solve difficult. He waited for years on the slim chance I'd come back and free him. If he was serious about finding me, he'd have already found a way to my world, and nothing would have stopped him." That's what I would have done for my child. Or Logan for his.

Doyle was silent for a breath. "You have a point, but the anger in your heart will only consume you."

"It already has."

...

Logan rolled over to an empty bed in a strange place. He had dreamed of Olivia, her soft skin, her warm embrace. The cranky mess she was waking up. The way she would walk for hours bouncing Ginny without complaint. Olie had protected her before Ginny even arrived in this world, had kept Lorraine from poisoning the growing life inside of her.

He knew Olivia's love of family was the reason she had suggested he give Lorraine another chance to be a mother to Ginny, but Logan couldn't. He could never let his small, innocent child be around the monster who tried to kill her.

He bounced his head against the pillow, shoving himself out of bed. No good would come of dwelling on Olie and how much he missed her.

He stepped out of the shower to a knock on his door. He opened it, not bothering to look at Hudson as he continued towel drying his hair, ill-fitting sweat pants slung low on his hips.

"I have procured us new clothing," Hudson said, bouncing onto Logan's abandoned bed with a shit eating grin.

Logan took the plastic bag, dumping the contents next to Hudson.

"I gotta say," Hudson continued, "I can't believe you passed on that fine piece of tail."

Olivia would have ripped Hudson apart for that comment. Logan just shook his head because at one point, he was the same way. A beautiful woman and no-strings-attached sex had been all he was looking for. He thought about trying to explain to Hudson the value of having a steady partner, but he shook his head. Logan had been alive long enough to lose interest in one night stands, even if it had taken a couple attempts at choosing a life partner to get it right.

With Hudson, it would all be a waste of breath.

Another knock and Jerry and Mark came in. "Free breakfast ends in thirty minutes. Let's move it, people."

Logan nodded. "Have you checked on Patti and Dillion?"

"Yes, they are getting dressed," Jerry informed him.

Logan pulled the tags off his clothing, changing in front of everyone.

Jerry laughed, prompting Logan to look down at the t-shirt he had just put on.

Hot! I ain't lion.

He raised his head, looking back at Jerry.

"That," Jerry said as he pointed, "is divine intervention."

Logan looked at Mark, who was also laughing behind a cough. Hudson just grinned from ear to ear. Logan thought about asking where he had found it, but his stomach made other demands.

"Let's go, I'm hungry," Logan commanded. Besides, they all needed a laugh.

Patti and Dillion were waiting for them in the hallway.

"Breakfast?" Logan asked. Patti had washed her hair; the dirt and grease gone, it bounced around her shoulders in thick curls. She smiled at him and nodded.

Dillion ran to him, hands outstretched. Logan obliged him, hoisting him up and resting him on his hip.

"You hungry, buddy?" he asked.

"I'm sorry, he's not usually so friendly." Patti cast a worried glance around with her son out of her arms.

"He's a natural alpha," Hudson explained. "He's drawn to Logan, to mimic his behavior."

Patti's step stuttered. "How can you tell?"

"He doesn't look away from my eyes," Logan stated. "Even shifter children feel the force of my beast and can't hold my gaze for long. He does it easily."

"Is that a good thing?" she whispered.

"Alphas carry far more responsibility than submissives. You are an alpha, also. It's hard to judge how powerful, but you will carry extra weight in the packs," Logan informed her.

"If I don't want to?" she asked.

"It's like a calling," Hudson explained, "to protect the others, to keep our packs safe. You can try not listening to it, but it will feel natural to help."

Patti nodded as they entered the elevator. "You explain it far differently than he did."

Dillion pulled at Logan's hair. "Brown!"

He smiled, "Good job."

Dillion pointed to his mother's hair. "Brown."

"Very good," Patti crooned to him. "You must have children."

"A daughter, she's seven months."

The doors opened and Logan inhaled the sweet smell of syrup and potatoes. Dillion wiggled and Logan set him down. He ran to the food, jumping at the counter. Patti was right behind, doing her best to wrangle him.

"Driving or flying?" Jerry asked around a mouthful of food, after they had sat down with heavily loaded plates.

Logan rubbed the back of his neck. "Patti, do you feel comfortable flying with Dillion back to St. Ann? I will have Alec, the Compass Alpha for the region, meet you."

She chewed on her lip, meeting Logan's gaze. He saw the terrified woman, but he also saw her beast step forward. "If you trust Alec, then we do as well."

Logan nodded, watching her turn her gaze away. He pulled out his cell phone, texting the information to Alec.

...

Logan waited until the plane crested the clouds before nodding to Jerry that they could leave.

The drive passed slowly. Logan was anxious to get back to Olivia and Ginny. His anger at his inability to fix Olivia was being taken out on Ginny through his absence, and it wasn't fair.

After passing the Kansas state line, they traveled another hour, arriving outside of the small town of Fort Dodge. It actually wasn't even a town, just a loose grouping of buildings. Jerry followed the directions spat out by the GPS until they were three miles from the soon to be departed.

"Same plan?" Mark asked, getting out of the SUV and stretching.

"Yes," Logan agreed, his beast anxious to be done with this. He rubbed his breastbone; something felt different.

He sniffed the air, pulling the scents deep into his lungs, sifting through the traces of blood, dirt, and power. The alpha for the rebels was here.

Logan smiled, straining his ears.

"What's so funny?" Jerry asked.

"I believe I'm evolving," Logan murmured.

"Evolving? What the hell is that?" Jerry asked.

Hudson and Mark shared a concerned look.

"It's a legend, just like mate marking. In times of great stress, our beasts will develop honed senses, far beyond those of a normal shifter," Hudson supplied.

Jerry grunted, "It's probably the succubus blood. All the vampires go fucking gaga for it."

Logan stilled in the tall grass, the flat land allowing a breeze to bring even more scents to him. He flexed his hands at his side. He needed to stay human to deliver the same warning as in Nebraska. Then he could free the animal inside of him.

"Stay behind me," he warned the others, before marching toward the compound.

Through the pack bonds, he felt Hudson's concern and Mark's determination. He idly wondered about what Jerry had said. He doubted it, though. Olivia's blood had been within him for months, and he physically felt no different.

Logan's sight picked up the dim outline of a fortress ahead, laid out in a square with sentry towers at each corner. He picked up none of the rancid odors from the first compound. It appeared the alpha was gaining funds, no doubt from his expanding pack. He'd never be able to maintain it, though. The tithe system only worked when an alpha allowed his pack the freedom to work.

There was no freedom here.

Logan could hear safeties being unclicked in the closest tower as the building solidified in his sight. He kept walking.

"Halt!" a voice boomed out. He kept walking.

"We will shoot!" A warning shot dislodged dirt by his foot.

Still he kept moving. He was Alpha and ruler of the packs for good reasons.

"Hear me well, if you fight me, we will kill you."

"Who the fuck are you?"

"The Alpha." He could hear the hushed whispers before him, the whisper of his backup moving behind him as he continued forging ahead. Without breaking stride, he shifted into his lion, shredding his pants.

"I didn't bring enough clothing," Jerry groaned behind him.

Shots rang out, but Jerry uttered a word and Logan's lion never felt the sting of the bullets. He charged and felt Hudson shift into a buffalo next to him, passing him to smash into the large wooden double doors. Hudson reared back, delivering a second blow, and they splintered against his massive weight.

Wolf shifters flew out. Hudson stepped back, a wolf between his teeth, the sound of its rib cage being crushed feeding Logan's carnal beast. Hudson shook his head, ripping the wolf apart before turning his attention to the others attached to his hide.

"Shit," Jerry said, before muttering another spell.

Logan cleared the distance between himself and the crushed doors, landing firmly inside the dimly lit fort. A wolf growled, lunging for his throat. Logan turned, snapping his jaws around its head, destroying the feeble attempt.

Another wolf lunged for his hindquarters and Logan kicked out, knocking the animal outside. It wasn't a killing blow, but he had time to rectify that.

Mark shifted and was defending him from the back while Jerry kept throwing magically charged bombs that sent the waiting wolves into the walls. Logan had no time to admire his handiwork as he took down wolf after wolf. Young and untrained, they fell easily at his feet, his paws becoming saturated with blood.

Logan huffed, his wounds healing, but his soul uneasy with the kills here. He turned to survey the damage, wanting the shifter responsible for this disaster.

If the pathetic excuse for an alpha thought sheer numbers would overwhelm him, he was wrong.

Hudson, make sure no one leaves here. I want the alpha, he sent through the pack threads.

On it, Hudson responded, before turning to check the perimeter.

Body after body fell, shifting human. They were younger and younger. It didn't stop him, though, didn't delay his life-ending paw swipes.

Turning and scanning the wolves hiding in the back, he shifted, blood dripping from his chin.

"Submissives, where is your alpha?" Logan boomed.

A few showed their teeth before cowering, none meeting his gaze.

Jerry limped up from behind him. "We should have brought Patti, at least she might have been able to talk sense into them."

Logan grunted, hindsight was always 20-20.

A wolf shifted back to human, panting from the change, unused to it.

"Patti?" he rasped out. A wolf snapped at him.

Logan leaned forward and snapped its neck.

"D-Dillion?" the submissive asked, chancing a look into Logan's caramel eyes.

Logan narrowed his eyes. He wasn't about to give away information on the two he had saved.

"Dillion is my son, is he alive?" the submissive asked.

"Yes, but the only way you live to see them is to show us the alpha," Jerry negotiated.

Logan growled. "Sorry, Logan," Jerry smiled. "I get all power hungry throwing magic around."

Logan turned, raising an eyebrow to the submissive as another wolf peeled back its lips, ready to pounce on him. Logan backhanded it across the room.

The submissive nodded, standing uncertainly. Mark went to him, still in his wolf, offering him support and a barrier to the others trying to attack him.

With the cracking of bones and a wail of distress, another shifter turned human.

"He will kill us all!" she screamed at their helper. "He is lying about Patti and Dillion! You are a fool!"

"Jerry, do you have a phone?" Logan asked.

"Yep." Jerry followed his train of thought, already dialing Alec. He put it on speakerphone.

"Hello?" Alec answered.

"Are Patti and Dillion with you?" Logan asked.

"Yeah, we are grabbing an early lunch. This kid is always hungry. Let me put you on speaker."

The submissive made a strangled noise, covering his mouth.

"Pepperoni!" chanted Dillion.

"Alright, how about some veggies?" Patti asked.

"Sausage!" Dillion added to his chant.

"Patti, I have a man here claiming to be Dillion's father," Logan began; it probably wasn't his brightest idea to do this in front of Dillion. Olivia would have known that. Dammit.

"Peter?" Patti asked, hopeful.

"Patti?" Peter asked, drawn to the sound of her voice.

"You're alive!" Patti squeaked.

"For now," Peter answered, casting a look to Logan.

"Don't fight him, Peter. He won't hurt you. He's taken great care of Dillion and me—food, clothing, even explaining about dominants and setting us up with a job and home."

Peter took another hesitant look at Logan, searching his face for betrayal. Logan found Olivia's voice haunting him.

They are terrified, Logan, having known nothing but pain and lies at the hands of this alpha. Show them why we follow you.

His own ego must have shoved its way in there. She'd never admit to following him.

"I'm not here to harm you. I gave my warning to the others. I want your alpha dead. I do NOT treat my people as he has done. We are pack, we are family, and we honor those bonds. So either make your peace with a new Alpha or make your peace with death."

Jerry patted him on his back, ending the call with Alec.

Several others began shifting back, the woman who called out to Peter lunging for him. Mark ended her swiftly.

The others bowed their dirty heads, panting from the pain of the change and kneeling, acknowledging him as leader.

"Alright, everyone follow us," Logan stated.

He nodded to Mark, who pulled Peter gently toward the door. Peter looked down at him, nodding, before turning. "This way," he announced in a trance.

Logan nodded. "I'll bring up the rear," Jerry said, giving Logan a look. He nodded, feeling a tug at his heart. Jerry wasn't officially pack, but he might as well be. He defended Olie and Logan both without fail. She had a gift for picking up the outcasts.

Peter cast a look behind him, waiting for everyone to follow them.

"Can I ask you a question?" he asked Logan.

"Yes," Logan grunted, wanting to get rid of the alpha.

"The al—" He stopped himself. "The guy who turned us said that I should be a dominant because I'm male." Shame laced his words heavily.

"It doesn't work like that. Many factors contribute to whether a shifter is a submissive or dominant; gender is not part of it." He reached out a supportive arm to Peter's shoulder. Peter jumped, looking back in fear. "There is no shame in being submissive. Our society is constructed to allow all members to have jobs that meet their desires."

Peter gave him a tentative smile and Logan knew Olie would have been proud.

"Patti and Dillion are going to be alphas. Alec will be setting her up with a job that matches her skills."

"Who is Alec?" someone from the back asked.

Peter turned right, ambling along and not checking corners. Thankfully, Mark was.

"Alec is the Compass Alpha for the East. He reports to me," Logan explained.

"I was a metal smith before all this," Peter admitted.

Logan nodded. "Olivia is going to be so excited," Jerry muttered from the back.

"Who is Olivia?" another voice behind Logan asked.

"My mate." His words were clipped.

"Oh." Peter looked back, sorrow in his eyes. "I'm so sorry. We heard she died."

"Nope, not dead," Jerry quickly answered. "Healing."

Peter nodded, surprised, looking back at the others. His steps slowed and he dropped a hand into Mark's fur before making the next turn, visibly shaking as he pointed down the hall to a steel door.

Logan pulled Peter behind him.

"It's operated by a switch from the inside," Peter whispered.

Mark growled, looking at Logan, feeling what he was going to do.

"Relax, Mark." Jerry threw a small bag at the door. "Cover your eyes!" he yelled as an afterthought.

Logan tossed Mark behind him, covering him and Peter with his body. Shards of metal sliced into his back. He hissed, straightening out, turning his back to the others. The metal fell out, clicking against the linoleum floor.

"Stay here," Logan commanded.

"Is he going to be okay?" Peter whispered to Jerry.

Jerry chuckled. "Don't let his kind demeanor fool you. Logan is the baddest beast there has ever been."

Logan smiled, shifting into his lion as he reached the door.

A snarling wolf lunged at him, larger than the others. Logan took the hit, letting himself be pushed back against the plush carpet. Teeth sank into his shoulder before Logan sliced down the wolf's side, opening four long, deep gashes.

The wolf yipped, jumping back, snarling still. Logan could make this quick, and after all the killing his beast should have been satisfied, but it wasn't. Logan wanted him to suffer, to bleed out slowly.

He stalked closer to the pretend alpha. Launching across the short distance, he sunk his teeth into the faker's shoulder, tearing out a chunk of muscle.

The alpha cried out, slicing Logan across his flank. Logan grunted, the wound already healing. The pretend alpha limped, his side healed but the missing muscle causing him pain. With a grunt, he retreated behind his desk and began to shift.

Logan followed him, watching as he pawed with his good hand to open the desk drawer.

"You are smarter than I thought," the ex-alpha hissed.

Logan gave him a carnal smile.

"But I don't fight fair." The pretend alpha pulled out a gun. Logan scented the same bullet that had torn through his mate.

The gun cocked. Logan let his beast take full control, launching as the gun went off. His teeth sank into his victim's head and he tore it free. It was too quick of a kill.

Spitting out the head, Logan pushed off the dead body, turning and landing on all four paws. His side throbbed, fresh blood leaking onto the carpet as he padded back to his party.

He shifted in the doorway, looking down at his left side and holding back a groan. There was a substantial hole. Cracking his neck, he pulled strength from the packs, using their energy to heal the wound. It shrunk in matter of minutes.

He looked into Jerry's eyes and nodded. It was done.

...

"The unicorns live under guard," The Magician stated as we stared into what I guess was a forest. Thick, tall trees, in hues of red and burnt orange, dotted the flat landscape before us, their leaves a dying brown.

"I suggest not killing them," he continued.

I turned, narrowing my eyes at him. He sounded like Logan and my heart constricted painfully.

"Fine." I bit out the word. "Let's just get this over with."

I stormed into the red trees, my clothing sticking to me uncomfortably in the humidity. I still charged on, having no idea where the hell I was going. Good news, it didn't matter.

A man as thick as one of the trees stepped out. I bounced against his solid chest, landing on my ass.

"You the guard?" I asked.

He nodded, a creaking sound coming from his neck.

I stood up, brushing dirt off my ass. "I need to see the unicorns."

"They do not wish to be bothered."

"Too fucking bad."

The guard tilted his head at me.

My father stepped up then. "We are seeking to speak to the unicorns regarding obtaining a rare and special object."

The guard frowned. "You wish for one of their horns."

My father bowed slightly. "Yes."

"No," the guard answered, and three more stepped out from behind trees.

I groaned.

116

"Please tell me we don't have to kill them for a horn," I groaned.

"No, they fall off every year. Similar to deer antlers," my father stated.

"Great, so is there anyone the unicorns will allow to visit?" I asked.

"No," the guard and my father answered in unison.

I groaned, "Great." The Queen was stellar at building relationships.

I pressed my lips together. "Sorry boys, this is going to hurt."

I punched the guard and screamed, pain radiating up my hand.

"Mother fucker!" I yelled, shaking my hand out, dancing back.

The guard cracked a smile, I think, before swinging an arm at my head. I ducked. No way in hell I was getting hit with one of those fuckers. I'd already been split apart on the ground, thanks.

His stiff legs took time to maneuver toward my new position. I smirked. Did I really have to best the guards? Or did I just need to be faster?

I shifted back out of range of another swinging arm. Finesse was not part of their skill set, either.

I cast a look at Doyle, who took a hit and was launched out of the forest. I ducked, dodging left and searching for my father. He wasn't faring any better.

"Magician, take care of Doyle, I'm going in!" I screamed at him.

He looked at me in shock and the guard fighting him landed a glancing blow to his side. I didn't stay around to watch any longer. Instead I charged forward. I twisted to the left when I felt the air shift with the guard's hands of stone trying to grab me.

"Trespasser!" the guards called out, the cry echoed by all the trees.

I pressed my hands over my ears, running. Now if I was a unicorn, where would I be? A white flank dashed in front of me and I bounced against it, landing on my ass.

"Ouch," I groaned.

A metallic purple horn was pressed against my throat. I backed away quickly, rolling behind a tree.

"What are you doing in our home?" he roared at me.

"I need a horn!" I yelled, peeking out the left side. A horn flashed close to my side. "Asshole!" I yelled.

"We do not serve you succubus whores!" he yelled at me.

Fucking hell. I peeked out the left side again, finding him waiting on the right. I launched before he could correct his mistake. I landed on his back, forcing my knees tighter on his neck than on anything else in my entire life. Haha, there's a whore joke in there.

"First off, fucker, I am not a whore." He reared back before galloping through the forest. "Secondly, I am trying to get off your damn world and back to mine!"

He stopped, skidding on the red dirt. That dislodged me. I flew forward, smashing my shoulder against an unyielding tree.

"Ugh." I rolled on my back, putting pressure against my shoulder, heaving a sigh.

"Get off our world?" he questioned, his pearl coat shining with glitter.

"Yep."

"How?"

"The Magician has a spell to take us out of here," I heaved, rotating my shoulder gingerly.

"Define 'us,'" he asked, black eyes staring down at me.

"Me, him, and Doyle."

He snorted. "But not us!" he bellowed.

"The portal won't be open long enough to get you through; we can come back for you after we are through, however," The Magician explained, escorted by the guards.

Doyle had a dried smear of blood by his temple. He nodded to me and I returned the gesture. Yes, we were beat up, no, we weren't done.

The unicorn turned his back to me. "You are the King of Liars!" he accused my father.

I stared at him. Great. What secret was coming out of the closet now?

"I did not lie to you. I did not know, there is a difference," The Magician answered.

The unicorn huffed, "The end result is the same, our packs are stuck in this barren wasteland!"

I groaned, standing. "Look, if you give us the horn, you have a chance at leaving here. If you don't, then you are stuck forever."

Flicking his tail, he turned his attention back to me. "What would you know, daughter of the liar?"

I stepped forward, pulling his head down by the horn. "I know one way or another, I am getting a horn to get back to my world. You are either on my side or against me."

He shook me off, laughing, "Tell your mother she has trained you well!"

I kicked his front leg; it buckled. "You will not compare me to her," I threatened him.

He stared open-mouthed at me. "You dare harm me?"

"I will harm anyone who stops me from leaving. Now choose, are you with us or against us?"

Probably not my best move, threatening the unicorns on their turf with their impressive guards, but I had a fucking point to make.

The unicorn blinked, and I daresay I saw the beginnings of fear. No one knows how to handle the crazy bitch.

"With you." His leg straightened up, healing. "Follow me."

My father looked at me, shocked. I ignored him, following the unicorn.

"I am Adair."

"Olivia," I responded, coming even with him. "Where is the rest of your herd?"

"Hiding. We knew what The Magician wanted. Why else would he venture here?"

I kept my silence. I could relate to the betrayal he'd suffered.

"How is the Queen?" Adair asked.

I growled. "On my shit list," I answered.

His head snapped to me. "Your mother?"

"Don't call her that. The bitch sold me into slavery and is only concerned about herself. If she had half a fucking brain, she would have gotten everyone out by now, instead of leaving her messes behind for her daugh—for me to fix."

Adair nodded, continuing on. "I didn't know."

"Now you do." It's hard to fake the kind of hate that flowed through my soul-body veins. The kind of hate that is etched into my very bones and defines who and what I am.

We reached what I thought was a shimmering pond, but upon closer inspection, it was actually a huge hole of horns.

"Wow," I muttered.

"Take your pick, Olivia," Adair instructed me.

I nodded, my hand resting on a honey colored horn that reminded me of Logan.

I held the horn to my father, who nodded. "You have chosen well."

I nodded, not daring to speak, taking my pack from Doyle and securing it gently.

"Okay, logistics. Where do you want to live?"

Adair looked at me for a long moment, probably gauging my honesty. "The rainforest."

I winced. "Yeah, that's being destroyed. Do you have any other options?"

"Blue Ridge mountain range in Tennessee."

I nodded. "Done. Now, do you harm humans at all?"

He stomped his front feet. "Only those who seek to harm us."

I nodded. "Any weird sacrifices, or killings?"

"We are a peaceful race."

"Okay great, I promised the mermaids they could come over first. After I finish with them, when The Magician is strong enough, we will call you."

"You are sincere," Adair stated, with a note of surprise.

"Yeah, I don't play games."

"You are scared," he muttered, stepping closer to me.

I clamped my mouth around the words that wanted to slip out, I am broken.

"We all have our issues, now if you could point us in the direction of the high desert?"

Adair led us to the opposite side of the forest. "We have saved days by this, thank you," my father stated.

Adair only grunted. I guess he was still sore about the past, couldn't blame him at all.

"This where I leave you," Adair stated, turning and blending into the forest.

I nodded, stepping out and away from the humidity, into a fucking blowtorch.

"Ugh, I wish I wasn't real again," I groaned.

"We are almost finished," Doyle encouraged me, smiling. "We are going home."

I smiled at him, damn sure we were.

My breathing hitched, a sharp pain slicing through my chest. I inhaled, pushing it away and shaking my head.

"Are you in pain?" my father asked.

"It's nothing,"

"No, it's our time, it's running out."

"Two more items," I told him, meeting his gaze. "Just two more." He nodded. I chose to ignore the fear and worry in his eyes. I hadn't made it this far to be cut down now.

Chapter 6

Logan rented out a ten-bedroom home for the submissives he had rescued, and even then people were doubling up.

Alec's Beta was on his way out to get everyone educated. Logan had already completed the blood ceremony to add them all to the packs. He rubbed his forearm, turning to Peter in the backseat, sandwiched between Hudson and Mark.

He had something to say, Logan could feel the pressure in his brain. "What's on your mind, Peter?" he finally asked.

"I — I should have told you sooner. I just — I just was worried you wouldn't accept me as pack," Peter ended in a whisper.

"Tell us what?" Hudson asked, turning to look at him.

Peter continued to rub the palm of his hand as Logan's irritation spiked.

"I forged the bullets that shot your mate," he confessed.

The blow hit Logan hard, knocking the wind out of him. Jerry's hand on his shoulder kept him from killing Peter, but a savage growl ripped from his throat.

"I didn't know what it was for," Peter sobbed.

Logan turned around, breathing, pushing his beast back down. Jerry removed his hand carefully.

"Where did he find the combination of materials to slow our healing?" Logan rasped, finally able to have a clear thought.

"He experimented." Peter's voice was soft.

Logan slammed is head against the headrest, unable to offer Peter forgiveness or comfort.

"Do not call him!" Anna's voice boomed over the car speakers.

"What the hell?" Mark muttered.

"I am in charge here, you will obey me," Anna continued. Logan heard the threat there.

"Touch him and I will skin you alive," he warned Anna.

"You sneaky little shit," Anna hissed.

"Olivia's missing," Tommy whispered, clearing his throat.

"What?" Logan's voice was soft.

"She was removed from the hospital over four hours ago and never delivered to us," Tommy continued on.

Jerry slammed the accelerator.

"Tommy, I want all video surveillance from the hospital and surrounding areas. I want every scrap of paper regarding her release from the hospital. Call Mercer and have him work it from his end. Call Mal, I want to know what she knows."

"Logan," Tommy urged, "I can't get ahold of Darren, and this bitch won't send someone to his house."

"Shifter matters are not ours," Anna dictated.

All Logan could do was breathe; it was either that or rip the moving SUV apart.

"Anna, you should run."

"You don't scare me, shifter."

Logan laughed, something he learned from Olie. "I will," he promised.

"We are thirty minutes out, Tommy," Jerry took over the conversation. "We will run by the house and check on Darren."

"No, check his work. I talked with Kass, she and the kids are okay." Tommy instructed. "I'm sending you the address now."

Jerry checked his phone, punching a few buttons as the guidance system took over navigation.

"Are you safe?" Hudson asked from the back.

"Yeah, for all her posturing, she hasn't hurt us," Tommy answered. "I'm pretty sure this is what Olivia was like in the beginning, also."

Anna huffed, "She's always had a soft spot for the unwanted."

Something inside of Logan snapped. "I don't know why Olivia chose you as her replacement, but it won't last."

"Oh yeah, what are you going to do about it? Her instructions are clear. I am in charge."

"While you live," Mark added.

"Try me, boys, the only one who has ever bested me was Olie," Anna challenged, flat and bored.

"Alright Logan, I've got massive amounts of video feeds to go through. I'm going to call Becky in on this," Tommy said.

"Use Gunner as well," Logan instructed.

"On it, let me know about Darren," Tommy asked.

"I will."

Ten minutes later, Jerry squealed to a stop in front of a one-story office building.

Logan hadn't been here before, why hadn't he? Darren was his brother.

Because he was still holding a pointless grudge from when Darren utilized Olivia to save Hannah, and in the process exposed the corruption in his ranks. He was a fool. Logan should have installed him back as the Compass Alpha for East.

He could still fix it, though. He opened his mind to the pack bonds, sifting through the emotions until he centered on Darren's. He was unconscious and inside.

Logan flung his door open, pounding up the concrete steps, slamming the glass door open so forcefully it broke, sending shards of glass onto the pavement under his feet. He cleared the front receptionist desk, turned left and slammed his shoulder into a vampire. Without preamble, Logan partially shifted, his right hand clawing down and through the vampire, splitting him in two.

Hudson charged past him, breaking down the door at the end of the hall where Darren was. Logan was just behind him, a vampire dying in Hudson's grasp, another vaulting through the window to escape.

Logan went after that one. "Keep him alive!" He yelled at Hudson.

His rational thinking was coming back; he needed intel. Why the fuck were vampires after Darren?

The vampire running away from Logan took a terrified look back at him. Logan launched, denying his beast the shift, his lion wouldn't keep the vamp alive. Gripping the back of his collar, Logan pulled him back, slamming the back of his head against the concrete.

Hauling him up by his neck, Logan dangled him there, the vampire reeking of fear.

"We didn't kill him," he whispered.

"I know."

Logan punched him and the vampire went limp. He dragged the body behind him, flinging him through the ruined window and climbing in after him.

Jerry looked over Logan and shook his head. "We need to get you shoes."

Logan looked down at his feet, crusted in glass and bleeding freely, before turning his attention back to Jerry, who held an ice pack to Darren's head.

He walked over to his brother, kneeling down, having no care for the glass slicing through his feet.

"Are you alright?" he asked, watching the goose egg on Darren's head slowly heal.

Darren nodded. "Yeah, I have no idea what they were after. They made an appointment and everything, sat down, started talking, and then wham. God, this is embarrassing, four vampires kicked my ass."

"Four?" Logan asked.

Darren nodded.

"Fuck, we missed one."

Peter edged toward the open doorway. "I'm sorry — sorry to interrupt, but Tommy is talking over the car." He held out Jerry's cell phone tentatively.

Jerry took it from him. Peter looked around and swallowed.

"Good job, Peter," Logan praised him. Peter straightened up, giving him a rare smile.

"They hacked Darren's computer and cell phone and stole one of his vehicles. I've taken the liberty of reporting it." Tommy's furious typing could be heard in the background

"Darren, why the fuck don't you have a better cell phone?" Tommy grumbled.

"Get him one, Tommy," Logan commanded.

"You don't have two kids to feed and a new business. Fuck, this is going to ruin me." Darren rubbed his forehead, the bruises gone.

"I want you back as the East Compass Alpha." Darren's head snapped up to meet his brother's gaze.

"What about Alec?" he asked.

Logan shrugged. "I'm going to offer him the West; if he wants it, the East is yours."

Darren's gaze swung to Hudson.

"Yeah, I kinda screwed up my gig," Hudson admitted.

"He's lucky to be alive," Mark clarified.

"Why?" Darren's light brown eyes bored into Logan's caramel ones.

Logan leaned back on his heels. "Because I removed you for the wrong reasons and I'm sorry."

Darren blinked a few times. "Okay, but only if Alec wants to move."

"That boy will be packed by tomorrow. He gets to spend his days on a secluded beach with women in bikinis?" Jerry finished by muttering a few words under his breath while holding Darren's abused head. "That should help with the headache."

Darren nodded. "Yeah, that's a lot better. Thanks."

"Easy Jerry, you've been hitting the magic hard the past few days," Mark warned, watching his boyfriend closely.

Jerry shrugged. "It's worth it. Just think how jealous Olie will be when we tell her about our escapades."

Logan smiled. She would be jealous she didn't get to kill the asshole that shot her.

"Peter, who shot the gun?" Logan asked, turning.

"The alpha," Peter answered easily. Logan nodded, he didn't know his name, and he didn't care enough to find out.

"Dammit," Tommy cursed, "whoever is loading Olie into the ambulance, with Darren's stolen car escorting them, isn't giving me a shot of his face."

"Male?" Logan asked.

"Yes, male, expensive taste, vampire," Anna's voice came over the phone. "Master Vampire."

"How can you tell?" Tommy asked, impressed.

"Look at his clothing; that's not off the rack, it's tailored, watch how it moves around his knee and ankle. That has to be a custom fabric to flow in that manor. As for vampire, watch his chest, it doesn't move with a breath. Also, he stands perfectly still, humans and shifters don't hold themselves in that way."

"Zachariah?" Jerry voiced Logan's suspicions.

Logan rubbed his temple. "We are coming to you. I need shoes."

...

The pain was getting worse. My breathing was labored, my skin felt on fire, and my head throbbed.

I landed hard on my knees, bracing my hands against the red desert. My vision blacked out.

"Daughter," my father whispered, running his hands over my face.

"I can't see," I whispered, feeling his hand on my cheek. "Am I dying?" Fear and pain coursed through me, making me weak.

"No," he offered, his voice raw. "Not yet."

"Doyle, take her back to my study. I can transport myself to the high desert," The Magician stated.

I felt his kiss on my forehead as Doyle picked me up. "Stay with me, daughter."

...

It was a cramped ride to the manor, for the vampires in the trunk that is. Hudson hadn't killed his vampire, though he had come very close. Darren took his own vehicle, which was left untouched, to check in on Kass and the children.

Logan had removed the glass from his feet, Peter was being transported to his child, and Jerry and Mark were on their way home. Logan went to Tommy's room, holding his shoes in his hand.

He sat on Tommy's bed. "Show me the video."

Tommy hit play, scooting back out of the way of his large monitors.

Logan finished with his shoes, leaning his forearms on his knees.

He saw the nurse wheel Olivia out, another accompanying her with the machines. They checked the paperwork handed to them by the Master Vampire, the main nurse flipping through the documents. It was dark. Even with the filtering Tommy had done, Logan couldn't tell much.

The paperwork was in order and the nurses walked away. Darren's black SUV led the private ambulance away from the hospital.

"Did you track down the private ambulance?" Logan asked Tommy.

"It's fake. I'm searching all stolen and recently sold ambulances and tracking down those that have LoJack, which so far has been all of them. What did you do with the vampires?"

"Blue took them to the basement."

"Oh geez." Tommy shook his head. "You should have waited on changing."

Logan stood, clasping a hand on his shoulder. "Good point. I just hope he hasn't had all the fun without me. Have you seen Anna?" Logan really wanted to beat a valid point into that red head.

"Naw, she went to the hospital to shake down some leads. She's not that bad, Logan."

"She's not Olie."

Tommy smiled sadly. "No one is."

...

I wasn't sure I was breathing any more or if Doyle was still carrying me. I was lost in an endless sea of throbbing pain.

...

Logan padded down the stairs to the scent of blood, a painful wail on the air.

He smiled, turning the corner. "How are they coming along?"

Blue used a rag saturated with blood to wipe off his blade.

"They belong to Tate's house." Blue cast him a knowing look.

"Then let's return them."

Blue returned Logan's smile, stowing his blades.

"Let me get the silver."

...

I could feel my heart struggling to beat, the death rattle in my chest.

"Logan," I whispered.

...

"Are you sure you don't want more backup?" Hudson asked, riding shotgun in the SUV. Blue sat smirking in the back, the thin silver chains around the vampires sending up tendrils of smoke.

"Don't tell me ye be afraid of a few vampires," Blue scoffed.

Hudson shifted in his seat. "A few, no, but an entire House full?"

Blue leaned forward, resting a hand on Hudson's shoulder. "Don't worry, I'll protect you."

Logan laughed, surprised, but a pang of longing hit him hard. That was a line from Olivia's playbook.

Hudson grunted, shoving Blue's hand off him. Blue sat back, laughing.

Logan rolled down his window at the guard gate.

"Logan, here to see Tate," he announced. He was looking forward to this fight.

"I'm sorry, you have been banned from the House."

"Huh, then what do you suppose I do with these two?" Logan asked, rolling down the backseat window.

"Shit," the guard muttered. "What are you two doing back there?"

The vampires shifted silently.

"You see we have a problem. These two attacked my brother and kidnapped my mate. So when I tell you that Tate will see me, I mean if I have to kill every vampire who crosses my path, I. Will. See. Him," Logan finished in a growl.

The guard looked terrified for a moment, but then straightened his back, opening his mouth to give a retort. Logan unbuckled his seatbelt, his hand landing on the door handle when the guard burst into ash.

He coughed, looking through the debris at Anna's emerald gaze.

"Tommy disabled security. They know you are here." She hit a button in the guard's station and the wooden arm rose, the tire spikes pulling into the ground. She disappeared before Logan could ask what the hell she was doing there.

He settled back into the seat, leaving his seatbelt off, slamming the SUV into drive.

"Did we know she was going to be here?" Hudson asked.

"No," Blue answered, clipped, drumming his fingers against the door handle. "I haven't made up my mind if I like her."

Logan cast him a short look as he pulled up in front of the Centennial House. "I do not. She lost Olivia. Some things are not forgivable."

Blue inclined his head, agreeing. Logan opened his door.

"You cannot park here. What the hell? How did you get past the gate?" the guard at the front door asked.

Logan landed a solid right hook, the vamp's head snapping back before he crumpled to the ground. The other guard pointed his gun, his finger on the trigger.

"Not another fucking step," he warned.

Blue landed an impressively high kick, followed by a left hook, dropping the guard to the ground.

"Let's go, these fuckers smell," Hudson complained, dragging the two bound vampires behind him.

"Really, Hudson, I didn't even get to properly play with them. I promise I can make them smell worse," Blue chuckled.

Hudson grunted, bouncing the vamps' heads against the concrete steps. Logan smiled, holding one of the double doors open.

"What the hell?" Hudson grunted.

Logan moved back in front of Hudson, Blue right beside him. Anna had quite the gathering, piles of ash at her feet.

"Looks like we missed the official greeting party," Blue muttered. Logan and Blue fanned out on each side of her. Logan didn't like it, showing her support, but he wasn't seeing any other options.

"You side with this monster?!" Tate bellowed, standing in front of his own support, the entire House, less the dead ones. His chest heaved, his body vibrating with rage.

Logan scanned the group behind Tate, looking for Mal.

"Please tell me you didn't kill Mal," Logan whispered to Anna.

"No, I warned her we were coming and to take cover," Anna answered, twirling a blade in her left hand. Logan took a second look at her, having seen that same predatory gleam and dexterity with weapons in Olivia.

Blue leaned forward, too short to be seen over Anna's head, looking at Logan with, Logan imagined, the same disturbed look he was trying very hard to cover.

"ANSWER ME!" Tate screamed.

Logan turned his attention back to the small vampire in front of him. He knew his eyes glowed with his beast.

"You will be the one delivering answers," Logan growled. Hudson dropped the two chained vampires in front of Tate.

"These two harmed my brother and helped kidnap Olivia. They belong to you." Logan's voice dripped with venom. His shoulders were tense, his beast not caring what Tate had to say, caring only for the taste of his blood.

"They aren't mine," Tate denied.

The captive vampire in front of Logan looked up at Tate with a smirk. "You deny your allegiance to the House of Zachariah?"

Logan kicked him, his heel connecting with the back of the asshole's skull, concaving it. Blood and brain seeped into the Persian rug under Logan's feet.

Logan turned his attention to the look of shock and horror on Tate's face.

"Someone killed the Executioner?" a voice whispered.

Logan's beast bellowed, "There will be silence!" His neck twisted, fur breaking out down his arms, his chest heaving with the effort of restraining his beast.

"Tate, I'd suggest a private meeting, before Logan and I kill your entire House," Anna said, her arms crossed over her chest.

Tate turned his attention to her, vibrating with rage. His eyes blazed, completely amber.

The vampire Logan had kicked pulled himself up. Logan kicked him again.

"Where is my mate?" Logan hissed. He held a hand up when Tate instantly opened his mouth.

"If the answer is, 'I don't know,' I will kill everyone."

"We will," Anna amended.

"I don't really think Logan needs any help in this state," Blue commented.

"Although Anna was doing a fine job on her own," Hudson smiled, adding his brilliant insight.

"He doesn't know, Logan," a voice called from behind him.

Logan growled, slowly turning. Raphael stood under one of the limited lighting fixtures, the glow casting his dark hair with a blue tint, his pronounced cheekbones giving him a sunken look.

Having made his grand entrance, he continued his leisurely stroll.

"We have been patrolling this House, due to the drought it has endured." Raphael raised a disapproving eyebrow at Tate before turning back to Logan.

"These two haven't set foot in here. Nor has anyone who left gone close to the hospital," Raphael finished.

Logan grunted, looking at Tate before turning back to the vampires in front of him.

"Do you want more time with them, Blue?" Logan asked.

"I'd love it. Since Tate is denying they are his, I do believe that makes them unprotected," Blue smiled.

"Zachariah will not be pleased," hissed the vampire Logan kept kicking.

Raphael bent down to the vampire, still on the ground. "Would you like to call him and inform him of such?"

The vampire's mouth sealed shut.

"Don't fret, I'll get it out of you," Blue promised. Logan was glad that smile wasn't pointed at him.

"That's it?" Anna asked, disappointed. "We still don't know where Olivia is."

Logan didn't need the reminder. He took a breath, turning to Anna. "The Oracle will."

Anna's eyes widened slightly. She opened her mouth to say something, but changed her mind, her gaze swinging back to Tate.

"Do not imagine for a moment this situation has been properly rectified. You have put ALL of us in danger with your poor allegiances and your inability to keep your House safe. You have made powerful enemies on this day," Anna regally informed Tate.

His disbelief was evident.

Hudson pulled up a vampire, Blue taking the other one.

"Let's go play, boys," he sang to them merrily.

With the vampires loaded back up, Anna stopped Logan. "I'm coming with you."

He grunted, "I don't need you to."

Her eyes flashed, before her gaze shot back inside the House. "This isn't over," she hissed at him.

Logan slammed the SUV door and revved the engine. Of course it wasn't.

...

Logan took Blue and the two vampires to the farmhouse.

Becky was waiting for them, smoking on the wrap around porch.

"Those things will kill you," Hudson commented, trying for a smile as he followed Blue inside with the vampires.

Becky's eyes flicked to him, her mouth blowing out the smoke as she held the door for them.

"Room four is clean, Blue," she called over her shoulder.

"My favorite, thank you darlin'," he called back to her.

"What's wrong?" Logan asked.

Becky's eyes flashed with emotion. "I can't find her," she confessed, her voice breaking as she flicked ash from her cigarette.

Logan reached out, resting a hand on her shoulder as she continued. "I've looked everywhere. I've scoured hours of footage, grainy to clear, enhanced images, focused on reflections, reversed images, looked for any deleted images. Nothing." Becky took another long drag.

"If she is gone, there is no one to protect us," she whispered, pushing away a tear.

"I'm still here, Becky, I will keep everyone safe," Logan tried to reassure her.

Becky looked at him, a sad smile on her lips. "Don't take this the wrong way, Logan. I appreciate your attempt at easing my fears, but your first priority will always be the shifters. Our band of misfits would be hard pressed to find our place within your packs."

He knew she was right, but he wasn't one to give up. Olivia wasn't the only one with a stubborn streak.

"Besides, she isn't gone. The Oracle will know where she is."

"Logan, you cannot go to The Oracle," Becky warned. "Your packs need you. If you both fall, the fucking vampires win it all."

Logan jerked his head at her words. "I don't like the vampires," Becky stated before flicking her cigarette away.

"It's not that, ..."

"He isn't going alone," Anna chirped up from the corner.

Logan groaned, turning to face her.

"Who are you?" Becky questioned.

"I'm Anna."

"Oh." Apparently Becky had heard of her. "Way to go, letting Olivia get kidnapped."

"Everyone's a critic," Anna mumbled.

Becky opened her mouth to say something else but Hudson arrived.

"To The Oracle, you say?" Hudson asked, exiting the screen door.

"You will not be joining us," Anna informed him.

Logan agreed, but he was curious.

"Why?" Hudson asked.

"The Oracle will have you for lunch. You are not strong enough to resist her allure," Anna belittled him.

"But you are?" Hudson tossed back.

"I have proven myself capable," Anna hissed.

Logan watched Hudson flick his eyes to him, restraining his annoyance.

"I need you to stay at the manor with the kids," Logan stated.

Hudson's eyes flared at that answer, Logan's beast stirring in response. Hudson was quick to look away.

"Lovely, now that's settled." Anna began walking. "We'll be taking my vehicle."

Hudson raised an eyebrow at Logan. He watched Anna's small form walking away with annoyance. She was testing him, and he'd bet money she knew it.

Logan tossed the keys to Hudson and followed Anna. The hellion wasn't giving him much choice.

He slid into the passenger seat, having just enough time to close the door before Anna gunned it.

Logan inhaled, his lion pushing to the surface.

"Stop. The. Car," he demanded.

"No, it's the best equipped vehicle. I need her weapons."

"You will not drive her SUV." Logan's claws extended.

"She didn't only belong to you," Anna hissed, taking her eyes off the road to glare at Logan for a moment.

"She is my mate!" he roared.

"Right, care to talk about how she entered into that role without her permission or knowledge?"

Logan growled, "If you value your life, you will stop speaking."

Anna smirked and Logan's claws dug into the seat, but she kept her silence.

...

Logan stood looking up at the sheer rock face, his foul mood riding him hard from being in Olivia's vehicle, not to mention the poor company inside of it.

"So you ready for this, big boy?" Anna taunted.

Logan gave thought to using his claws to score the gray stone; he could see still the marks from his first visit here with Olivia. Given that he needed The Oracle's help, he decided it would be in his best interest not to upset her.

His hands found the holds from his earlier visit easily. He assumed it was the magic. Anna huffed next to him, her shorter legs making her work harder.

Good, she deserved it.

He still didn't understand how Olivia had ever befriended her or had faith in her to run the Council. Nor was he asking. He preferred her labored breathing to whatever tactless observations she would make.

Halfway up, Logan's beast pressed close to the surface, anxious to have his mate returned to him. He cast a look at Anna, surprised she was keeping up so well, her long fingers moving easily from hold to hold.

He grunted before returning his attention back to his climb.

A few moments later Logan stopped, quieting his breathing, hearing a voice. He looked to the stone in front of him and above him, seeing no faces in the rock like he and Olivia had encountered.

He opened his mouth to ask Anna if she also heard it, but the words died on his lips. Several rock faces were surrounding her, whispering words the wind took away from him his exceptional hearing. She kept climbing, her jaw clenched, eyes narrowed.

Logan debated calling down to her, deciding not to. Whatever demons she had, they were hers.

After several more long minutes, Logan's fingers curled around the base of the arched opening and he pulled himself flat along the gray surface. He turned, keeping his stomach flat against the rock, reaching a hand down to Anna.

She grasped it and he hauled her light weight up next to him. Her chest heaved with the exertion.

"I hope you have hidden reserves, that is how we leave as well," Logan warned her, or rather reminded her, since she had been here before.

Words were beyond her as she sucked in air desperately. Logan grunted, a smile playing over his lips, enjoying her silence. He rolled away from her, standing before turning right down the long, smooth hallway. He expected taunting, as Anna had endured during the climb, but nothing came for him.

That was cause for alarm.

He heard Anna's steps behind him as they entered the large, domed cavern.

The Oracle sat facing away from them on a stone, backless couch. The arms curved upward, decorated with intricate carvings.

"Much is amiss," The Oracle stated, her voice so different from what Logan remembered.

"The broken child has returned," she continued, inclining her head slightly towards Anna, still not averting her gaze from the ever-changing rock wall in front of her.

Anna crossed her arms over her chest, a sneer on her face, ready, no doubt, with something foolish to say. To Logan's surprise, the only movement from her mouth was the grinding of her jaw.

Logan turned his attention back to The Oracle, who had turned to face them, resting her delicate stone chin on her hand. She was adorned in a flowing

Greek dress with a thin band around her throat, bracelets dangling from her wrists.

"Do you remember what I said to you last time?" Still her attention was only for Anna.

Anna raised her chin. "I do." Her voice a whisper.

The Oracle nodded, staring at Anna intently. "You are not the one I hoped to see here."

Anna bristled at the open insult. "I am all they have." Logan wasn't sure who the "they" were supposed to be. The kids had him, Ali and Grant.

The Oracle tsked, tilting her head. "The broken Seven returns."

Logan looked at The Oracle, surprised by the name she used to address Anna and confused by the term broken.

Anna took a step forward, before remembering herself and pulling back. "I am the same as Olivia."

The Oracle laughed. "I wish, dear girl. Olivia embraces her damage, it's what pushes her, what drives her. She has accepted her blood lust and revels in it. The past may have a hold on her, but your past is going to destroy you."

"I. Am. Fine." Anna hissed.

The Oracle twirled a strand of hair around her stone finger. "Your future is littered with choices. Your salvation or your damnation lies here."

She uncrossed her legs, the fabric flowing around her, resettling to give the impression of knees under her dress.

"You have come about Olivia," The Oracle stated, acknowledging Logan. She stood, crossing the room in one fluid movement to a drink cart. Logan couldn't say if it had been there before and wondered what a being made of stone would drink.

A stone glass made its way to her lips before she turned back to Logan. While he found her delay annoying, he heeded the warning Olivia had given him before, The Oracle was not to be trifled with.

"The events unfolding are bleak, indeed," The Oracle hinted yet again.

She sat back down on her stone couch, resting the cup next to her.

"But you are not here about future events, only your Mate."

Logan nodded. He had spent the drive here carefully choosing the wording to ask The Oracle where Olivia would be.

"I need to know where and when I can rescue Olivia." He hoped it was the right language, simple seemed to be better.

The Oracle picked up the glass again, touching it to her lips before resting it on her knee, tapping her index finger against it.

"Under normal circumstances, this is where I would play with your emotions. Question if you actually believe she lives, and if you are strong enough to save her." The Oracle sighed, her chest moving in sync with the exhale.

Logan was growing anxious, but he kept his silence.

"However, I fear for our future." She shook her head, tendrils of stone hair bouncing as she did.

"Here is what you need." She waved a hand and Logan's sight was taken.

He felt his knees hit the stone and Anna's arm around his shoulders.

He saw Olivia on a table, men in surgical masks and gloves surrounding her naked form. Anger coursed through his blood and he roared.

"Pay attention to the details," Anna whispered, close to his ear.

Logan tore his attention from his mate lying prone on the stainless steel platform to the building: no windows, gray concrete floors, dust collecting in the corners. The vision changed again, flinging him to what he assumed was the exterior of the building. Logan spun in a full circle, seeing thick trees surrounding the structure, the grass growing wild, weeds climbing up the cracking concrete face.

The fading painted sign on the door gave him hope. "Cooper's Mechanical," he said out loud for Anna's sake.

As Olivia had described to him previously, it was like Logan was looking at his phone calendar.

"Twelve hours from now," Logan grunted out, the pressure in his head lessening as his vision forced its way back. He blew out a breath, giving himself a minute to regain his equilibrium before he tried standing.

He didn't brush off Anna's arm like he wanted to. Perhaps he needed to be a little kinder with her if The Oracle's words held any truth. While he might not understand everything she said, he knew it all to be the unbiased facts.

"We need to get going," Anna warned him, worry and fear playing across her features.

Logan nodded. He thought about bringing up the issue of payment in the form of a memory, but he chose not to. If she was willing to give the information freely, he was going to take it.

The Oracle said nothing more, watching them leave.

...

Anna was faster going down than Logan. Swinging from the hand holds, she dropped the final few feet. Logan landed after her, making the short walk to the already running SUV.

As he clicked his seatbelt in place, Anna put Olivia's SUV into drive, carefully turning around before getting back on the gravel road.

"Do you know about her past?" Anna asked softly, obviously rattled from The Oracle's words.

"Olivia's?" Logan clarified, though he didn't really think they were talking about The Oracle.

Anna nodded.

"Pieces, it's not something she enjoys speaking about. Now that we are mated, I have felt the shame and misery she holds onto when she remembers it."

Anna only nodded, chewing on her thumbnail before drawing a breath.

"She's the only reason I made it out of there alive. What they made us do—" Her voice cracked before she reassembled her composure.

Logan debated, reach out or shut her down? The Oracle's words sounded in his ears, salvation or damnation.

His own capture and torture wormed its way out of the locked box he tried to keep it in.

"We have all done things, been forced to do things, we are ashamed of. Olivia tells Mindy all the time, just because they took your body, they didn't take your power."

Anna didn't look at him, nodding and rubbing at her eyes. He hoped it was enough.

Logan sighed, rubbing his forehead. "I need to make calls. Are you alright?"

Anna nodded, clearing her throat, "Right as rain."

Logan nodded, pulling out his phone and dialing Tommy. He answered instantly.

"What did she say?"

"Olivia is being held in an abandoned building named Cooper's Mechanical. Can you find it?" Logan asked.

He heard the keyboard clicking in the background. Anna shifted in her seat and he put the call on speakerphone for her benefit. Once Olivia got back, she was going to explain to him what the hell she was thinking when she wrote that will.

"It's in a small town called Blue Ridge in Alabama, outside of Montgomery. Drive time is eight hours, flight three," Tommy rapidly spoke. "What else did she say?"

"Nothing about Olivia. There were some vague references to the future being bleak."

"That's helpful," Tommy grunted.

"Right," Logan agreed. "Alright Tommy, I need to make more phone calls. Have you heard anything from Becky on the vampire hostages?"

"Only that Blue has outdone his own creative techniques, and she had to stop watching the video once he started feeding them each other's entrails."

"That is creative," Logan grunted. Olivia had trained him well.

"You want me to call the plane and get it ready?" Tommy asked.

"I'm not sure you have authorization for that."

"I do. I added myself to all your online accounts."

"Tommy, don't go spreading that around."

"Got it, boss."

Logan hung up, calling Hudson.

He answered shakily, "What's up?"

"Doing okay?" Logan questioned.

"Great, just watching the kids. Please tell me you have a new task for me."

"Call everyone. We know where Olivia is being held."

"Everyone?" Hudson asked.

"Everyone. Even Mal and Raphael. I want every asset we have ready to take off in an hour." Logan ended the call. He rubbed his chest, a piercing sensation growing from between his shoulder blades to his sternum.

"What's wrong?" Anna asked.

"I don't know. I just—" Logan clutched his chest, coldness seeping into him.

"No, oh by the Gods, no," she muttered.

Logan let out a ragged breath.

"It's Olivia, isn't it?" Anna whispered.

Logan grunted, bearing down on the sensations, refusing to believe she was dying. The Oracle — The Oracle never said Logan would find her alive; rescue, that was the word he'd used. It was implied she would be alive, yes, but he had never clarified it.

"Anna, what if The Oracle is sending us to pick up a corpse?" Logan asked.

She looked over at him, startled. "You used the word rescue..." Her voice trailed off; she was probably following the same line of reasoning Logan had.

"Shit, call Hudson back," she said, her tone suddenly forceful. "Our flight has to leave immediately. We can have the others follow behind us. Tell him to bring the entire armory."

Logan nodded, making the call. She was right, not that he had plans to admit it.

Chapter 7

The worst of the pain edged away, clearing out of my head like fog lifting away, only to heighten my awareness of the agony that remained.

I groaned, reaching up to cradle my pounding head.

"Olivia, are you ready?" my father asked.

I groaned again, such an intelligent response.

"We don't have much time," Doyle warned.

"Olivia, grant me permission to put you into this orb," my father implored.

I cracked my eyes open, seeing the small, empty glass orb.

"I won't fit," I grunted.

"Daughter, please," my father whispered.

I blinked, hearing the pounding on the door, the screaming of my mother.

"Permission granted."

What the fuck did I have to lose, anyways?

...

Logan, Anna, Hudson, Mark and Jerry stood outside the building from Logan's vision. They had arrived in two rented SUVs after the short flight.

"I don't suppose she gave you any hints on what's inside?" Jerry asked, adjusting his leather cross body bag.

"No, what is in your bag?" Logan questioned.

"Spells and potions. Plus some explosives." He shrugged on the last part.

"We are ready. There is no more time to waste. I will go first, follow at your own risk," Anna announced before sliding off into the shadows. She was silent, even to Logan's ears.

He followed her, not about to be last to this party.

...

Cramped wasn't the right word. I didn't have long to focus on the sensation before it felt like my father had thrown the orb. If I'd had a stomach, which in that cramped form I didn't, I'd have lost the contents of it.

Spinning, around and around, until I wished I couldn't feel a damn thing. It occurred to me now what a vulnerable position I had put myself in. I had just willingly shoved my soul or essence or whatever the hell I was made up of into this thing, at the mercy of The Magician, my father.

That should count for something, right? There should be some inherent family trust, even for the one who gave me to Selena.

There wasn't. I feared I had made a mistake.

Finally, it ended and I was back to feeling cramped. I could almost make out sounds and muffled voices, but it was all too far away to focus on.

...

The door broke in easily under Anna's kick, old rotted wood splintering willingly from the doorframe. She moved to the left following the swing of the door, while Logan took the right. He inhaled once as both of them scanned the dimly lit room. Boxes and crates littered the dirty concrete floor. Hanging overhead were large industrial lights, many of them broken.

"Vampires," Logan warned, before moving to the first stack of boxes and kicking it over.

Anna had gone with leather, like Olivia always did, with an impressive arsenal strapped to her. She pulled her sword first.

Logan had chosen gray sweats, they would be easy to shred when he decided to shift. Vampires, like cockroaches exposed to light, scampered out from their hiding places, swarming Anna and Logan.

The first vampire came at Logan, fangs bared. Logan reached out, crushing his head. His other hand partially shifted, claws extending and slicing off another cockroach's head.

"Mark, you keep your furry ass where I can see you!" Jerry yelled.

A vamp latched onto Logan's shoulder as he turned to see Jerry launching a blue bottle into the horde of attacking assholes. It splattered, sending indigo smoke up into the air. The vampires continued their advance, heedless of the smoke. Not one made it through.

"Nice job, Jerry," Logan complimented the mage.

Jerry smiled giving a small bow.

Two more vampires latched onto Logan's back, fangs and claws cutting through the cotton sweatshirt and into his back. Turning both his hands into claws, he reached back, pushing each digit through the vampires' necks and yanking. Both heads came off in a bloody spray.

Hudson had shifted, protecting Anna's back while she sliced through the horde of vampires descending on them.

There were too many. Logan knew it. He felt it in every fiber of his being. The Oracle must have known this awaited him. Perhaps that was the reason for her melancholy; she knew if Logan stayed with her timetable, Olivia would be dead.

With the choices he had made instead, it was possible they all would be.

Logan's body shifted as the next three vampires came at him, his bones popping. They tried to take advantage of his shift. As his paws hit the ground, Logan bent his knees, using the momentum of his shift to toss the vampires over his shoulders. He walked over each them, his claws slicing through their chests to pierce their hearts.

He ripped upward, roaring on his hind legs. The numbness in his chest stopped spreading, but it was still there, still lingering.

Jerry threw another jar, the same blue smoke dusting the vampires rushing down the stairs from the upper floor. Logan took a guess the smoke wouldn't hurt him and tore up the stairs, following the trail of vampire dust.

He huffed, clearing the debris from his lungs before entering the first room on the left, which smelled like Olivia.

His lungs refused to take another breath. Padding into the deserted room, he looked down upon his mate's body on the metal table. No machines helped her breathe, no IVs delivered fluids. He laid his head upon her chest, willing to hear her heart.

Nothing.

Her body was littered with red, angry welts. Next to her sat a tray of hospital grade knives and tools.

"Logan!" Jerry called out behind him.

He didn't feel the vampires on him until Mark tore them off, yelping in pain. He should have moved, should have protected his pack, but he could only stare at the closed eyes of his love.

It was all lost.

He didn't want to go on.

The weight of the vampires on his body, tearing into his flesh, was welcome.

...

I came to screaming, feeling my father above me blending the globe of my soul back into my body. I could feel the small chunks of glass sliding along my chest before they fell to the ground. My body, she was beat the fuck up.

I yelled again, more annoyance than pain this time around.

I sat up, carefully, my back protesting the movement. I looked down at myself sitting on a cold metal table. My body was littered with a multitude of slices, varying in depth, some crusted over, most still bleeding slowly.

"What the fuck?" I muttered.

"Daughter, I fear we don't have time," my father rasped. I turned to look at him, hunched over, leaning heavily on Doyle.

Doyle inclined his head to my right. I turned, seeing shifters and vampires locked in combat. In the center I saw Logan's hide, covered in blood.

"No," I whispered, my right hand landing on an impressive array of shiny and sharp objects. I was flinging blades before I reached him, my fingers plunging through the chest of a vampire to shred her hearts with my bare hands.

This was berserker.

Another vampire attacked from my left, slamming into my shoulder. I slashed out with a saw, slicing across his jugular. I didn't have time to finish the kill before fending off another attack.

"Olie, here!" I turned, seeing a familiar face.

"Anna?" I whispered, reaching up to take the sword she had flung at me. Its weight was familiar. I looked at the handle while I carved a vampire's head in two.

"What are you doing with my weapons?" I yelled. She yanked her own, well her borrowed, blade out of a vampire's chest as he turned to dust.

"You cannot be serious right now?" she asked me, breathless. We moved back to back, our training kicking in even after years apart.

"We have to get to Logan," she demanded.

"I know," I agreed. My left side was on fire and it was slowing me down. Mark and Hudson were with Logan, but it was going to take all of us to get out of here alive. For every vampire I struck down, another two replaced them.

"DOWN!" Jerry screamed.

Anna and I turned in to each other, both of us crouching down, our arms over our heads.

The explosion rocked the room, filling it with screams.

I heaved a sigh, pushing back up to standing.

Whatever Jerry did had cut the number of vampires in half, but it still wasn't enough. I lifted the sword, my arm protesting its use, to fend off another attack.

I was slowing down. A vampire got a cheap shot in across my face. From the center of the room, Logan bellowed, standing up on both his back paws, shaking off the attached vampires.

"Show off," Anna muttered. I gave a short chuckle, ducking under the punch aimed for my nose and swinging the sword wildly, connecting with his neck, thankfully.

Bones crunched and screams ripped from throats as the shifters made short work of the remaining vamps. I sagged against Anna, my blade falling from my hands.

"Shit," she whispered under my weight.

"Olie, Olie honey, can you hear me?" Jerry yelled in front of my face.

I nodded, "Yeah I haven't gone deaf, thanks."

His worried gaze combed over my multiple lacerations before it swung back to my father and Doyle.

"Are they friendly?" he whispered.

I nodded, speech requiring too much energy.

"We need to get out of here," Mark said, coming up next to Jerry. "I can hear the sirens."

I nodded. "Dad, Doyle, let's go," I commanded. We were on my turf now. I'd have gladly kissed the ground under my feet, but I wouldn't have gotten back up if I did. Besides, it was heavily coated with vampire ash.

Anna helped me stay upright. I searched for Logan in the mess of boxes, finally catching his gaze. I couldn't help the smile that sprung to my lips.

"Olivia, be careful!" Hudson warned, warily backing away from the bloody lion.

My brow drew down as I slipped my arm off Anna. "Get everyone out of here," I commanded. I didn't check to see if she was listening. I had absolute confidence in her.

I took a pain filled step, a slice on my calf causing me to limp.

"Logan," I tried. His raw sienna gaze hadn't left my own. His shoulders stiff, he was frozen in place. Only his lion head moved as he tracked my progress closer to him. Blood pooled down my body, making my feet slippery.

"Logan," I tried again, adding more force into the command.

Still nothing, no acknowledgement, no movement.

"Motherfucker, change forms now and get over here and help me!" I yelled. I had no idea what was going on. What I did know was that my unconscious body had somehow ended up in the hands of some slice-happy vampires.

He blinked.

I huffed out a breath, anger turning to hurt. He was all I'd wanted while trapped in the other realm, what kept me going and fighting to get back. Did he not feel the same? I reached for the mate bond. It was weak to my inspection, but he tilted his head at that.

I could feel the beast radiating off him, could see the animal and not the man reflected in his gaze. There was a chance I had lost him in what I was assuming was a rescue attempt.

I ground my jaw together. He was going to have to kill me to get rid of me.

I took another step closer to him; he growled softly.

"You are not going to hurt me." I sure hoped he wasn't going to. I pulled on the mate bond again, in my mind's eye surrounding myself with it.

He lowered his head, showing his teeth.

I took the final few steps, closing the distance between us.

"I need you. This shit isn't over." It was the pain that made my voice shake, not the emotional mess inside of me.

I laid a hand on his head, reaching my fingers down through his thick fur to brush his skin underneath.

He roared, pulling away from me. My hand stung as if burned. Black spots danced in my vision and I crashed against a discarded box, wooden splinters finding a home in my already tortured flesh.

"Olie," Logan whispered, pulling me toward his naked form.

"Logan," I breathed his name out, exhaustion and pain causing tears to slip down my face.

"Shit, I went beast, I, I didn't know you."

"It's okay," I whispered, breathing in the scent of his skin, my cheek pressed against his chest.

"Where are the others?" he asked, scooping me up.

"Outside, Mark heard sirens."

My eyes closed, but I felt him nod as he jogged outside. "They are close," he agreed.

The night air was crisp against my skin, the shiver causing a whine of pain from my throat.

"Hang on baby, it's going to be alright." There was the Logan I had come to depend upon. I reached for our bond, finding it heady and strong. His love washed over me, followed by his relief and utter joy.

"Let's go!" Anna screamed from the passenger seat.

Logan didn't waste any time, getting into the empty back seat, eyeing Hudson in the driver's seat.

"My father?" I asked.

"Other car," Hudson answered, spraying mud as we followed the other SUV. "Doyle damn near didn't fit."

I nodded, enjoying the feel of Logan's arms wrapped tightly around me, but knowing my wounds needed to be looked at.

"I thought I'd lost you," Logan whispered against my oily hair.

"Come on. It'd take a whole lot more to kill me than a few gunshot wounds."

He chuckled against my neck, his arms impossibly tight. It hurt, but I didn't care. I had missed him so damn much.

A throat cleared in front of us.

Logan didn't release me.

"You need to tend to her wounds," Anna reminded him.

Logan huffed, sitting me next to him before reaching over the seat, searching for the right bag. I leaned my head back, exhaustion setting in.

"We need to stop for food," Hudson warned.

"Drive through for now," Anna commanded. "We can stop once we put some distance between us and this place."

Hudson grunted his compliance. I wouldn't call it agreement.

"Who are those people with you? You called him Dad?" Anna asked me. I opened my eyes, tilting my head to look at her.

"We are from an alternate world, where the pure blood succubi and incubi, along with their supporters, were banished by the witches."

I watched her shocked expression, her crystal blue eyes rounding.

"Yeah, they traded us to Selena."

"For what?" she hissed.

I shrugged, regretting the movement. "I don't know, but my father is a Magician. I inherited those powers, but he's locked them up somehow. Which explains why I was able to manipulate the Puppet Master's magic and throw fire around."

Logan pressed a cleaning cloth to my side. "OW!" I hissed.

He smiled, actually he hadn't stopped smiling. I found myself returning the gesture.

"You two need clothing," Hudson said as the lights of a town came into view.

Logan reached back again.

Chapter 8

Jerry found us an out of the way motel with an attached diner.

I carefully got out of the SUV with Logan's help. His own wounds had healed, but I could feel his hunger through the bond, partially for me, mainly for red meat.

"I've got them grilling every piece of meat they have," Mark said at my door.

I nodded in my black shirt and blue shorts.

"And grilled cheese, veggie quesadillas, and dessert, lots of dessert," Jerry added, also smiling.

"How do we handle Doyle?" I asked.

"We were waiting for you. Your father isn't very talkative," Mark muttered.

I huffed, "That's because he's an asshole."

Logan helped me walk to the backseat of the other SUV. I looked in, seeing my father, with Doyle crammed in the back.

"How do we handle Doyle?"

"I don't believe he needs handling."

My brow furrowed. "Can you disguise him?"

"No, I don't have the strength."

I growled. "But your friend can," he continued.

"Jerry?" I asked, surprised.

The Magician nodded.

You don't trust him, Logan spoke to me.

I don't.

"I can feel your distrust, Olivia." My father commented. I checked my guards, finding them gone.

"What the fuck?" I whispered, a hand going to my chest, the air leaving my lungs.

"Easy." Logan supported my weight, leaning me against the side of the SUV.

"My guards are gone!" I whispered.

"What do you mean?" Logan asked.

"How I protect others from feeling everything I do. My guards, my walls, my barriers, they're all gone."

Logan's brow furrowed as he looked down at me before shaking his head. "It doesn't matter. You'll get them back or rebuild them." He cradled my face. "All that matters is that you are here and alive."

His love overflowed the mate bond, warming my soul and reaching my toes. I took a worry-free breath, nodding.

"Whoa." Anna turned the corner, putting up a hand to shield herself.

"My guards are gone," I told her.

She nodded. "Probably because you were so close to death." She shrugged, "We've seen it before."

I nodded, she was right, we had. I took another breath, clearing the fear from my system.

"Jerry," I breathed out, straightening, pooling my reserves of strength. "We need Jerry to get Doyle out."

Anna nodded, heading into the diner.

"You are in pain," The Magician noted.

I huffed out a pain-laced breath. "What was your first clue?"

"You've learned to control your influence?" he pushed on. Clearly, my pain was not a priority.

"Yes, we all have. It's how we survive. We aren't as large as the shifters or the vampires, nor as strong. Being able to blend in has kept us alive." Hadn't we already had this conversation? It seemed I wasn't the only one who had trust issues.

"But you run The Council?" Doyle questioned. "And are mated to the Alpha?"

Observant minotaur.

"Yes, we have a secure future now, but nothing is guaranteed."

Jerry rushed to my side. "Are you okay?"

"Yes, can you work with my father to create a way to cloak Doyle?"

Jerry blinked at me before looking in the back of the SUV and then back to me.

"He's a magician," I told him.

"The minotaur?" Jerry asked in disbelief.

I laughed and it hurt. "No, my father. He drained himself coming here, but he said with your help he can cloak him." I watched the play of fear and curiosity contour Jerry's features.

The darkness made me sway. "Dammit, you need to get off your feet," Logan hissed, picking me up, careful to observe his surroundings.

"Go. I'll handle this," Anna said, before turning her icy blue gaze to the backseat.

I nodded, leaning heavily on Logan.

"She is different now that you are here," he muttered in my ear, his arms wrapped strongly around me.

I huffed, "She was probably worried I'd die and make her run the Council."

Logan said nothing, but through the bond I could feel his annoyance at my statement.

He set me down at a table, moving to the windows to draw the blinds down. A pale, shaking waitress in a yellow apron the same color as the walls stepped up hesitantly, her note pad shaking in her hand.

"Can—can I—I get you something?"

"Is anything ready yet?" I asked hopefully.

She shook her head, looking over at Logan.

"Can you go check on the steaks? We'd prefer them bloody," he commanded her.

She nodded, tripping over her tennis shoe clad feet to get away from us. I groaned, my body certain it was on fire. I raked a hand through my hair. "Oh, that's disgusting."

Logan looked at me. "You're beautiful."

I couldn't help my answering smile; at least there were no cuts on my face.

Jerry and my father walked in with a large, hairy black man. I blinked before I turned my attention to Jerry, who was being helped along by Mark.

"Are you okay?" I asked as he sat down near me. Logan kept standing.

Jerry nodded. "It was pretty terrifying. I've never wielded my power like that before."

My father and Doyle sat down at the table to my left. Doyle looked down at his hands, turning the digits around for inspection.

Hudson and Anna came in, her face flushed. She snarled when he tried to touch her. Huffing out a breath, she sat heavily in front of me.

"Food?" she questioned.

The waitress appeared, arms loaded down with food.

"Put the meat here." I indicated the seat next to me. Logan stalked toward her, surprising her from behind. She yelped before scooting away.

"I hope she comes back with more," I groaned.

Thankfully, she brought more and more food to us, until I was certain there couldn't possibly be any left in the kitchen. When we all had eaten our fill, I asked...

"What have I missed?"

Throats cleared. "Are you sure now is the best time for this conversation?" Anna asked.

I narrowed my gaze. "Yeah, I'd really like to know how I went from shot in front of the courthouse to cut open on a metal table."

Logan shifted in his seat. "Zachariah took you from the hospital."

"I was having you moved to the mansion," Anna said.

"With no security?" I asked, annoyed.

"I used his brother, Darren." Anna indicated Logan.

"Zachariah had his goons there. We got there just in time," Logan answered, wiping his mouth.

"You certain it was him?" I asked.

"He was spotted on the security cameras when you were taken from the hospital," Logan stated. I could feel his unease.

"Good enough for me. Is he the one that shot me?" I asked.

It was Hudson's turn to shift uncomfortably. "No, I missed a clan of shifters who had gone bat shit crazy in my territory—uh, what was my territory. But don't worry, we took care of them."

I nodded. "Who is taking over the West?" Probably not something I needed to worry about.

"Alec, Darren is being reinstated in the East."

My eyebrows rose. "Glad to hear it."

"The Centennial House merged with Zachariah's House." My head jerked to Anna, my eyes rounded.

"Tate did what?" I hissed out.

"I forgot about that," Logan muttered. "Zachariah starved them into it."

"Starved them into it?" I repeated, slamming my fists on the table.

"I offered them an alliance, help. Tate refused." Logan shrugged, yawning. Well fed, he would need to rest now to recover. I could use some sleep myself.

"Do you have a check?" I asked the waitress, who was watching us from behind the bar.

She nodded, giving me the total. Someone had Logan's wallet and dished out the required bills plus tip.

"Thank — thank you," she muttered.

I stopped in the doorway. "Hey, we will be back for breakfast, so please restock." She nodded adamantly. I guess it was a good tip.

Logan carried me up the stairs. "I can't believe Tate merged with that asshole. What a pathetic leader," I grunted.

"I agree. Hudson has been in touch with Raphael."

I yawned, "Good. We'll need to pull Mal out before we attack."

Logan set me down, unlocking the door. "Attack?" he asked, guiding me in and locking the door behind us.

I assumed the others went to their rooms.

"Shower?" Logan asked. I nodded. While I'd have liked for the reason Logan was in the small pink tub with me to be romantic, the truth was I was having issues standing.

We fell into bed together, our bodies needing to touch to be reassured this was real.

"I was done back there," Logan whispered, my head on his chest.

"It was just shock," I told him.

"No, Olie. When I saw you there, dying, cut open, I wanted to die, too."

"But Ginny?" I asked.

"I forgot about it all. The kids, Tommy, Ginny, the packs, everyone who needs me. I could only feel the pain of losing you and it consumed me. I would have died if my beast hadn't taken over. I would have let the vampires take me."

I had no words. I had no idea how I would have reacted if our positions were reversed. I wanted to blame it on the mate bond, but the fact his beast took over killed that idea.

I shifted, looking up into his caramel gaze, reading the self-doubt there. I felt it through our bond and I smiled at him.

"You did it, Logan. You kept The Council and the Shifter Nation running while I was gone. The kids are all alive, I'm assuming." He huffed a laugh out. "I'm alive, too. You rescued me, my white knight in shining armor."

Logan laughed, nuzzling his head into my shoulder.

"I love you, Olivia."

Stroking my fingers through his hair I whispered, "I love you, too."

Chapter 9

I slept well, even with the lumpy mattress and noisy air conditioner.

The door to the room opened and I rolled over, watching Logan walk in and drop a white plastic bag on the bed next to me.

"Clothing," he told me. "Come on, let's go eat."

I scooted out of the dingy sheets, checking my wounds. They were still red welts. I had been hoping for only scratches, but the pain was greatly diminished.

I dressed quickly before we made our way downstairs again. The diner was busier, with a few patrons in the booths. We claimed the same tables, spreading out. The same waitress greeted us, looking exhausted.

"No rest?" I asked.

"My kid is sick," she shrugged.

I made an understanding noise before we ordered.

"How's Ginny?" I asked, turning to Logan.

"Good, I haven't seen her much since you were shot," Logan answered.

I rubbed the bullet marks on my chest.

Anna pulled down my shirt, looking over the forming scars.

"You've never scarred before," she commented.

"I know." I smacked her hands away.

"You are weak," she continued.

"Let's advertise, shall we?"

She pulled back, her hands held up, submitting. "How long do you think it will last?" she pushed.

"A few more days at least. Her body is still re-bonding with her soul," my father commented.

Anna turned her attention to him. "Are you my father as well?" she asked him.

I swallowed, turning to look at him.

"No. But you and Olivia share the same mother."

Anna looked back at me. "What's our mother like?" she asked, a dreamy glint creeping into her gaze.

"She's the reason people call us demons." I hated to crush her dreams, but she had to know the truth. "We didn't get along. I would have killed her, given the opportunity."

Anna pulled back as the waitress started bringing our massive food order. "You can't kill her until I meet her," she said, taking a bite of her French toast.

"I make no guarantees."

We ate in silence, but I knew what needed to happen.

"We flew here," Logan began, sensing my mood shift through the bond. "I've called and they are ready to leave when we are."

I nodded. "I need another few days to heal and gather my executioners, but we are going after Zachariah."

"And Tate," Anna added.

I nodded, not liking it. "And Tate."

...

The flight back to St. Ann was short. I couldn't wait to get back to the mansion and the kids.

We pulled up in front of our home to cars I didn't recognize.

"Who is here?" I asked, slipping out of the SUV.

"I don't know," Anna said, pulling a blade. I needed to get my weapons back or call Myrtle. I'd probably just call Myrtle.

The front door opened and Tommy ran into my arms.

"I thought we'd lost you," he whispered, his arms tightening around me.

"Come on, Tommy. I assumed you, at least, would know I'm harder to kill than that." He nodded against my chest, taking a ragged breath, his tears falling.

"It's okay, buddy. I'm here and I'm not leaving."

"That's good, cause Anna is an asshole."

"I heard that," Anna muttered.

"You probably deserved it," I told her.

She shrugged, not denying it.

"Who is here?" I asked Tommy.

"Everyone. All the executioners are back, Raphael and his crew as well. They have a lot to tell you," he said, shifting to my side. I slung an arm over his shoulders, wanting him close.

"More than Tate and Zachariah merging houses?" I muttered.

"Yeah, apparently Zachariah has been turning vampires and forcing them rogue. Which Raphael won't tell us how is done."

We walked up the stairs. "Fuck," I hissed.

"Are you going to tell me?" Tommy asked, raising an eyebrow.

"No. There are some secrets that need to be kept."

We pushed into the house, ending the conversation.

The kids rushed into me, knocking the wind out of me. Logan put a hand on my back, steadying me. I couldn't help but laugh, feeling their emotions raw against my own. Their fear coated the back of my throat, piercing worry hitting me hard in my gut. I pulled on the strength of Logan behind me, pushing the love, the complete dedication to them and their protection.

"I'm back and I'm insulted everyone thinks a few bullets are enough to kill me," I teased. A few tear-stained eyes looked up at me, relieved.

"What now?" Tommy asked me, stepping back.

I wanted to answer that now I was loading up my weapons and killing Tate and his entire fucking House, but I wasn't foolish enough to think I was sufficiently healed to tackle that hornet's nest.

"I need to rest and plan." The truth ground raw against my ego.

"I want to be involved," Tommy demanded.

I nodded, laying a hand on his shoulder. "Of course, but I don't even have a step one as of yet."

He lifted his head defiantly. I pulled his chin back down, looking into his mocha gaze.

"I'm still the boss and I'm still in charge."

He blinked, nodding, pulling back from my gasp.

"I'm going to my office. Raphael, Logan, Anna, let's go."

"I would have hit him," Anna muttered, as we made our way upstairs.

"He's been hit enough in his lifetime."

"He's defiant. He hacked into several vehicles to listen to our conversations," Logan added.

"Did he leak information? Did he cause problems? Or did he just listen and help?" I asked, pushing open the door to the office Logan and I shared. Okay, it was really his office. I had claimed a chair, but at the moment, I needed the small conference table for this meeting.

Logan cleared his throat. "He just helped. Except he did leak Hudson's browsing history to his girlfriend."

I laughed. "He must have found something good, and Hudson must have pissed him off."

"Yes and yes," Logan smiled.

I poured myself a glass of bourbon before sitting down. I pressed the cool liquid against my forehead. "Enough about Tommy. Get me up to speed. Raphael, you first."

He leaned forward, his hands interlaced, elbows on the table.

"As Tommy already told you, Zachariah is making rogues. What he didn't inform you of is that he's doing it in semis that are circling the city."

"Circling the fucking city?" I slammed my drink down, sloshing the amber liquid over the sides.

Raphael's black eyes stayed calm as he continued, "We've tracked down five vehicles so far, taken down one. I want you to see inside."

I nodded. "Done. Have you located Zachariah?"

Raphael shook his head, leaning back, crossing his arms over his chest. "No. He went underground after your kidnapping."

I groaned.

"Not surprising. He let himself be caught on camera." I turned abruptly to Anna.

"Shit," I groaned. "Yeah, killing off the Centennial House is part of his plan."

"There are innocent vampires in that House," Raphael stated, his face placid.

"There are innocents everywhere, that doesn't stop them from being killed in the crossfire," Anna snipped.

"What do you want to do, Olie?" Logan asked me, scooting his chair closer to my own.

I shook my head. "Zachariah's House is based in Europe. It makes zero sense to travel there and kill them all, not to mention we took out a sizable chunk at the abandoned building where they were holding me. Now that he and Tate have joined Houses, he knows I'll go after Tate. And maybe that's enough." I turned my gaze to Raphael.

"Killing off the leader will make all those vampires, innocent and not innocent, Masterless. That is a fate often worse than death," he told me, information I already knew.

"They can join other Houses," Anna offered.

"Who would take them in? They'd be leftovers of a diseased and fallen House," Raphael countered.

"In case you missed it, that's kinda what we do here. Keepers of the misfits," I snapped at him, my pain tolerance and patience dropping to dangerously low levels.

"We can't take them all in," Logan whispered to me.

"I know," I answered. "Can Tate break from Zachariah?" I asked Raphael.

He shook his head. "No, the joining is airtight."

I closed my eyes for a moment, knowing the decision I had to make. Logan slipped a hand onto my knee, squeezing gently. It stung; I wasn't fully healed.

Raising my lids to reveal my sea green gaze, I pinned Raphael with it. "Tate made his decisions. I will take his and Zachariah's heads for kidnapping and torturing me. He is guilty by association."

"Those that would stop you?" Raphael asked.

"The kill is mine, by right and Council Law. Anyone who stands in my way will suffer the same fate as them."

Raphael nodded. "There is one additional issue to address."

I should have known. With vampires, nothing is as clear-cut as it seems.

"What?"

"I'd like permission to set up a secondary House here, since I am spending so much time helping you."

I gave him a disbelieving look. "You don't need permission from me. You need it from the resident vampires."

"Morgan has already given his approval."

I sighed. "And with the removal of Tate and Zachariah, my approval is enough. Well played, Raphael. You have my permission."

Logan growled in annoyance. I turned to him, his gaze locked onto Raphael's. "Anything else?" I asked, feeling my body tiring. This weak shit sucked.

Logan turned his raw sienna gaze to mine, his anger replaced by warmth.

"We left your father alone with the children," he reminded me.

Anna and I both shot up. "Shit!" I yelled, running from the room. Okay, it was more like hobbling.

Logan chuckled from behind us, "I can hear them." He yelled after us, "They're fine!"

Anna was poised looking down upon the first floor, an unreadable expression on her face. I probed with my unguarded senses.

Feeling my intrusion, she indicated with her chin the scene below. I leaned heavily on the polished wooden banister. Doyle had his illusion removed, the kids touching his horns, fur and feet. His voice rumbled as he answered their questions, but I couldn't make out what he said.

My father sat on the blue and white striped couch. Tommy was next to him, rapid firing questions at him. I could see The Magician's mouth moving as he answered, but couldn't hear what he was saying either. I wanted to; from the intensity in Tommy's stare, I was certain I'd find the answers intriguing.

"We have parents," Anna whispered.

"We have parents," I confirmed.

"Does that change anything?"

I shook my head. "Everything."

She nodded. I straightened up, patting her shoulder before heading back to the office.

"I have one additional question," Raphael began.

I huffed out a breath. "What?"

"I can feel your emotions."

"That's not a question," I told him.

"Are you influencing me?"

"No. Getting shot shattered my guards. It will take time for me to rebuild them."

"It's unnerving. I'd suggest keeping yourself unguarded in that manner when you deal with Tate."

I nodded, "Thanks for the insight."

"I will be taking my leave. Would you like me to leave anyone as guards?" Raphael asked.

Irritation spiked through the mate bond. "Thank you for the offer, but I think we have it under control."

"Tomorrow, we will see the trailer you have confiscated," Logan demanded.

Raphael nodded. "Of course. I'll text you the address."

I nodded, leaning against Logan once Raphael left.

"You need to rest," he whispered, his arms coming around my shoulders.

"I know. I need to eat, too, but I want to see Ginny."

We exited the room. I cast a look at Anna, still watching The Magician and Doyle.

"She always wanted parents," I told Logan.

"Did you?" he asked softly.

I shook my head. "No, because if we had parents, they were either dead from Selena or had given us to her. Turns out it was the latter."

Logan pulled me close to his side, feeling my pain at being abandoned.

"Maybe that's why you save all the children, on some level you knew."

"Maybe," I whispered. "I don't think I can forgive him for it."

"No one said you had to."

Logan opened the door to Ginny's nursery.

"He's an important asset. I need to get along with him." That was the last thing I was able to say to Logan before Ginny screeched in joy.

...

I fell asleep on the floor watching Ginny play. Rolling up, I groaned, rubbing the kinks out of my back.

"Hungry?" Logan asked, rocking, a sleeping Ginny on his chest.

I nodded.

Carefully, Logan laid Ginny down, covering her with a blanket before we walked out, grabbing the baby monitor.

I rolled my head on my neck as we tramped down the stairs.

"Do you have a plan?" Tommy asked me, jumping in front of me in the kitchen.

"I'm going to kill Tate and Zachariah."

He nodded.

"What about the semis with rogue vampires?"

"I don't know. We are going to see the trailer tomorrow."

"I want to come with you," he rapid-fire demanded.

"You have school and homework tomorrow," I reminded him.

"I can miss it."

"No, you can't. Tommy, there is a reason I fight as hard as I do. It's to give you, each of you, an opportunity to have a normal life. To be able to choose your life and not have it choose you. You are going to school, and when I need help, I will let you know."

He didn't like that answer, but he accepted it, going upstairs.

I blew out a breath, watching him, hoping I had done the right thing.

Logan rubbed my shoulder, feeling my uncertainly, steering me toward the breakfast bar before heading to the fridge.

"Grilled cheese?" he asked.

"Perfect," I agreed.

"Is my phone lost?" I asked, thinking I should call Kass.

"Yes, we will get you a new one," Logan commented.

"Did you tell Kass I'm back?"

"Yes, I called Darren while you were sleeping. They'll be over in a bit. Alec is moving out, and I want them moved into the Compass house. It has better security."

I nodded.

"I need to call Myrtle."

Logan laughed, "What more could you possibly need?"

"Anna needs her own weapons. I want mine back."

He laughed, sliding his phone over to me, shaking his head.

"Logan," Myrtle answered hesitantly.

"She's back!" I yelled at her.

"Lord in heaven, woman, that shit is not funny. I thought for sure he was calling to tell me..." Her voice trailed off.

"Seriously Myrtle, it was a few bullets. Good news, I'm not that easy to take out."

"What was I thinking?"

"Your sarcasm has been noted. Anyways, I need weapons."

"Glad to hear you haven't let a little near death experience slow you down."

"They're not for me."

"You want me to bring a selection to the house?"

"Yeah, the works."

"Is it ever anything less with you?"

I thought about Raphael and the semis circling the city. "Never." I ended the call, pushing the phone back to Logan.

He pushed a plate toward me with two sandwiches. I inhaled the first one, slowing down for the second when my stomach cramped. Apparently, not eating for almost two weeks would do that to me.

The door opening had me turning. Kass set Hannah down, coming to embrace me. "Don't do that shit again."

I laughed, "I'll try."

"What the hell happened? Logan said your father is here?" Kass asked, astonished.

"Yeah, he and Doyle the minotaur made it through the portal with me."

"How?" Kass asked.

I sighed. "We had to go on a goose chase for the needed supplies, and I learned that mermaids and unicorns are real. The unicorns are assholes."

"Mermaids?" Logan and Darren asked in unison.

"Yeah, and I promised I'd bring them and the unicorns over to this world."

Logan set the frying pan in the sink with a thud. "You think that's wise?"

I sighed. "Possibly not, but I needed their help. There is no reason I'd have to follow through on it, except that I gave my word, and I do feel partly responsible, since my insane mother got them shoved into that hellhole."

"It wasn't pleasant?" Kass asked.

I shook my head. "No, everything was red, all the damn time. Plus, since my soul was separate from my body, it was hard to navigate and stay corporeal. The food was awful and the company, worse. I'm so glad to be back in my own body."

Kass nodded. "There are more of our kind, though?"

"There are, but they are loyal to their Queen and I have no plans to bring them over," I answered.

She nodded. "It's strange to think there are others like us out there."

"They're not like you," The Magician announced. I turned, looking at him with a raised eyebrow.

"Kass, meet my father, The Magician," I introduced them.

"What do you mean they aren't like us?" I asked.

163

"You were raised in the human realm, with their morals and expectations. The court in the Succubus Realm treated humans like play things, which is why the witches banned them and their supporters."

Kass nodded. "I suppose it's for the best they are trapped."

"Why didn't the witches just kill them?" I asked.

"Too powerful. One couldn't get within ten feet without being influenced by them, something you are experiencing now."

I groaned, "Yeah, don't remind me. My guards are all jacked up." Not that I had been spending much time fixing it. I wasn't sure I had the energy to do so right now. I'd rather have my body focus on healing than shielding.

Kass nodded. "What's your plan on the unicorns and mermaids?"

"I don't have one. I'm trying to deal with one fire at a time. Besides, I doubt Dad has recovered from bringing us over."

He nodded. "It will take me additional time. Your friend Jerry has provided me with herbs that will assist in the process."

"Good. Do you need any weapons?" I asked.

He raised an eyebrow at my question. "Are you expecting trouble?"

"We always expect trouble. It's how we stay alive and keep our charges safe," Logan informed him.

I nodded, setting my jaw.

"I see. You have cultivated a loyal following in your empire," my father commented.

I wasn't sure how I felt about the words "following" and "empire." "We protect ours. If you are going to stay here with us, I expect the same from you."

"I am not to be protected?" he questioned.

Logan scoffed, "You are powerful, the powerful protect the weak."

He nodded. "We will remain here for a time. There are still promises to be fulfilled."

I nodded. "One crisis at a time." He was going to leave? Already planning on leaving? Fucking hell, if I felt like I was trusting him or getting mildly attached, then those words were a powerful reminder not to.

"What is the current crisis?" he questioned.

"I need to hunt down and kill the vampire who kidnapped and sliced on me."

"Excellent, I look forward to it."

I couldn't help but smile at his bloodlust.

"We both need a few more days to heal and regain our strength. It's going to be bloody."

"I don't believe things end any other way with you, daughter."

I cracked my neck, I couldn't disagree with that.

Kass and Darren didn't stay long. The kids were tired and they had lots of work to handle at the new/old house.

Logan and I retired. Ali and Grant had set up rooms for The Magician and Doyle. I hadn't had much time to talk with them; hopefully, all was going well.

Falling into bed, I gave thought to being intimate with Logan, but my body was already shutting down. Dammit.

Chapter 10

Dressed in my own jeans, black shirt and leather jacket, I stowed my new phone in my back pocket.

"I can't decide," Anna lamented.

"We are just going to check out the rogue semi," I told her again, standing in the driveway of the mansion as she rummaged through my weapons stash in the back of my SUV.

She gave me a disbelieving look and couldn't help but laugh. "I saw what you are carrying," she told me.

I huffed, pulling my jacket over my twin guns and dagger, wishing I had that short-lived duster to cover my throwing knives on my thighs.

"I'm a little paranoid right now," I shrugged. "At least I left the crossbow."

"True." Anna made decisions similar to my own, opting for one gun and two daggers.

We climbed into the other SUV, where Logan, Doyle and The Magician were waiting for us. Apparently, my vehicle still smelled, whatever.

"Ready?" Logan asked, looking at me in the passenger seat.

"Yep." I ran my hands over my weapons again. He drove away from the mansion, using the directions Raphael had sent over.

We weren't taking the whole gang. I had a bad feeling about this trailer, and I wanted to keep information within a small circle. Here's hoping I could trust my father. I'd had Becky monitor the camera in front of his room overnight, and she said he'd never left.

"How long have you been the Head Executioner?" my father asked.

I blew out a breath. "Seven years, I think," I answered. It wasn't an anniversary I celebrated.

"At least," Anna agreed.

"When did you get free of Selena?" he asked.

I shifted, not wanting to have this conversation. Logan placed a hand on my knee, picking up on my mood. Hell, the whole car could, but still The Magician pushed on.

"When we were sixteen," I answered, my voice and emotions turbulent.

"Sixteen years," he repeated in wonder.

Anna and I were both silent for the remainder of the drive.

We were outside the city, and I was wondering how Raphael had gotten the semi down the narrow dirt road we had just bounced along.

The light from the partially cloud-covered sun filtered through the trees, casting eerie shadows on the silver trailer.

"You came," Raphael said. He didn't sound surprised.

I raised my eyebrow at him, waiting for him to explain.

"It could easily be a trap," he continued.

I laughed, "You looking for a fight?"

Raphael shook his head, his dark locks glossy in the ghostly afternoon light. "No, I just find your choices interesting."

He was working on my last nerve.

"Open the trailer, the Executioner does not have the patience for this." Raphael waved his hand, walking away from the swinging doors.

I smiled, so there was one benefit of being unguarded.

I stood next to Logan as the doors swung out. My stomach dropped, my half smile disappearing.

Sunken eyes regarded us, beating against the clear cages, no blood flowing from the broken bones as they fought for food.

"There are no magical restraints," I commented idly, looking over their ankles and wrists.

"He was starving them," Raphael commented, anger lacing his words. "Not enough to force humans into being vampires, and rogue, but starvation just the same." He shook his head in disgust. His morality was interesting for a vampire so old. I wondered if he remembered the succubi living in this world, with the unicorns and mermaids.

"The cages are small," Anna noted, interrupting my musings.

"To hold more." I took Logan's hand, getting into the cramped space. I ran my fingers over the thick plastic doors. The rogue in question rammed the cage.

Doyle and my father stayed outside the trailer.

"Twenty." Raphael confirmed the count I had just taken. "Twenty rogues. What on Earth and all the heavens and hells is he doing? Why does he need this? They cannot be controlled."

I shook my head. "You said they are circling the city?"

"Four others, yes." Raphael confirmed.

I nodded. "He's getting ready for an attack."

"But he can't call them off; they will turn on him as soon as on his enemy, who, I assume, is you," Raphael observed.

I pulled out my phone, calling Tommy, knowing he would be about home from school.

"What?" he growled at me.

"I need your help."

"Finally," he exhaled.

"The four semis circling the city are housing twenty rogue vampires each. I'll send you pictures of the exterior and license plate of this one. See if you can track down the rest."

"On it."

I looked at my phone, annoyed that he had hung up on me.

Logan was working on the electronic interface toward the front of the trailer. I left him to it, turning to Raphael.

"How can you tell he turned humans and isn't making rogues of established vampires?" I asked.

Raphael shook his head. "If each container has the same number, we are looking at one hundred rogues. If that number were missing from local Houses, the Vampire High Council would have been called on already." He shook his head, "No, he's taking humans."

"You should have Tommy check for missing persons as well," Anna said.

I nodded, texting the request to Tommy. His attitude had me worried. I can't say it was worse than mine, though, which had me worried even more. I wanted a life better than my own for him. Maybe it was a bad idea getting him involved in hunting down the bad guys. Since he was at the mansion behind his computers, I didn't worry about his physical safety.

I hadn't given enough thought to his mental welfare.

"Shit," Logan hissed.

I turned to him, Raphael and Anna crowding around him in the small space.

"What's wrong?" I asked, trying to look at the computer screen.

"It's a countdown," Raphael muttered, backing up a step and running a hand over his face.

My brows drew down. "Countdown to what?" I snapped.

"Releasing the rogues," Anna said as Logan continued to type furiously.

My breathing increased, my mind repeating Anna's words.

"Four trailers filled with rogues," I whispered. "He's not attacking me. He's going to kill off the entire city."

Logan turned his caramel gaze to me and I felt his beast pulsing within. "There is no kill switch that I can find."

I exhaled. "Let's get this trailer to the Farm and have Becky take a look at it. How much time do we have?"

I pulled out my phone, texting Becky.

"Five hours," Logan stated.

I dropped my phone against the metal floor. "WHAT?"

"Five. Hours." Logan repeated.

"What do we do, Executioner?" Raphael asked.

I turned, looking at him. His angelic brows were drawn in defeat, porcelain skin etched with a future he had seen before.

Not on my fucking watch.

"How many of your people are here?" I asked him.

"Thirty," he answered rapid fire.

"Logan, who is still in town from guarding the mansion?"

He shook his head. "Only a few. I've sent most back home."

"We have to protect the children," Anna whispered.

"Agreed. Raphael, get your people to the mansion. Logan, call back everyone you can." I turned to Anna. "The executioners are all in town. They will keep the kids safe," I reassured her.

She nodded, worry and fear playing across her face from memories we both wanted to keep buried.

"What about everyone else?" Raphael demanded, his dark eyes clouding.

"We need to organize them, get them centralized so we can protect them." I was thinking out loud.

"Doyle and I can assist," my father offered.

"Great, I was counting on it," I answered. Yes, I had trust issues with him, but he was powerful, and I was stationing him where I needed it the most.

"Such a brilliant plan," a voice spoke over the laptop Logan had just used. "Too bad you will never see it come to fruition." I turned slowly, seeing

Zachariah's face. My own contorted in disgust. Large, dark eyes regarded me from unblemished skin.

"Raphael, it is such a tragedy you will die here with your demon whore. I had plans for your House," he continued on.

"I'll never join you," Raphael hissed, jumping easily back into the trailer, stalking toward the screen.

Zachariah just laughed. "They all claim that at first, but look at Tate. I took him down easily enough, and that wasn't even my best work." He continued, smiling regally, "Now, I'll be sure to take wonderful care of your darling succubi babies. I've heard their blood is divine. I'm thinking of opening up a blood barn for the shits." He sneered the last word and I lunged at the screen.

"Over my dead body!" I screamed. Logan caught me around my middle.

"With pleasure." The screen went dark and I let out a snarl. It was echoed by hydraulics as the cages swung open.

The rogues were on us in an instant and we were right in the thick of it.

"Seal the doors!" I yelled at Raphael, closest to the exit. We had to keep them contained. A few managed to escape, but Raphael leapt out after them. Between him and Doyle, I had no worries. A rogue attached to my shoulder, another on my forearm. A torn appendage flew my way, probably Logan's handiwork.

My father listened, closing the heavy doors. I heard the metal slide clunk into place.

I grunted as another rogue latched onto my back. Ugh. I did not need this shit. The quarters were close and guns were out. I tried pulling my blade, but the rogues on my arm and shoulder weren't cooperating.

With a grunt, I rammed my body back into the thick plastic cages. I succeeded in breaking the hold the rogue had with his teeth, but his claws were still firmly attached to my back. I slammed back again, looking down at the trail of blood running down my forearm, jaws gnawing on my already delicate flesh.

I rammed a third time with a scream of outrage and annoyance.

Logan ripped the rogue off my back, its claws slicing through my flesh as he tore its head from its body. I was slightly annoyed that I needed the help and tore my forearm out of the mouth of the second rogue, reaching for my blade and slicing off her head, before plunging the silver into the hearts of the asshole attached to my shoulder.

With a grunt, I flew forward as another one attached to my neck. I smacked my head against the plastic, wrenching my arm at an impossible angle to stab into what I was hoping was a vital piece of body.

Its grip loosened, so I turned in the tight confines, wrenching my blade up and turning the vampire into dust. This had to be the worst place logistically to get attacked. I flung myself again at the rogue attached to Anna's back, slicing through his hearts before I rounded on the next one trying to take a bite of my neck.

Logan tossed a rogue at the roof, bending the rogue in half and denting the trailer. I groaned, wanting to shut my abused body into the plastic container and let Anna and Logan handle it, but I didn't. I turned, ripping my blade up and across the chest of the next rogue that came at me.

Logan ripped four rogues apart, spraying the trailer in additional dust. I coughed, blinking the decayed vampire bits out of my eyes.

"Open the door," Logan commanded. I felt his arms come around me, inspecting my body.

I hurt. I laid my head on his shoulder. The door flung open and we all piled out, sucking in dust-free oxygen.

I stumbled down the tall step of the semi before leaning against the SUV and sliding down, spitting out chunks of vampires.

Logan pulled the first aid kit out of the car, bending down to wrap my forearm in gauze.

"You need to stop getting hurt," he warned me, his fear of losing me riding our connection hard.

"It's going to get worse before it gets better, Logan," I told him. I wasn't weak and I met his gaze to prove the point. He stopped wrapping, rubbing a thumb against my dirt stained cheek.

"We have four hours," Anna said, re-sheathing her blades. "I knew I should have brought the dual swords."

I grunted, she was right on both counts.

I searched my pockets one handed for my phone, flipping through to dial Becky's number.

"Boss," she answered.

"I need you to get to my location as of yesterday. Bring everything, we have four trailers of rogues and four hours to figure out where they are and a way to destroy them."

Silence.

"Becky?"

"Rogues?" She whispered.

"Yes."

"How many?"

"Twenty per trailer."

"Four of them, wi—with twenty rogues?" she stuttered.

I hissed as Logan tied my gauze. "Keep it together, Becky, none of us will get out of this if we lose our shit."

She laughed hysterically. "Right, I'll be right there."

Logan helped me stand, pulling out his own phone and handling his business.

"Call Darren and Kass, they have to get themselves and the kids to the mansion." Logan nodded in agreement, the phone pressed to his ear.

Raphael took in the remains of the trailer. "Remind me not to piss you guys off," he muttered.

"You should see us with dual swords," Anna huffed.

"Four hours," I whispered. "How the fuck do we save an entire city in four hours?"

"We have to take down the trailers at their locations," Logan advised.

I nodded, calling Tommy back.

"What?" he answered.

"Do you have the trailers?" I asked.

"Not yet, you haven't sent me the pictures," he reminded me.

"Shit," I hissed. "The trailers are set to a timer to release 80 rogues on the city."

Again, silence. I put him on speakerphone, snapping the pictures and sending them.

"How—"

"Enough, I've sent you pictures. We are on our way to you. Get me the info, now." I hung up and proceeded to dial every executioner we had.

...

Thirty minutes later, the mansion was swarming with cars, vampires, and shifters, and my executioners were lined up inside the high voltage fence, ready and waiting for the coming attacks.

I threw my door open as Blue came up to the SUV. "Myrtle is an hour out with the machine guns," he informed me.

I hissed, "Get them here now." I only knew of four trailers, that didn't mean there weren't more.

We marched into Tommy's room.

"What do you have for me?" I demanded

His fingers were flying over the keyboard. "The semi is registered to a shell company. I can't find any others registered for that company."

There went that lead.

"Becky is going over the trailer now, but the parts aren't anything special. Nothing that we can use to track down the others with," Tommy continued.

"Three hours and thirty minutes," Anna reminded me.

I didn't need the countdown.

"What about everyone else?" Tommy asked, stopping his fingers over the keyboard and turning to me. "What if I can't find them in time and they are released?"

I squatted down in front of him. "You and everyone here are safe. I'm doing all I can to make sure we save as many as possible."

"Which is?" he demanded.

I stood back up, rubbing my sore forearm. "We are going to see Tate."

"Olivia, you are not strong enough," Logan warned me.

"I'm injured, Logan, and undoubtedly not at my best, but I refuse to hide. Zachariah brought this fight to me, and I plan on finishing it."

"It's my fault," Tommy said.

"How could it possibly be your fault?" I asked.

"When I skipped school and Gregory kidnapped me," he reminded me.

"That wasn't your fault, Tommy. I pissed him off by not letting Gregory beat the shit of the Blake while Tate did nothing. He took you as punishment for my actions."

"None of that matters. Zachariah planted Angelina here to seek out Blake so they could ingrain themselves in Centennial House. This was planned, we just happened to get in their way. Keep working, we will protect all those we can," Logan reassured him.

I nodded. "Let's go kill Tate!" Anna cheered.

"I want my double swords," I complained.

"Me, too."

Fifteen minutes later, Anna and I had changed and better equipped ourselves and were waiting outside.

"Who do you want to take with us?" Logan asked.

My father and Doyle walked out.

"I want you two to stay here. You are my last line of defense if anything gets inside of this house," I told them, checking my clips and ammo in the back of the SUV. I was desperate if I was putting my trust in my father, but whatever his faults, he was powerful.

My father regarded me, saying nothing. Finally, "You are worried."

"Very," I agreed, forgetting my emotions were broadcasted for all.

"I will protect the children," Doyle promised solemnly.

"Thank you." I turned to my father expectantly.

"You would die to protect them," my father announced.

"Yes," I agreed, my patience running out along with my time.

My father nodded. "I will do all I can."

It was the best I was going to get from him.

"Thank you. I'll be in touch."

I turned to Logan as they went back inside. "I want Anna, who do you want?" I asked.

"Darren, there is no one I trust more."

I nodded. We gathered our small group and piled into my SUV, Logan taking the wheel. It still smelled.

"What's the game plan?" Darren asked from the passenger seat, looking back at me.

"Kill Zachariah and end this," I wished out loud.

"Ha," he answered.

I gave him a rueful smile. "We need information. If we can find a few of Zachariah's vampires to question, that would be ideal."

"Are you going to kill Blake?" Logan asked me.

I jerked my gaze to his in the rear view mirror. "I — I haven't even thought about that."

He shrugged, "We can now."

I nodded, thinking. "We can, but we have more important things to do than settle an old score. Besides, I'd rather take my aggression out on Zachariah."

"No one is going to talk to us," Anna said. "I already killed a few of them off."

I raised an eyebrow at her. "Impressive. What else did I miss?"

She shrugged, "Nothing worth mentioning."

"We need to get Mal, if we haven't already," I added.

"I asked Raphael to obtain her, but I didn't see her in the mansion," Logan commented.

It was another twenty minutes to the Centennial House; we had two hours and forty minutes left.

But who's counting? I was ignoring the dread in my stomach and the what-ifs pinging around. I had no use or time for them. I had to protect those I cared about. I would try to save the rest, but I didn't see this ending any way but bloody.

"We should call Mercer," I said as we made the final turn to the Centennial House.

"And tell him what?" Logan countered.

"That he and Mindy need to get to the mansion." I pulled out my phone for a quick text. It would be met with questions, but I didn't have time or answers for him right now.

Hopefully, he'd listen blindly to my orders. I sighed, leaning forward to look at the guard station as Logan rolled to a stop.

"It's empty." Logan confirmed my observation.

"Why would they leave it empty?" I mused.

"They've pulled all their resources inside, just as we have done, to protect everyone. They know what is coming, Olivia," Anna spelled it out for me.

I smiled at her. "I doubt they know we are coming."

She flipped her short red hair over a shoulder. "That much is true."

Darren looked back between us, clearly worried.

175

Logan put the SUV in park. "I don't want to shred the tires or take Tommy away from his current project to override the security here."

"You should turn it around in case of a quick exit," Anna advised.

I nodded and he did as she requested.

With a last check to our weapons, Anna and I exited the vehicle. I imagined we looked similar, with our jeans, leather jackets, dual swords, guns, and throwing knives strapped to each leg. The truth was, I liked her being back. She had taken a different path when we escaped, and I respected it.

But having her fighting at my side was reassuring. She had been the only person I could count on for so long, and maybe after the betrayal by Grams, I needed that. My gaze swung to Logan's ass. I had that trust in him, too. My fear melted away as I felt his answering emotions in the mate bond.

I pulled a blade, twirling it around and using the handle to knock on the tall, solid doors. "Come out and play, Tate, or I'm coming in!"

"Please tell me we have explosives," I whispered to my crew.

"I'm insulted you think we need them," Darren countered.

I laughed before pounding again. "Come on, Tate, you don't want me destroying your doors with what is coming."

The door creaked open and Mal's face peered out. "Go home, Olie, protect those you love," she hissed at me. Not exactly sure how I felt about that warning coming so late from her.

Logan caught the door, forcing it open with one thick arm.

"That's why we are here, my dear," I informed her, hands braced on my hips. "We've come to pay our debts."

Mal shook her head, looking back up the stairs. I couldn't see who or what was there.

"I'm not leaving him," she whispered harshly to me.

"Define 'him,'" I tried.

"Tate." Her voice broke over the single word, a pink tear slipping down her cheek. "I love him."

I exhaled. "You know what is coming." It was a statement, but I waited for her to nod. When she did, I shook my head sadly.

"That's a terrible life decision," Anna commented.

I couldn't help but agree.

Logan stepped forward, laying a thick hand on Mal's shoulder. "You saved my daughter, we will do the same for you."

What he didn't say, and what I felt in the mate bond, was that it would be with or without her consent. I silently sent my approval. Mal's shoulders relaxed.

"Do you know where Zachariah is?" I asked.

Mal shook her head. "He met with Tate before you were taken. That's all I know."

"TATE!" Logan bellowed.

"Where is everyone?" I asked as Logan marched to the stairs.

"Down below for safekeeping," Mal said, rubbing her arms in a worried gesture.

I nodded, following Logan. He had stopped at the top of the steps and I could just see his hazy outline.

"Did you know he planned to take Olivia?" Logan asked as both Mal and I made our way to him.

Mal gasped and I held her firmly in place. Logan had Tate pinned to the wall with a clawed hand. I can't lie, that was hot.

"Yes," Tate wheezed out. He might not have needed oxygen to breathe, but he did need it to speak.

"We need him alive to answer our questions," I reminded Logan.

"You said you would protect me!" Mal screamed.

"We did and we will. We made no promises when it came to Tate. He sided with the enemy, Mal, certainly you can see that," Anna scolded.

Mal pushed against my restraining hand, trying to get to Tate.

"Don't, Mal," I warned her. "He is going to die."

Her gaze jerked to my own. "What?" she whispered.

"Tate just admitted that he knew Zachariah was going to take me."

Mal blinked at me, her brow drawn down, one broken exhale escaping before she looked back at Tate, sadly shaking her head. She stopped fighting against me, turning to sit on the top step, her shoulders shaking with soft sobbing.

I turned to Tate, all my humor and kindness draining from me.

"Where is he?" I demanded of him.

He shook his head. I ground my jaw, crossing my arms over my chest, thinking.

"You are just going to kill me," Tate wheezed, all the fight leaving him.

"You are a pathetic excuse for a Master Vampire. Leaving your entire clan at the sadistic hands of Zachariah. Did you even bother to fight him? Try to protect your House? Or did you just roll over and show your belly?" I sneered.

"Easy for you to say. You kill everything and love nothing. You have left a path of destruction in your wake and what is coming now is all your fault."

"Clearly, because I forced him to create rogues and lock them in trailers."

"No, because you killed his son."

"He took Tommy. Unlike you, Tate, I protect my own. Now, are you going to start talking, or I am going to start carving?"

He closed his mouth, not saying another word.

Logan tore his talons through Tate's neck, letting him sink to the floor. Tate clutched the healing pieces of flesh before tackling Logan around his middle.

I drew a sword, but Darren stopped me. "He needs this."

I raised a questioning eyebrow at him and he continued, "He needs to punish the people responsible for hurting you."

I relaxed my stance, watching Logan shove Tate's head into the drywall.

"So what do we do after he kills him?" Anna asked me, leaning against the railing.

"See the rest of the House, I guess. They will have felt Tate's death," I answered.

"That doesn't mean they will be any more cooperative," she anticipated.

"I know, but do you have any other ideas?" I countered.

"He's not going to be in the city," Anna guessed. "He left part of his House here, thinking they would be safe, but he won't take risks with his own safety with the rogues."

I locked my jaw; she was right.

"Or he left his House here because he felt perfectly safe and is also hiding here," Mal spoke up.

We all turned to her, with the exception of Logan, who had torn off Tate's arm.

"What do you mean?" I asked her.

"Zachariah had renovations done to the west wing. He said it was to remodel it based on his tastes, but what if he built in a safe room?" Mal continued. "He was very secretive, and the supplies being brought in, they didn't make sense for a remodel."

"Is Angelina with everyone downstairs?" I asked.

Mal blinked, surprised by my question. "I don't know."

I looked at Logan, his beast pushing at the seams of his clothing, fangs descended in his mouth and over his lips.

"We don't have time to wait for him to finish," Anna stated.

The snapping of Tate's head leaving his body had all of us turning. Logan stalked toward us in a cloud of Master Vampire ash.

"Let's go," he said around a mouthful of teeth.

I blinked at him, shocked. "You killed him, already?"

Logan raised an eyebrow, fangs retreating in his mouth. "Yes," he answered.

"But he was a Master Vampire." I was having a hard time with this.

"Are you doubting my skills?" Logan teased.

"No, but ... okay, maybe a little," I stuttered.

"I'm evolving," Logan finally confessed.

"What does that mean?"

"That I eat Master Vampires for breakfast," he grinned.

Mal made a pained sound, covering her mouth. I pulled her to me. "Keep it together. We still have to save the city." I was starting to sound like a damn comic book.

Unlike the heroes those brightly colored pages display, I didn't think we were going to be successful. I pushed my mind away from that depressing train of thought. The humans were not my responsibility to keep safe, and this was undoubtedly a vampire problem, but I couldn't stand by and let innocent people suffer.

"How do you plan on getting into the lower levels?" Darren asked.

Mal clutched her chest, taking a moment to pull herself together. Crap, we probably should have kept Tate alive a little bit longer. I laid my hand on her arm, pulling in the overwhelming sorrow that was trying to shut her body down. She gave a small whimper, her own hand latching onto mine.

There are no adequate words for the loss of a loved one. Even a dumbass loved one.

Mal slipped down, sitting on the step, folding into herself, rocking and whimpering softly. I pulled what I could. Vampires are linked to their Masters, connected and grounded through them. The loss of that is terrifying.

"We need Raphael," I said to Anna, still drawing from Mal.

She nodded, pulling out her phone, which I'm guessing I was paying for.

Mal cleared her throat, rubbing her forehead. "I felt his life force end," she whispered.

I turned to look at Logan, feeling his annoyance pressing against the bond.

"We need to identify those who are grieving versus those who are mildly upset. That will tell us who belonged to who," I told him.

I wasn't sure we had the time. I had stopped counting.

"We don't have time," Logan voiced my thoughts.

I stood, feeling Mal gain control over her emotions.

"I'm open to ideas," I countered.

"Let's go bomb the west wing," Anna said with a shrug.

"Let's," I agreed.

"Olie," Mal said, shocked.

I turned to her. "We are running out of time. A bomb won't kill Zachariah. We don't have time to hunt around through the house."

She nodded, her mind clearly preoccupied with other things.

I turned to Anna. "Do we even have explosives?"

"Yes, I added them to the SUV."

"That seems a little dangerous," I told her.

She rolled her eyes at me. "You never did like explosives."

I couldn't disagree with that.

"What about everyone down below?" Darren asked.

I groaned. "There are benefits to keeping them contained. We don't have the time to sort through who is trying to kill us and who will come over to our side."

I had been below the Centennial House on a variety of occasions. They had a very nice apartment for kidnapping people, huge training rooms with elevated windows, and the security hub for the entire house.

"Can you hear them down below?" I asked Logan.

He shook his head. "No, it must be soundproofed."

I nodded.

"We have bigger issues, let's leave them for now." I turned, heading to the SUV.

...

Between killing Tate and setting up the charges, we had lost another forty minutes. We had two hours left.

So I was still counting.

Each passing minute dimmed my hopes of being able to walk away from this unscathed.

Raphael had arrived and we were all outside behind the SUV, waiting for Anna to finish twisting wires together. I liked weapons, but explosives made me nervous.

Mal and Raphael were talking in soft voices I was trying not to overhear. I wasn't successful.

"Joining my House will help ease your pain," he told her.

She nodded, rubbing her eyes before dropping her arms across her chest.

"Nor will you be Masterless," he reminded her. Not a good position to be in within the vampire world.

Again she nodded, looking down at her hands, fidgeting.

"Olivia can't protect you forever," he pushed on.

"Hey asshole, yes I fucking can," I told him.

Raphael gave me a pointed look. I closed the distance between us. "Look, Mal, this is the best option I see for you. The good news is that the protection Logan and I have granted you won't go away with you moving Houses."

Her gaze jerked to mine.

"Olivia is correct. The protection we have extended is for your lifetime." Logan came to stand behind me. "And for the record, Raphael, we can protect her forever."

Raphael gave a disgruntled snort.

"The point being, if Raphael turns out not to be the moral and ethical good guy we think he is, I'm not above killing him," I finished.

"Me either," Logan added.

"Really? This is how you treat your allies?" Raphael asked us, annoyed.

"This is how we treat those we have sworn to protect," Logan informed him.

"I am trying to help your friend. I don't have to offer her a place in my House," Raphael countered.

I raised an eyebrow. "Moral good guy," I reminded him.

"You are testing the limits of my morality," he huffed.

"I'll do it," Mal said softly. "I wish I had time to mourn," she finished sadly.

Raphael nodded, lifting her chin up. "You will, we just have to survive what is coming."

She nodded, trying bravely to give him a smile.

"Alright, hold on to your asses!" Anna yelled, hitting a button.

I pulled Logan down behind the SUV, covering my head.

"Geez, Olie it's not that big of an explosion," Anna reprimanded me.

I lowered my arms, glaring at her. "You are the reason I don't like explosives."

She laughed, explaining to the others, "One time I added too much powder."

"I lost all my hair!" I yelled at her as we surveyed the damage.

She continued to laugh. The west wing slowly caved into itself.

"Perfect!" she congratulated herself.

I turned to Logan, who was smiling at the wreckage, shifting his legs longer and thicker.

"Can you hear him?" I guessed as to why he was smiling.

He nodded, turning to Darren, who began shifting in turn. I hadn't heard them speak. Actually, even with my guards down, I hadn't heard any of the shifters' thoughts. That was an interesting tidbit to file away for later inspection.

I saw the rubble shift and almost took off running after Logan and Darren.

"You going to let them have all the fun?" Anna asked.

I shrugged, "It seems like a lot of work."

Her gaze cut sharply to me. "Not advertising," I warned her. My body was still sore and while I wanted to go after Logan and prove I wasn't the weaker partner in the relationship, my ego was going to have to admit that for the moment, I was.

She nodded, saying nothing as we watched Logan and Darren kill a few vamps, their spray of ash mingling with the settling dust.

"They're starting to come up," Mal said, wiping her face clean. I smelled fresh blood and I hoped she really had joined with Raphael.

"Do you have any issue if I take in others?" Raphael asked me.

"No, just don't let them interfere with killing Zachariah," I told him, pulling a sword and moving in front of the pile of rubble formerly known as the west wing of the Centennial House to protect Logan and Darren's flank.

"What's going on?" a blond vampire yelled, pointing at Logan. "They can't do that!" he screamed.

"Listen and listen well. Your Master Tate is dead, and Zachariah will be suffering the same fate for abducting me and attempting to kill me," I bellowed over the hundreds of vampires. I didn't actually need to bellow.

Blondie sneered. "The Vampire High Council will not stand by while you kill two Master Vampires."

"I certainly hope not. I'd appreciate their help in cleaning up the mess they have left me with. Not to mention the rogues," I countered.

Blondie shifted at that reminder, scanning the area around us. "What do you know?" I asked, laying my sword point against his neck.

"Nothing I will tell you, succubus whor—" I sliced his head clean off his shoulders before he could finish the last word.

"That seemed a little rash," Mal said at my side.

I shrugged. "Anyone else want to volunteer information?"

"We don't even know what is going on!" someone yelled. "Our Master is dead!" another sobbed.

I blew out a breath. "Alright, listen up. Zachariah has four trailers, each filled with twenty rogues that are set to be released onto the city in less than two hours."

Shocked whispers met my announcement, but not everyone shared that shock. "Now if you have information on what is going on, I highly suggest coming forward."

Not a soul moved. I grunted.

Raphael stepped forward and I moved back. By all means, get these assholes to give a shit.

"You will all be Masterless before the day is done. Those of you who choose to fight with us to save the humans and Supernaturals alike from the rogues will earn a place in my House."

That got their attention.

"I'm going back where it's safe," one said, moving to go back into the house.

"Whatever," I hissed, annoyed.

I turned to see Logan and Darren hauling Zachariah over the rubble. I moved toward them, my sword still drawn.

"Easy, Olie," Anna warned, my blood thirst coating the air.

I snarled as Logan shoved him to his knees. "You will pay for this," Zachariah laughed, a thin tendril of blood at his temple.

"Call off the trailers," I demanded.

He laughed again, the blood running down from his temple disappearing as he healed.

"I can't. I made certain that no one and nothing could stop the retribution you so justly deserve."

"Please tell me he is lying." I looked to Logan, Darren, Mal and finally Anna.

"I don't scent a lie," Logan said softly.

"How do we save them?" I whispered.

Zachariah laughed, an insane sound. "You can't. That is the beauty of my design. The untold deaths will fall onto your head! You will lose everything!"

I lifted my blade, but Logan beat me to it, ripping off Zachariah's head.

"That was my kill," I reminded him, irritated at his swiftness in ending the asshole's life. Zachariah was a major pain in my ass. I wanted some drawn out torture.

Logan shrugged, unconcerned with my annoyance. "You can kill the next Master Vampire. Besides, keeping him alive with part of his House behind you was asking for him to escape."

I ignored the wailing behind me, trying desperately to scrape together a plan. Time was running out and I still had an entire city to try and protect.

"Alright, I have a plan. We are going to commandeer a news station and get a warning out. I can't find the damn trailers, but I can try and get the humans organized. Now, I'm open to suggestions on where to herd them to."

Okay, herd, not my best choice of words.

"The sports stadium," someone called out. "It's centrally located, with large parking lots, and enclosed."

I chewed on my thumbnail. "Alright, get there. I have a news station to hijack."

...

In the SUV, I called Tommy, relaying our plan.

"So you want me to hack into all the news stations, cancel their programs and run whatever you are recording?" Tommy asked me.

"Yeah," I answered, wondering if I had finally hit my boy wonder's limits.

"Done. Call me when you get there," he commanded. Not really sure I liked his tone, but I had bigger issues.

"What's our time?" Darren asked.

"I don't want to know," I groaned.

It was less than two hours, I knew that.

Logan drove. Raphael and the rest of the cooperating vampires went to the Garland Arena. I wasn't sure it was going to be enough room. Besides that, how did I get an entire city there in under two hours?

I rubbed my forehead and Logan drove faster, feeling my angst, actually the entire car felt it. I gave thought to shoring up my guards, but my body needed the energy more than I needed to contain my raging emotions.

"If I was Zachariah, I'd be sure one of those trailers got dropped off right by the mansion," I said, thinking out loud.

Logan growled.

"I was thinking the same thing," Anna said, turning to me.

I met her icy gaze. "They have the panic room," she tried to reassure me.

"And the electric fence," I added.

"Protection wards," Anna said.

"Don't forget the people we left behind. Jerry, your father, Doyle, and an entire brigade of vampires and shifters," Logan reminded us.

"Plus the executioners," Darren supplied.

"They alone should hold the line," Logan stated.

"I know. It just doesn't feel right not being there to protect my house," I muttered.

"Our house," Logan corrected.

I had no response for that. It was ours, but I still felt the burden to protect it falling on my shoulders.

"Hey, I wouldn't have left Ginny there if I didn't feel she'd be safe," Logan tried again.

I nodded, chewing on my thumbnail.

"He'll send the others where they will do the most damage, the heart of the city," Anna guessed.

"That's that I would do," I answered.

...

We pulled up outside a news station. I was expecting security, but we drove right up to the front doors, no one stopping us.

Logan didn't bother to find a parking spot, throwing the vehicle into park before we all emerged. I could imagine what we looked like, two females sporting weapons at every angle and two pissed off linebackers flanking us. At least we'd had extra clothing so the linebackers weren't naked.

We pushed through the glass doors and people stopped to stare.

"Where can I get on TV at?" I asked a slack jawed man in front of me.

Open-mouthed gawks met my question.

"This way," Logan said, turning to the right down a hallway. "I can hear them."

Shifter hearing, gotta love it. We followed Logan, humans getting out of our way, pressing themselves against the gray walls.

"I thought it would be fancier," I muttered to Anna. She just shrugged as we pushed through the final doors and into the newsroom.

Heads turned to us, angry glances thrown our way with whispered demands.

I kept walking to the petite woman in the brown dress and the man in the navy suit. I could scent their fear, or maybe that was Logan's sense of smell I was picking up on, either way I didn't stop until I stood in front of them.

"What do you want?" the brunette asked.

I turned to the camera, looking at the red dot.

"Are we live?" I asked.

"They're trying to cut the feed, but Darren is dealing with it," Logan said, coming to stand next to me.

I nodded.

"My name is Olivia. I am the Head Executioner for the Supernatural Council and you are all in danger. In an hour, four semi-trucks filled with twenty rogue vampires each will be released into the city. We are asking everyone to get to Garland Arena. We have protection set up there."

"What are rogue vampires? I thought vampires were friendly?" the brunette squeaked.

"Rogues vampires no longer possess rational thought, they are driven by the need to feed and cannot drink enough," I answered, turning to her. Logan adjusted me so my back wasn't to the camera.

"You can't stop it?" the man demanded.

I shook my head. "I tried. There was no failsafe built into the vehicles. I don't have time to track them down, nor do I have any additional leads. I can only try to minimize the losses."

"Why?" the brunette whispered.

I shook my head. "I don't have a good answer for that. I can tell you the one responsible is dead."

"Who is protecting the stadium?" the man asked.

"Vampires," I answered.

"Vampires!" the brunette screamed. "I thought they were coming to kill us?"

"Rogues are coming to kill you, the vampires are trying to stop it," I clarified. "Shit, did we call Tommy?" I asked Logan.

He nodded.

"Why are you people still here?" I yelled. "This isn't a joke. If you stay here, you die!"

"How do you kill a rogue?" one of the guys behind the cameras asked.

"Beheading is the fastest way. If you can shred both hearts, that will work as well," I answered.

"What about fire?" he asked.

"It has to be a steady steam for a long period of time. Their flesh heals just as quickly as it burns," I told them with a shrug.

"What about those who want to fight?" he pushed on.

"The rogues are fast, deadly and fueled by the need for blood. They retain their vampire speed, hearing, and sense of smell. Sneaking up on them is impossible unless they are feeding, and even then, as a human, your chances of not becoming their next meal are slim. Get to the stadium, we can protect everyone there."

The room began to clear out, but not everyone left. I wasn't foolish enough to think that everyone would listen, but I had done all I could.

Darren exited the top rows. "Tommy has the feed running continuously and on all channels."

I nodded. "Let's go to the stadium."

Chapter 11

When we arrived, Raphael was outside, setting up patrols.

"More Supernaturals have stepped forward to help after your TV appearance," he informed me.

I nodded, seeing sirens gearing up in bulletproof vests. It was good they had the extra protection; fighting wasn't their strong suit, but I appreciated that they wanted to help.

"Is that Myrtle?" I asked as a purple head of hair peeked out.

"Yes, she is making a fortune right now," Raphael admired.

"Sneaky troll," I muttered.

"Resourceful," Anna stated.

I shrugged, feeling good with my weapons collection. I didn't need the shiny knife I saw her wave around. Clearing my throat, I turned to Raphael. "So, what's the plan for patrols?" I asked.

"We have enough manpower for a ten-mile perimeter to bring in stragglers. I don't anticipate the stay here to be long. The rogues won't attempt to hide. It should be over relatively quickly once we know their locations."

Logan nodded. "Agreed. We need to have teams ready to go once we find out where those locations are."

"I was hoping you and your band would take a hot spot," Raphael said.

Logan nodded. "We move quickly and the girls can ride us."

"Not to mention we are the best killers," Anna bragged.

I laughed, "Bloodthirsty much?"

She shrugged, noncommittal. "You going to get the knife Myrtle keeps flashing around or am I?"

I laughed, "It's all yours."

Police sirens had all us all turning. In my emotionally open state, I felt the anger they were pushing off.

"Strange," I muttered. Logan inhaled the air, coming to stand next to me.

They stopped their cars in a barrage of squealing tires. I stepped forward for a closer inspection. An officer threw open his door, pulling a bullhorn out.

"You are all trespassing. Leave peacefully and no one gets arrested."

My mouth literally dropped open.

"We have to shut him up," Logan hissed, storming over there.

"Be careful!" I warned.

I wasn't walking into a volley of gunfire.

"I need to speak with you," Logan stated, not slowing his gait when the officer landed a hand on his weapon.

"Come, Olivia, I'll block you," Raphael said, standing in front of me. I grunted my thanks before we walked.

"I told you, Governor Hash has demanded you and your freaks leave. There is no credibility to this threat you have fabricated."

I moved from behind Raphael. "Proof?" I yelled. "You want proof?"

The officer adjusted his stance, thumbs settling into his work belt. "Yes, your word isn't good enough."

"We don't have the resources to take him to the trailer," Raphael reminded me.

"It doesn't matter, we killed those rogues. All that is left behind is—" Screams interrupted me. Terrified, soul-numbing screaming.

"It's too soon!" I yelled, pulling a blade.

"By the Gods," Raphael cursed, at least I think that was a curse. He didn't waste time, though. "Logan, you and yours get to the north, start at Hardwater and Edge and work back."

Logan nodded, apparently not having issues taking orders from a vampire. That was nice, unexpected. I checked the bond and felt his change.

"If you have family who aren't here, get them in here. It's your only bet," I told the officers. The blood had drained from their faces as they listened to the fighting.

"What, what will guns do?" asked another officer, coming to stand next to the frozen first.

"Not much, you have to hit both hearts or shoot off their entire heads. Swords are your best bet, but they are fast, so much faster than you." I shook my head sadly, seeing the truth of my words registering in his eyes.

He blinked, his resolve gaining strength. "Can they get through the cars?"

"The glass will be easy for them. But they won't be thinking like rational beings, so you should be able to outrun them or run them over with your vehicles," Anna added, coming to stand next to me.

I pulled the bullhorn from the trembling fingers of the officer. "Get your families in here. Shoot for the head, try not to get out of your vehicles."

It wasn't enough, but it was all I could do.

Logan felt my resolve and nodded, letting the growing lion inside of him out. It was only a moment of snarling and the tearing of clothing before a furry lion stood next to me. With a huff, I stowed my blade, sliding onto his back.

"You can't be serious?" Anna asked as Logan began moving forward.

I shrugged, "You can walk."

Logan loped ahead and I heard her cursing. Nestling my fingers in his thick coat, I fought the urge to lean down and wrap my arms around him. I still needed to stay alert for attacks, and survivors.

We ran into no rogues but many humans. We told each the same thing, to head to the stadium, quickly. From the lack of screams around us, we hadn't hit a hot zone.

"Damn," I said, sliding off Logan's back.

What? he asked.

"I was hoping for some action," I admitted.

He shook his head.

"Can you talk to all the shifters like that?" Anna asked. We hadn't talked about my mate mark, but I assumed she knew.

"I used to be able to read their thoughts, but since I've woken up, I haven't heard them."

She nodded. "That's a cool power."

"I'd rather stay out of their private thoughts, actually." Although it had come in handy saving Logan. "Besides, it was a drain on my shields. I had to constantly block against it."

Anna nodded as a family of four came out of a building. The mother had her arm slung around a child no more than eight, while the father held a toddler.

"What do we do?" they whispered.

Logan lifted his head, scenting the air. I listened intently but didn't hear anything.

"Come on, come with us!" Anna yelled, picking up on something I wasn't.

They made their way to us, trembling at the sight of two large lions. Anna positioned them in between us and I felt the air change. That was new.

"Incoming," I warned her, pulling a sword.

She did the same as we turned our backs to the family between us.

"What's — what's coming?" the father whispered behind us, clutching his small child to his chest.

"Rogues," Anna answered. I couldn't see her, but I imagined her stance looked similar to my own, ready and waiting.

I finally heard them, sliding over metal with their claws, snarling and hissing before they emerged into the deserted street.

"Come to momma," I encouraged. They didn't need it, didn't slow at seeing us, but instead charged our group with renewed speed.

I didn't count as they spilled out from the alleyway, but I did draw a second sword. Darren snarled and we all took a step backwards to protect the humans.

I swept up with a blow across a rogue's chest, not a killing blow, but the downward sweep I followed with chopped its head off. I ducked under the next rogue's attack of claws to my face, using my swords as scissors to chop its torso from its body.

It was hard to tell genders in their beef jerky state. I carved my blade along a vertical line through its chest to be sure the job was finished as it flopped around on the ground before exploding in ash.

Still in my crouched state, I drove my left sword up, slicing through the next rogue, hitting tough skin and brittle bones until dust rained down around me. I followed the movement of my sword, standing up before I changed directions to swipe the head off of another one.

My side was killing me. Reaching down, I felt my warm blood spilling out. Some rogue had gotten a lucky slice in.

With a grunt, I swung my sword over my head, pushing the pain away to carve, slice, and dice to protect the family behind us. I should have counted; I think I took out twenty on my own.

I coughed out ash, squinting around at the deserted street, listening to the absolute and eerie silence. I groaned, wanting to sit down on the pavement, actually lying down sounded better. I did neither, turning to check on the family.

They were trembling, crouched down with their children clutched tightly in their arms.

"Alright, let's get you guys to safety," I said, trying to push assurance in my words.

They nodded, standing slowly.

You are hurt, Logan said.

"I know," I grunted, looking down at my now sticky side. "Let's get them to safety and we can deal with it."

He huffed, not liking my answer. He bumped my hip with his shoulder and I slid on his back, grateful for the help.

"There has to be only one left," Anna surmised.

I looked up at her, blinking. "What?"

"The trailers, if there really were only four, we just took out one, there was one at the stadium, and we're assuming one at the mansion, so there should be only one left," Anna explained.

I grunted, "Hopefully. It would be nice to think this was all over and I could go home and sleep."

Home, the word rebounded. I reached for my phone, calling Tommy.

"Olie, are you okay?" he answered.

"Yep, we are good. How's everyone there?" I asked.

"Blue is hurt pretty bad, but your dad and Jerry are working on him. The trailer dropped the rogues off right outside the mansion."

I cringed.

"Any other causalities?" I asked.

"Not that I can see, we haven't been cleared to leave the safe room."

"Good, stay safe. There should only be one trailer left unaccounted for."

...

We arrived back to the camp with a whole horde of survivors, some with bloody reminders of the rogue assault. I slipped off of Logan's back with a groan. He shifted into a sexy naked man, picking at my shirt.

I wished it wasn't to look at my wound.

"It's not that bad," I told him.

He looked up at me. "You need stitches."

I groaned, "Let's get them now. I'm not really sure how I feel about having scars."

He looked at me, surprised, walking through the masses gloriously naked. I tried not to snarl at the few women and men who gawked at him, I wasn't successful.

Myrtle saw us coming and cleared a cot for me, sitting me down roughly before probing my side.

"Get clothing out of the brown box, Logan," she commanded him.

Logan grunted before strolling over to the box, pulling on a pair of gray sweats. The stares didn't diminish. I suppose seeing a man turn into a lion and back would have that effect.

Blowing out a breath, I winced as Myrtle shoved me roughly on my back.

"Sorry kid, I don't have time for my usual bedside manner."

"That's assuming your usual bedside manner is an improvement," I grunted at her.

She huffed out a laugh. "That's true, and since I haven't worked on you before, you will just have to take my word, it's better."

I hissed, pressing an arm over my eyes as she began to clean and sew. Logan's hands stroked back my hair as he whispered sweet words to me.

"You brought in quite a few survivors," Myrtle commented, trying to get my mind off the steel poking into my flesh.

"Any word on where the fourth trailer is?" Logan asked.

I cringed; Myrtle was not a delicate seamstress. Her stitches better be fucking fantastic for this amount of pain.

"Yes, they dropped it outside the Governor's offices. He wouldn't allow anyone to leave and seek safety. Hundreds are dead due to his ego."

"I should kill him," I grunted.

"Too late, one of the rogues got to him." I jerked as she tied off the thread.

Sitting up with Logan's help, I looked around at the humans, dazed, bleeding, but helping each other. I hoped the human Hell did exist, and that Hash was now there, enjoying a variety of perverse tortures.

"Go home, Olivia, take care of your own." Myrtle gave me a firm pat.

I grimaced, looking at Logan, who nodded his agreement.

Chapter 12

We arrived to the sidewalk and yard being hosed down by Hudson, completely in the nude. His body was littered with healing wounds.

"Hey boss!" he called out, like he hadn't just gone a few rounds with rogue vampires.

"What are the casualties?" Logan asked.

Hudson's face fell, his gaze turning to me. "Blue is stable, but it will take time for him to heal. We lost three vampires and two shifters. The human losses are far more substantial. Did you hear one of the trailers was dumped off in front of the Governor's offices?"

"We did," Logan confirmed.

"I haven't heard about the fourth one," Hudson continued.

I pushed by them, letting Logan get Hudson up to speed, and into the house. I nodded my thanks to those who had put their lives on the line to protect my family.

Tommy ran into my arms as soon as I cleared the living room. Ali and Grant were behind him, breathing out a relieved breath at my appearance. I held on to him until he pulled back, remembering he was a teenage boy who didn't need anyone.

"Is it over?" Ali asked.

"I think so," I told her.

She breathed out a sigh. "Alright, let's get things cleaned up," Ali said, soothing children as she passed.

...

It was early the next morning when our doorbell rang. We had put everyone up at the mansion for the night, and Logan and I had kids camped out all over our floor.

We had given up our bed to three of the older teenage girls, nesting down with the younger kids in a heaping pile of comforters and snuggles.

It was just what my healing body needed, although sex would have been a pleasant addition.

Logan lifted his head at me, a question in his eyes. "I'm not expecting anyone," I told him.

He nodded, shifting kids off him gently before we stood as a unit, making our way downstairs, me in my sports bra and shorts and Logan in his own black gym shorts.

I picked up a gun, clicking off the safety, from a hidden fingerprint safe behind a vase. It really shouldn't come as a surprise that I had high-tech safes hidden around the mansion.

"Do you really think you need that? Whoever it is rang the bell," Logan asked.

"I'm still weak," I hissed at him. "It makes me feel better."

Logan grunted, "I'm right here."

I cut him an annoyed glance as he unlocked the door and turned off the security alarm. It certainly wasn't a dig at him. I just liked my firepower and had trust issues, and currently performance issues as well.

Logan opened the door and I jerked back, surprised. "Mercer," I said, stepping out of his way, "please come in."

Mercer took in our attire and my gun in one sweeping gaze.

"What's wrong?" Logan asked, scenting emotions I couldn't.

"Olivia, I need you to—" He stopped, running a hand over his face.

Mindy pushed the door open, coming to wrap her arms around my legs. She was eight or maybe nine now, but I picked her up easily, okay my stitches pulled a lot, as I did it one-handed because of the gun.

"She's dead," Mindy whispered into my ear.

My gaze jerked to Logan as I asked her, "Who, sweetie?"

"Grams," came her broken whisper next to my ear.

My arms held her tighter. Logan reached out to cup my face; I hardly registered that he was saying my name or taking my gun from me. All I could hear was Mindy sobbing above my own ragged breathing.

"No," I whispered.

Mindy's sobs increased to wailing, a broken cry issuing from my own lips.

Logan's arms were around me, guiding me into a chair. He tried to pull her from my arms, but neither of us was letting go.

Logan stroked my hair, rubbing Mindy's back. I bowed my head into her shoulder, my chest heaving from my own tears.

"What happened?" Logan asked, I assumed of Mercer.

He sniffed, clearing his throat. "She was meeting with Hash at his office. The entire building was decimated."

"What do you need from us?" Logan pushed on, keeping his head.

"I can't locate any of her family. I assume Olie has everything in order," Mercer finished on a whisper.

I tried to stop crying and regain my ability to speak. "Get Ali and Grant—" I had to stop. I pressed my lips together to stop the sob. Swallowing hard, I squeezed out, "They have everything."

Logan nodded, clearly debating on leaving me. I shook my head and he went.

My emotions were broadcasting and I heard doors opening. The kids filed downstairs, and I didn't know how to handle any of it.

...

We buried Grams next to her husband and child in a small cemetery outside of St. Ann. She might have been human, but to me, she would always be a Supernatural. I sat there dressed in black, next to Logan and all the children, and felt nothing. A coldness had seeped into my body, which helped me re-build my guards, but did nothing to help me connect with the kids. I should have been there for them. I should have supported them, but I found myself unable to do much.

"Olivia will be reading the eulogy," the minister or pastor or whatever the fuck he called himself stated.

I stood, smoothing out my dress, standing behind the podium, looking over Grams's chestnut coffin and so many eyes looking back at me.

"Grams was born Gretchen Master in a small town in Kansas. She grew up on a farm, enjoying the outdoors. At the age of nineteen, she fell in love with and married Kent Graw. Their son Danny was born eighteen months later." I cleared my throat, willing the tears to evaporate. "Three years later, she lost them both to a home invasion, and traveled down a dark path of drug addiction and prostitution. But she, she still cared. She still loved and she, she still, tried."

I wiped my tears away, glad I hadn't bothered with makeup. "That's where I found her. I spent three weeks getting her off the drugs, at one point handcuffing her to a bathroom. And from there, we built an empire."

There was a lot I could have said about that empire, but I moved on.

"Even though our paths had separated, she remains in our hearts the woman who helped us, who listened to us, who loved us when we were not so loveable. And that is who she shall be, forever."

I found Logan's gaze, my heart torn apart by every tear the children cried, by the pulsing loss and grief that rolled over me in painful waves. He nodded, giving me a small smile. His unconditional love pushed into me from the mate mark. I knew it was there, but in my cold and detached state, I couldn't respond.

...

After the funeral, Kass had organized a dinner, or meeting, or wake, or whatever it was called, for people who wanted to sit around and talk about Grams. There was supposed to be something therapeutic about it.

I ended up on the roof of Halfling, hiding. Logan knew where I was; when I heard the door open, I assumed it was him.

Instead, a sniffling Tommy came over, sitting heavily down next to me.

I knew he blamed himself for it. I blamed myself for it. Neither of us was right.

"It was Zachariah," I said softly.

He sniffed, his head hanging low, nodding at my words.

"He must have sent those threatening pictures to Grams, encouraged Hash to pursue her politically, and kidnapped Blake's niece," I told him.

Tommy shook his head. "I skipped school."

"He wanted Blake and Angelina to wed. To entrench himself in The Centennial House. I was in the way."

"This isn't your fault," Tommy said, turning to look at me.

"Nor is it yours," I told him.

He looked away from me, neither of us believing the other.

He cleared his throat, pulling himself upright. "What's next?"

I looked out across the skyline of St. Ann. "I need to unlock my magic, bring the unicorns and mermaids over."

"Have you given thought to properties?" Tommy asked, drying his eyes, steel resolve replacing his grief.

"Isolated for the unicorns, high male population for the mermaids."

"There are no male mermaids?" Tommy asked, surprised.

"I don't think so. The mermaid I met said they need human males to procreate."

He nodded, no doubt thinking.

"What about Anna?" Tommy asked. I felt his mixed emotions.

"I don't know. She's welcome to stay, but I doubt she will."

He ground his jaw, looking at the skyline with me. "So this is our new normal? Logan, Anna, Ali and Grant?"

I nodded. He turned to me. "What about the damn vampires?"

I groaned. "I don't know. The human government is going after them exceptionally hard. I imagine we will hear about it."

"Logan did kill two Master Vampires, which is impressive, by the way."

I nodded. "He's evolving, getting stronger. No doubt, the vampires will see him as a threat."

"You are a power duo and now you have access to other dimensions. You are both threats."

I nodded, reaching over to pull him close. "I don't want to think about that now."

Tommy rested his head against my shoulder and we sat in silence.

So much had changed in a short time. I had gained a father, lost my adoptive mother, regained a sister, and survived a mass slaughter attempt. I would be lying if I claimed to have processed it all. Sitting in the dying light with Tommy snuggled up against me, I knew one truth.

We were going to be fine. The makeshift family I had created would survive this and thrive.

Connect with Me!

Thank you for reading Death of a Succubus! I greatly appreciate your support and I whole heartedly hope you enjoyed it. If you did, please consider leaving me some love on the platform you purchased on.

Facebook: kimbairauthor

Instagram: KimBairAuthor

Email: kimbair@proton.me

Website: www.kimbair.com

Telegram: kimbairauthor

Join my mailing list to be first in the know www.kimbair.com

Thank you and happy reading!!

More books by Kim Bair:

Dead Shifter Walking, The Succubus Executioner Book 1

Demigod Down, The Succubus Executioner Book 2

A Witch's Fury, The Succubus Executioner Book 3

A Council of Betrayal, The Succubus Executioner Book 4

Death of a Succubus, The Succubus Executioner Book 5

Legacy of the Succubus, The Succubus Executioner Book 6

Creation of the Dual Shifter, The Dual Shifter Executioner

The Mel Files

Andy's Origin, The Andromalius Chronicles

www.ingramcontent.com/pod-product-compliance
Lightning Source LLC
Chambersburg PA
CBHW022103170626
46808CB00002B/566